THE
WORK

THE WORK

A novel by Maria Meindl

Stonehouse Publishing
www.stonehousepublishing.ca
Alberta, Canada

Stonehouse Publishing Inc. is an independent
publishing house, incorporated in 2014.

Cover design and layout by Anne Brown.
Printed in Canada

Stonehouse Publishing would like to thank and acknowledge
the support of the Alberta Government funding for the arts,
through the Alberta Media Fund.

Government

National Library of Canada Cataloguing in Publication Data
Maria Meindl
The Work
Novel
ISBN 978-1-988754-16-1

To Rolf: all yours.

PART I

Rate My Prof

Rebecca Weir
Humber College, Toronto
Producer: To End All Wars Inc.

Course:
The Stage Manager as Co-Creator
Overall Quality: 1.5
Level of Difficulty: 5
Would take again: N/A
Hotness: 1

See how other students rate this professor:
09/30/2011: *AWFUL*
Spent 2 dyas in Weirds class. That was a mistake but im leving it. Not surehow old she is. Green hair.

06/12/2011: *AWESOME*
Professor Weir teaches the art of stage management from her thirty years' experience in what she calls The School of Life and it has served her well. She is always organized and prepared and demands the same. I would highly recommend this class to anyone who wants a career in the demanding but fulfilling world of theatre and dance.

06/08/2011: *AWFUL*
Deadline Nazi.

05/04/2011: *AWFUL*
Green hair. Anal.

07/05/2010: *AWESOME*
Stage Management is a job I would not want, EVER, but my marks

went up from following her schedule template. Funny stories also.

07/02/2010: *AWESOME*
I have never met anyone this organized in my whole, entire life. You will die listening to her stories. She is a major person: committees at school, plus the head of a company and won a volunteer prize. She is boss of *To End All Wars*. Interesting and dedicated prof.

06/15/2010: *AWESOME*
Am I the only pervert rating her for hotness? Tall and rocks heels. Green hair.

05/15/2008: *AWESOME*
Basically I feel like one course with her is all you will need, ever. You walk in there in September and then suddenly it's May and if you are still alive you know you are good.

04/12/2008: *AWFUL*
Confisgate my phone OCD witch.

06/16/2007: *AWESOME*
She teaches you the morals of your work. You must die at 4:30 p.m. and your show still goes on at 8. Remember someone can come along and replace you at any time. If someone is really having trouble she will help you but DO NOT SLACK OFF IN EVEN SO MUCH AS YOUR MIND. She will know it and you are dead.

1984

It's over. Rebecca arrives at the church basement which served all summer as a rehearsal hall. Slipping past the beige-paneled meeting room, she glimpses dozens of people milling around, giving each other orders as they string up balloons and streamers. She heads for the washroom marked "pastor," locks herself in and leans against the door, makes a bargain: one hour at the cast party, one beer, one plate of food, a few hugs. Then she can go home.

But first she will need to change. She slaps the dust off her jeans, then heaves her knapsack onto the counter to retrieve the shirt which is balled up at the bottom. The slinky fabric is unfamiliar to her touch and she sets it aside with her fingertips. She removes her "South Pacific" T-shirt and the tank top that serves as underwear, rinses out her armpits and dries them with rough paper towel. Deliberately, she pushes the knapsack aside so that she can see more of herself. Her face is pink, her nose peeling from the sweltering Sunday matinees, and her hair is coming loose from the coated elastic which grips it in a ponytail looped back on itself. "Smile," her sisters used to tell her. "People will think you're no fun." But Rebecca isn't inclined to smile for no reason. Now, she looks at her taut breasts, her strong arms and muscular belly. There is a lot *of* Rebecca. The phrase, 'big boned' has dogged her since childhood. But for a change she doesn't mind. Big might be good. There is potential in this body, though she can't think for what.

Rebecca has never actually worn the top. Her cheeks are flushed as she slithers into it. It has a wide-open neckline just like – okay – the poster for *Flashdance*. She drapes it so as to leave one shoulder bare. The elastic has fallen out of her hair and she tosses her head to make it look fuller. No. This has to stop.

Actresses – Amanda Garten, for instance – have to look at themselves in mirrors all the time. In preparation for being looked at by others. It's part of the job. Rebecca is not an actress and never will be. *"What a feeling!"* she sings in a mocking whisper, crossing her eyes and pretending to stick her finger down her throat, reminding herself who she really is.

A stage manager! It was on the weekly cheques she has received since May, on the posters and program the company had specially printed, sparing no expense. It was on the door of her church-basement office. It sang in her mind through the hour-long journey on the bus that got her there each day and through the weekly conversations with her sisters that – until this summer – had always made her feel she was wasting her life.

For the two lonely, fragmented years she has lived in Toronto, Rebecca has struggled to keep busy. Every time a job ended, she felt as if a crevasse in the earth had opened up instead of a week or two of free time. Her strategy was to say yes to everything, including hanging lights in a mosquito-infested Quonset hut in Muskoka, breaking down the stage of an old opera house and rubbing the edge of each board with graphite to reduce squeaks, trucking in supplies for a Dutch performance artist who covered herself in ketchup and rolled around in sawdust under a highway overpass, getting rid of the mess before the flies arrived, and spreading out a new load of sawdust the next afternoon.

Then came *South Pacific*, a production of The Simcoe Thespians, who had been putting on shows every summer for fifteen years in a park in North York. The budget was enormous for some reason, affording a professional crew and choreographer, well-known actors in the lead roles, a live band, and new sets and costumes. At the first read-through, Rebecca learned why the show's coffers were so rich. Among the first to arrive was Amanda Garten, cast as Nellie Forbush. She was closely followed by an older man whose face Rebecca instantly recognized: Leon Garten. *Garten* ... of course! He owned two theatres in Toronto, not to mention a chain of drug stores and a television station. Clad in pink pastel stretch pants and a shirt in a deeper shade, weighed down by the hockey bag he carried on one shoulder, Leon kissed Amanda at the door and waved her off: "Leave it to me, Doll. Go!" He heaved the bag onto a chair then took out a white baseball cap with "*South Pacific* 1984," embroidered on the front. The bag contained enough caps for the cast and crew and a matching set of T-shirts. He put on one of the hats and busied himself organizing the shirts on a row of chairs near the door.

Amanda approached, her attention fixed sincerely on Rebecca. She had a loose-limbed way of moving, like a pre-teen girl. Her fine hair was cut short for the role of Nellie, the wisps around her temples highlighting her enormous, widely spaced eyes. "Amanda Garten," she said.

"I know." Rebecca brushed a heat-swollen hand on the back of her jeans before enfolding Amanda's cool, dry one. "Would you like to sit down ...?" Rebecca pulled out a chair and tucked it in.

"Thank you!" Amanda said, as if she'd been given a treasure. Yet it was clear she could not imagine things would go any other way.

At the start of the read-through no one appeared to notice Leon, but Rebecca watched the realization spread around the group, each back becoming a little straighter, each voice a little more distinct as its owner tried to capture Leon's attention. Rebecca looked over at Leon, curious to see which actors he was watching, and found him smiling at *her*. Flustered, she busied herself with her notes.

South Pacific was hard. Somehow, she had to blend the efforts of amateurs, professionals, and the numerous hangers-on who just wanted to be part of the excitement. Miffed at being cast in minor roles, the Thespians' founding members would regularly interrupt rehearsals to ask about their costumes. A clique of young actors monopolized the kitchen at breaks. Their eruptions of laughter created a kind of shield around the coffee urn; anyone who dared approach would do so gingerly, as if walking in on a top-level meeting. The young ones were always the last to return to work, prompting the veterans to sigh loudly and glare in Rebecca's direction. Then there was the lighting designer who flew in from New York for four days to take notes. Except that given the Thespians' meandering pace, it was the wrong four days.

She made it work. Rebecca saw to it that they all walked around in a perfectly functioning world whose mechanics they never noticed. But the people who matter have noticed. One day when Leon was there to watch a rehearsal, she approached the coffee machine (ostensibly to check the water level but really to allow the less assertive cast members to gain access to it in her wake). He was standing with Richard – the director – hands clasped atop their ample bellies, absorbed in earnest talk. Rebecca heard Richard say: "Incredible. She doesn't miss a beat." Leon nodded, rubbing one thumb rhythmically on the other. "Very good," he said. "Very good." He turned and smiled at her and she blushed, not realizing he had known she was there. For one, sweet moment she allowed herself to think the compliment might be for her. Then she got back to work.

And now it's over.

Moving from the bright hallway to the party room is a shock to her eyes. The room is lit only by candles. A large area has been cleared – presumably to make a dance floor – and the insect-like drone of *"You Should be Dancin'!"* by the Bee Gees pulses from the speakers. She grimaces. *What senior citizen picked the music?* An orderly lineup of people snakes past the food table with its mountain of cocktail shrimp, jellied salads and cakes on raised platters, while another crowd gathers around the fortress of liquor boxes on the opposite wall. Total strangers. God, she hates cast parties! And why did she decide to wear this pornographic top? She adjusts it so that the low part is in the back, locates the clock and calculates how soon she can decently go home.

Through the dimness of the room it seems to Rebecca that a ray of moonlight now moves toward her, in the form of a diminutive woman with silver hair arranged in a bun. This can only be Amanda's mother. She wears a trim, white pantsuit and a triple strand of pearls. The woman meets Rebecca's eyes after scanning her body like a tree. That glance contains a lightning exchange of understanding. This woman has noticed Rebecca, noticing *her*, noticing Rebecca's height. Seamlessly, she adjusts. "I'm looking for the girl who's as talented as she is statuesque," she says, with a lilt in her voice that Rebecca cannot place at first. Then she realizes it is the remnants of an English accent.

The woman introduces herself as Sylvia Garten. "Leon wanted to come himself, but there's a dinner for the Foundation. He asked me to give you this while he delivers his words of wisdom to the Board!" From a jeweled clutch she produces a business card and hands it to Rebecca. "There's a girl: Martie Solomon. In the office. Here's her number. This week you'll have a haircut, get a little something new ..." she plucks at her own collar, "Wednesday, Thursday you'll call her. She's expecting you."

Rebecca feels the card soften as sweat coats her palm. She can't think of an answer, but Sylvia looks at her steadily until she grasps the situation. This is business. This is good. And Sylvia is going to stand there, staring at her, until she gives the correct response. She answers, "You know, I don't have a good hairdresser. Your hair is lovely. Can you recommend someone?"

Sylvia gives an almost imperceptible nod, then jostles her hair roughly. "For this frizzy mess, I have a girl come in. Amanda and I: we look the same no matter what we do. But Martie goes to John, at Le Coupe. He's for the business girls."

"Le Coupe."

"Le Coupe, in Yorkville. With fine hair like yours you need a really good cut."

"Amanda is wonderful. A star. And easy to work with. Of course, those things go hand in hand."

"Puh! Puh! Puh!" Sylvia turns her head from one side to the other and makes as if to spit out something disgusting. She soon recovers, though, and addresses Rebecca gravely, "I warned Leon he should get a woman to direct her. This Richard got the bank managers and schoolteachers up singing and dancing but with Amanda he was too smitten. There was no way he could bring out her best."

"You mean the review ...?"

Sylvia shakes her head and looks heavenward. Under the headline, *Garten Scion Disappoints,* it condemned Amanda's performance as half-hearted, and pointed out that RxWorld was first on the list of sponsors for the show. "No one paid attention," Rebecca assures Sylvia. "The seats were full every night."

"God willing ... God willing... Next week ... I guess you know ..."

Rebecca shakes her head.

"She's going to try her wings, in New York!"

No, she doesn't know. Rebecca feels choked. Evidently, she means nothing to Amanda – to any of them – but manages, "Well she really should; she's so gifted."

Sylvia raises her hand, deflecting the praise. "She's been involved with this ... experimental ... business. They think it's a revolution but we had it years ago. After the war we had it. In England. Even then it was nothing new. You see, Leon has done well because he understands how to lift people's spirits. And all this *experimentation* ... it just makes everyone worry! It will never really take off. But now, maybe ..." She gives Rebecca another significant look, then shakes her head. "Enough of me. Dinner's waiting. Let me guess. There'll be a chicken breast, a scoop of rice and seven spears of asparagus. You: you'll stay and have fun with your friends." She shimmies her hands on either side of her face, batting her eyelids as the opening notes of *"Stayin' Alive"* burst forth on the speakers. Rebecca sees hours of relentless work in the gesture. This woman was once a dancer. Rebecca leans toward her. She wants more of Sylvia, wants to hear her story, but Sylvia is turning to leave.

"Call Martie," she says. "My husband likes to give people a chance."

Rebecca watches Sylvia for as long as she can. Now, she is all the more eager to go home, to contemplate the memory of their conversation in solitude. But Sylvia has given her an order, phrased like a prediction: *You'll stay and have fun.* She goes to put the card in her front pocket of her jeans then realizes it will get crumpled and switches it to the back.

She crosses to the table which is serving as a bar. Salvaging a lone stubby from a forest of imported beer bottles, she opens it by pressing the crimped edge of the lid against the table. She clutches it against her stomach, taking the odd, nervous sip. She feels chilled. All around her people are laughing and talking. How do they manage to navigate from one group to another? What do they think of to say? Rebecca likes working conversations, working jokes; even flirtation is possible in the context of work. Once the job is done she feels lost. She thinks of the card in her pocket. Maybe this means the end of those terrible gaps in her life. No! Mustn't let her hopes get too high.

She hears a voice beside her: male. "Anyone know where I can get a *real* beer around here?"

Rebecca turns, adjusting her gaze to meet someone much smaller than the voice led her to expect. The top of his graying head is level with Rebecca's chin, yet masculinity rolls off him like a smell. He *does* smell of something – an earthy, skin-and-breath smell that anyone else would have tried to cover up. Not this man, though. He wears it boldly. Everything about him is bold. His personality takes up all the space his small body does not. She hands him her beer, her mind watching her body, which acts on its own. He tips back his head, gulping again and again as half the contents disappear down his throat.

"That's better." He raises the stem of the bottle towards her, a salute. He puckers his forehead, deepening the lines in an already grave face. His glasses, held together at the temple with a paper clip, draw attention to his constantly-roving eyes, which glance at Rebecca briefly then return to scanning from one corner of the floor to another as if searching for something.

"I'm Marlin," he says at last, transferring the beer to his left hand

and extending his damp right one for her to shake. "Marlin Lewis."

Of course, she has heard of him. "Maverick" was the term a reporter used to describe him last year when a company he had worked with imploded. After enjoying a successful tour of Europe and Asia, that is. Rebecca has no problem with mavericks, but the way she's heard actors talk about Marlin makes her want to escape this conversation immediately. They say: "I spent a few months with Marlin," or "I need to pay Marlin a visit." They might as well be talking about a drug dealer and/or Helen Shakti, the naturopath they all seem to share who – from what Rebecca can gather – makes a point of starving people, breaking up their relationships and turning their skin yellow before they run out of money and give up. Rebecca is so, so glad not to be an actress, not to have to submit to these upheavals. Her life feels precarious enough. Yet Marlin's gesture of freeing up his right hand makes her pulse quicken. It is chivalrous – touchingly so in someone wearing broken glasses and a frayed tee shirt.

"Rebecca Weir." He grasps her hand in a way that *makes sense* of her. She feels taller, more solid on her feet.

Marlin stands back, squinting as he looks up at her. "You look like you're in charge here."

"Not really."

"Come on, admit it. You're not like *them*, Rebecca. What are you doing here?"

"I'm the stage manager. Or was. The show's over."

"That much seems clear." He grins (or is it a grimace?) and takes another swig of his drink. Rebecca's eyes feel moist. She realizes that her mouth is open. Marlin breaks their gaze abruptly, frowning at the floor as he scans it.

He's with her again. "Come journey with us."

Rebecca shakes her head.

"Confused? Of course. You've just spent four months watching over a corpse."

"*South Pacific* was –"

"Written in 1925 –"

"– 49!"

"Very good! My point is that it's not *now*. Do you know where the word 'rehearsal' comes from?"

"French. *Repetition*," she answers proudly.

"Exactly. And it's no accident that the English version includes the word 'hearse.' That's not Theatre and that's not The Work. I have a company: SenseInSound. We gather. We journey. Every moment is new. Every moment is *now*. You can be part of it. If you're willing to risk."

Rebecca backs away. "I'm busy."

"Sounds like all the boys want to dance with you, Rebecca!"

"This is not a high school dance."

He grins again. "Could have fooled me. What comes next?"

She takes her right hand to her back pocket, but can't remember if the card is there or on the left. "I have prospects."

As if in answer, Marlin draws closer and she feels his heat and smells his peaty smell, overlaid with beer. "I see you here," he says, positioning himself beside her, not quite touching. "Just here." Together, they look out at the room. The candles and music seem friendly now. "I don't consume people and spit them out again. That's not The Work. Only in intimacy can we truly risk. Risk is what keeps us alive. And we all yearn for it, Rebecca. Even you."

Rebecca's gut twists. He's too close; he's seeing through her – or claiming to – which amounts to the same thing, since – it's now clear – she knows nothing about what goes on inside herself. *Walk away*, she thinks, but before she can put this idea into action, Amanda appears from the crowd, wearing a black top and jeans, a nicer black top than Rebecca's, a sequined one, with a single gem on a chain around her neck, and matching earrings and high-heeled sandals with little rhinestones. Marlin's face closes. The part of him that was open to Rebecca, closes. The moment before Amanda and Marlin touch each other stretches out. Or Rebecca stretches it out in her mind by resolutely not relating one piece of information to another. Marlin has mixed her up. She has no idea how she feels but knows she doesn't want this: for Amanda to belong to him, or he to her. Until they touch, the connection between them is still in doubt.

They reach for each other, tears starting in Amanda's eyes. There's a story there which Rebecca is not privy to, yet she feels the brew of sadness and desire, anger and forgiveness that enfolds them. It leaves her outside yet captivates her completely. Amanda places herself between Rebecca and Marlin, tucks herself into the crook of his arm. She is actually smaller than him. They belong to the same, refined breed. She closes her eyes, takes a deep breath, and when she opens them, includes Rebecca again. "I'm so glad you're still here. I wanted to thank you for everything you've done. I know it wasn't easy to pull together this – this crowd – but you've done it. Really. You're the best."

Marlin kisses the top of Amanda's head, whispers, "Let's get out of here." They turn away, arms linked, tiny hips touching, a matching pair of dolls. Alone again, Rebecca steadies herself against the table, thinking of the way a kite buffeted by conflicting winds can skid violently to the ground. Then Amanda is back. She places a hand on Rebecca's arm. "I know Marlin can be difficult to understand, but his work ... The Work is changing lives Rebecca. Once you've experienced it you'll never be the same. Go tomorrow. It's at Eastern Avenue and Leslie. People will show you the way. Please help him. He needs you ... *I* need you. Journey with them. Promise me you will!"

Gesendet: 20/12/2011. 5.07 a.m.
An: director.graddrama@UToronto.ca
Von: AmAndAm@gmail.com

Betreff: The Truth

Dr. Charbonneau, I have nothing to tell you.

There were plays. Read the reviews. There are children: two.
Grown. Maybe they'll talk to you. Gerrard Space is still there. Go
and see it. My story? A blank. The Work meant living in the eternal
Now, one day barely connecting with the next. There was no story.
Search Kevin Purcell. Search Victoria Fodor, Connie Herbert, Portia Bianchi. Gaëlle Mercier. We used to search *for* people. Now
that polite little preposition is gone. We just search them, without
a warrant. And find what? Yet another performance. For the now-
non-paying public on the internet.

Search Rebecca Weir. She's the one you need. We all do.

Yours truly,
Amanda M.

1984

At 9:45 on Labour Day morning, Rebecca hurries down Leslie
Street from Queen. For a change she didn't enjoy the ride on the
streetcar and wished the subway were open at this hour to get her
across town quickly. The western part of Queen Street is familiar.
On days off she has made a point of walking to Parkdale, seeing in
person what she's read about in the news. Patients released from the
psychiatric hospital have settled in overcrowded rooming houses
nearby. When they have places to live at all. Rebecca has come to
recognize the man who arrays tins of soup beside him on a bench
outside the library, the woman who paces in front of a convenience
store as if waiting for important news. It no longer startles her to
hear someone deep in conversation with a friend she can't see. She
must train herself *not* to be startled, by this or anything else she
might find in her city.

This morning as the streetcar travelled downtown, she noticed
that a couple of new restaurants had opened, replacing a fabric
store and a greasy spoon. The word "trendy" is often used to describe Queen Street West. Rebecca does not understand what the
word means; only that it doesn't describe her. Then they passed
City Hall, and Eaton's. There was still so far to go! The streetcar
continued through an area that seemed a mirror of Queen West,
the buildings diminishing in size as they left the downtown core

behind, but it was less crowded and less … self-conscious. The ragged combinations of leather jackets and trailing shirt-tails that she saw on Queen West looked like they had taken hours to assemble. And even the men wore makeup! Was it the quality of self-regard that made Queen West "trendy?" Here, the sidewalks were empty except for the odd man lurching around still drunk from last night. There were variety stores with rusted signs, a coffee shop with neon glowing half-heartedly in a dusty window. Rebecca was frightened. Self-regard also meant people were looking around them, keeping track. Here, she was anonymous. Toronto could ambush her with its vastness, its sudden changes. How much further would she have to go?

On Eastern Avenue she finds houses, factories and variety stores, a clump of one kind of building, then a clump of another. The street keeps changing its mind about what it wants to be. And garages. So many garages. This is not an area for pedestrians. She examines the sides of hydro poles, hoping to find a poster, but there is nothing. The factories on the south side look uninhabited with their dusty windows, stained walls and empty parking lots.

Maybe she's got the date wrong; maybe this Journey business is tomorrow. Rebecca feels exposed. And guilty, as if trespassing.

Marlin said, *I see you here, just here.*

Amanda said, *He needs you.*

She keeps walking. Rebecca discovers the triangle of streets where Eastern Avenue divides. There's an abandoned red brick building, three stories high. A man and woman drive up on bicycles, dismount and lock them to a pole. They move elegantly, as if this were all a dance. Rebecca is intimidated by this couple; their spare figures bespeak discipline, or lack of appetite. Yet they are the only ones who can help her find her way.

"Excuse me!" Rebecca calls. "I'm looking for the Sound theatre."

"*Sense*InSound," says the woman without stopping what she's doing. "This is it. Come with us. Hurry. We're late."

It is ten a.m. *I was here fifteen minutes ago!* Rebecca assures Marlin, in her mind. She follows the couple into the building. In the front entranceway, she is met by the reek of urine, a force field. She has the urge to go no further, but the couple keeps going, not re-acting to the stench. She follows. They climb a few steps and find the remnants of a wired glass door at the top. Squares of it cling to the mesh and crunch on the floor under their feet. After this: a hallway with grey, peeling walls and doors every ten feet or so. They pick their way past caches of beer bottles and pizza boxes. Rebecca draws shallow breaths so as to inhale as little as possible of the smell. The hallways are a labyrinth. As they go past doorways, whiffs of various chemicals fade in and out, the remnants of what-ever businesses lived and died in these rooms.

They pass a freight elevator, its wooden grille smashed, and beside that, another door, glass intact, with a stairwell beyond it. It grows hot, then hotter, then airless as they climb. At the top is one enormous room. There are no walls at this level, only columns. Light creeps in through streaked and sometimes boarded-up win-dows. Rebecca's skin is slick with sweat, but at least the smell is fad-ing. In the very middle of the floor is a ladder leading to a hole in the ceiling. The man signals for Rebecca to go first. Her breath catches as she feels a rung strain under her feet. The word "insur-ance" swims in her mind.

How much hotter will it get? How much less air can she stand? Emerging at the next level Rebecca gulps the breeze that floods her lungs. Sun flows in from a skylight directly above. Broken windows on all sides leave the wind free to gust in.

Disinfect entranceway.
Cut mesh and line hole with duct tape.
Clear first-floor hall to stairwell.
Check to see if second-floor windows will open.
Make new ladder.
She loves this place.

The couple she arrived with bustle over to one end of the room where about fifteen people lie on quilted moving blankets on the floor. The man signals with a tilt of his head for Rebecca to follow, and from his silence she understands she is to be quiet. He hands her a blanket from a stack and points to an empty area at one end. "New people start there," he whispers. The couple busy themselves getting their own blankets and arranging them near hers.

Rebecca doesn't do this type of thing.

Where is Marlin? Glancing around furtively, she recognizes his figure at the other end of the room. He paces up and down, muttering as if berating someone in an urgent whisper. She can't approach now to ask him what he has in mind for her to do.

Marlin's T-shirt clings to the taut muscles in his chest and shoulders. A pair of white pants are tied low around his hips with a drawstring. As he moves, an intimate sliver of belly appears, then disappears again. There is a catlike grace to his steps as he places each foot down in a studied, deliberate way. Even in this private moment, he might as well be on stage. Marlin *inhabits* his body in a way that inspires awe in Rebecca. So – she realizes – do the couple she has just met. And so does Amanda, now she thinks of it. All the nooks and crannies, not only of their bodies but of their very selves seem to be familiar territory. They feel comfortable in a world of emotions and desires that Rebecca cannot even begin to navigate. And she does not possess – what? The courage, or even the ability to change that.

No one else looks in Marlin's direction. No one else is even standing up. Laying down her blanket, Rebecca takes her place on the floor.

They just lie there.

And lie there.

She imagines herself being squashed under the weight of the humid air above her. When she gets up she will be flat, like a cartoon character after a landslide. It brings a kind of madness, not to know what is going to happen or how long the waiting will last.

They lie there.

Rebecca becomes aware of the breathing of the people around her. The air, which seemed fresh, now begins to give up its subtle smells. Dust: the dust of neglect which has gathered in this long-empty space, the dust of desiccated wood, and the grime from the cars and trucks whizzing by outside. And there are all the chemicals downstairs, diluted by time but ever-present as an undertone.

Rebecca's hand sneaks out to the side of her blanket and touches the floorboards. There is rough, worn-down wood, punctuated with the occasional broad-headed nail and something else. Tiny spikes are sticking up out of the floor. *Insurance.* She runs her fingernail over one of the spikes. It is too hard to be a splinter. It is metal. *Tetanus.* She longs to take a proper look but knows this must not be allowed.

Wanting to look when she's unable to look makes her feel even crazier. She retracts her hand and places it on her stomach for a moment, then links the other hand with it and moves them higher, to a point above her breasts. Then she separates her hands and puts them down by her sides again.

The floor hurts. She needs to pee.

"Stillness." Marlin's voice breaks in just as the feeling becomes unbearable. "Stillness is the hardest thing to achieve, yet it is essential to The Work. We will not begin to move until we find stillness." It is her, Rebecca. She is the one not being still. She should not have moved her hands. Rebecca blushes hot and presses her hands on the floor by her sides.

"So, we begin."

Marlin stops talking. Rebecca hears him circulating among the rows of bodies. She wants to raise herself on one elbow and find out where he is.

Heads down! She is in school, now. Someone has been bad, and they all have to put their heads on their desks. Miss Graves walks between the rows, occasionally smacking her ruler next to one of them. Rebecca's ears hurt in advance each time Marlin's footsteps approach, preparing to hear a thunderous crack. There is no floor under her any more. There is no loft, no dusty breeze. There is the desk, her folded arms against her forehead. There is the teacher approaching and receding, the anticipation of shock twitching up and down her back. There is the shallowness of her breath, the fear.

Pee. She needs to pee. And it is back: the feeling of hot pee leaking down her thigh and dripping into her shoe. And the complete, scarlet humiliation that made her curl into a ball and not speak to anyone for the rest of that day. No one was able to convince her to sit up straight until it was time to get on the school bus and her sister dragged her out indignantly by the coat-sleeve, muttering "space cadet!"

Is it happening now? Or is this a memory she is feeling, as *if* it were now? Rebecca's muscles clench and twitch with the desire to curl in on herself. *Stillness is essential in our Work.* Marlin said to be still. She is still, or at least makes herself *lie* still, but that, Rebecca knows, is not what he meant. She is doing it wrong. She *is* wrong, for having so many thoughts crowding her mind. Rebecca's head pounds, her ears rush. The floor hurts. Her bladder feels like it is made of molten metal. If it hurts, that meant she didn't pee just now. Good. But how long will this go on? The classroom. Needing to pee. Maybe all the kids are in trouble because she peed. For Rebecca it is all part of one experience; she cannot remember what was cause, what was effect, what was then, what is now. There is only this feeling of humiliation, and it has to do with her body, and waiting for a blow.

Marlin's voice: "On the floor, we're all children. Paupers and kings, black and white, red and yellow, woman and man: we're all the same. Renew your acquaintance with the floor. Feel it supporting you."

He can see through her. Rebecca clings to his voice, longs, in the silences, for him to go on speaking.

"Everybody: as the next breath goes out, make an earth sound. Earth sound please." Rebecca takes a bigger breath than usual, but a silent one. That is as much as she can muster. Now, she remembers where she is. A rehearsal hall – yes, it is – albeit an illegal one with smashed windows. And these are actors around her, filling the space with their grunts and growls, taking away the air she needs. Gritty, barbaric sounds rumble around her. Rebecca has to struggle to keep from clenching her fists; her jaw clenches instead. Actors can follow their impulses. She can't. They'd probably even pee at this moment, let it all out. Rebecca would never do a thing like that.

That's what makes her a servant and them the masters. That's why she thinks about tetanus and broken ladders and cleaning up years' worth of dirt in an entranceway that others walk right through. She is too busy fixing things to growl.

They'd win any battle, these people around her. If it came to hand-to-hand combat Rebecca knows they would fight to the death, while she would hold back and let herself be killed. It seems, all of a sudden, as if she *were* in combat: for air, for the right to make sounds. She is losing.

"Bring it down please. Very nice. Quieter now, bring it down. Air now. Simply air." Marlin breathes audibly. "Yes. Air sound now. Yes."

The feet are coming nearer. Rebecca finds it hard to draw breath, and she realizes she is trying not to cry. Marlin's feet stop next to Rebecca. The frustration of not being able to make a sound rises inside her, the loneliness of not being able to share it. She is falling, helpless, into a deep well of feelings she has known all her life. Tears drip on either side of her face. Relief and shame are one, as her bladder lets go, too. All that work to hold it in a little water. Why? Why not simply do what she must do?

Marlin kneels and passes an astonishingly soft hand over her hair. Stroking it back from her face, stroking her tears out of the way. "Now," Marlin says, "A simple sound. Ahhhh."

Air surges into Rebecca's lungs and a gutteral *Ahhhh* is heard around her. She cannot claim it as her own; it is too elemental, too ravenous a sound. Yet she partakes in it. It enters her as much as it leaves her; it is as much hers as it belongs to all of them.

"Yes." Marlin says. "Everyone, please."

"Ahhhh." Her breath is theirs. Her breath is her own. Rebecca is sobbing. Marlin stays beside her. He sees her need, forgives her for it. He stays with her until she's finished crying, then says, "Connie, Bill: make her comfortable will you?"

Rebecca feels strong arms roll her to her side. A dusty-smelling blanket is moved under her head, another heavy one placed on top of her. She is dripping with sweat, her jeans warm and pungent. The woman she met this morning lies in front of her and the man curls around her from behind, legs conforming to the bend of Rebecca's knees, one arm draped over her waist. Their sweat mingles. Nothing is expected of her. She rests between these two people as if they were all animals in a barn.

The session continues. Sounds go from low and bestial to sonorous, to birdlike, then back down again, but they seem less threatening, now. She is one of these people, one *with* them. A sweet, nourishing sensation approaches. Rebecca has felt it before, but cannot remember when. It is sound, refreshing sleep.

The man behind Rebecca gently rocks her shoulder, and the woman turns and whispers: "We're finishing up!" Rebecca sits up groggily and they remove the blankets around her. Everyone is stacking blankets in orderly fashion in the corner.

"You did great today," Connie says. "Your first day. Had a breakthrough."

"That was good?"

"Yeah, I know it can be uncomfortable at first. But it comes around to everyone eventually. And when it happens to you, it's good for all of us." Connie pulls a long-sleeved shirt out of her bag and hands it to Rebecca.

Tears cloud Rebecca's vision as she ties the shirt around her waist, concealing the wet spot on her jeans. Connie rolls up her blanket. "We can wash this at home." Rebecca just nods, too tired and grateful to feel ashamed.

Bill says, "We all give a donation …" A line of people are putting money in a cracked pottery bowl next to the stack of blankets. Rebecca panics: she has nothing! She is a thief, stealing this … Journey, as they call it … stealing it from Marlin. She reaches in her pocket and produces a tissue, tries again and finds a mashed twenty-dollar bill she forgot ages ago and obviously laundered. She feels blessed. She hands it to Bill, who nods and takes it to the bowl.

Connie explains that they often meet for breakfast at Gale's restaurant down the street. Cheap food. Clean bathroom. "He doesn't mind if we rush in after the Journey to use it."

"A bathroom would help ..."

"Well," says Connie, "the guys have it easy as usual. They can just unzip anywhere and let it go." They laugh. Together.

One by one, the others file down the ladder. Marlin paces back and forth some distance away. No one says goodbye but they all glance his way before their heads disappear into the hole. Rebecca follows suit, just as her foot seeks the rung that will take her eyes below floor level. It only takes a moment, long enough for her to glimpse Marlin's silhouette as he turns to walk the other way. *I see you here.* Rebecca sees it too: somewhere between the powerful voice and diminutive body, between the eloquent words and the paper-clipped glasses, she might just find her place.

Google Books

Motherdreams: Stories of Love and Loss
by Constance Herbert
Fanshawe House, 2010
320 pages
GET THIS BOOK

Acknowledgments

This is a book for, by and about women, yet my biggest thanks go to two men.

Bill Stronach: you were my friend, then my sweetheart, then my lover, then my friend again. Now you're my husband – and all the other things, still. When you kissed me behind the portable in Grade Four I punched you and my own hand bled. Your kiss felt like home, yet I felt like you had stolen something. Later, I realized it was choice. My course in life had been set too early. And yet, sitting beside you outside the Vice Principal's office that afternoon, our hands found each other, and I knew who I was: the person who holds hands with you.

For all we have been to one another we never became parents. And the way we helped each other through it has made this book possible.

Marlin Lewis: what can I say? It is your gaze I miss most. You watched us with the love we all wish our parents could give us, but often could not. We were free to explore, yet we were never alone. It was that gaze that helped us see ourselves. In a life that felt con-fined, you showed me there was always space: for more learning, more growth. You pushed Bill and me over a precipice. By letting go, we found solid ground. By befriending with the seeds of human aggression, we truly found a way to end all wars.

This is a book about letting go of the dream of motherhood. My own story of multiple miscarriages is only one small part. There are stories by women who gave up their children for adoption, some who lost children to death and family rupture, some who could not conceive to begin with. Gathering these stories and telling my own I kept hearing Marlin's words.

[pages 4-320 are not shown]

1984

All mine, Rebecca thought, closing the door of her new apartment behind her. During her time in the city she had moved from one boarding house room to another as properties were sold, roommates came and went, cockroaches infested and exterminators tried, with their peppery-smelling sprays, to get rid of them. To no avail. Rebecca chose rooms in the large, Victorian houses near the university campus. They were full of students who had nothing in common with her. The rooms were also overpriced but, never wanting to invest the time in apartment-hunting, she kept taking the first place that came along. Rebecca walked the creaking floors every night, working as hard as she could the next day, step by step getting good enough, she did not know for what.

But after signing her contract with the Simcoe Thespians, Rebecca got up her nerve to answer one of the ads in the back of a newspaper she pored over every week. *Now: Toronto's News and Entertainment Voice*. Just like *The Village Voice* in New York! This newspaper was about everything she aspired to in her new city. Calling the number in the ad made her part of the world of grungy sophistication it offered.

Venturing west of her usual stomping ground, she found a place on Shaw Street, north of Bloor. It consisted of one room with a closet, a bathroom and a galley kitchen. The bathroom tiles were coated with mold, the tub, tacky and stained. On all the walls, yellow paint showed through a peeling layer of white. Work would make this place hers. For the first week she cleaned, repaired and painted, sleeping on a camping mat on the floor and going for meals to a nearby diner on Bloor Street. When the parquet had been glued down and shined, the kitchen covered with a new layer of press-on tiles, the bathroom scrubbed free of its stains and smelling like bleach and vinegar, it was time to buy furniture. Rebecca made a trip to the Goodwill warehouse. The store was full of gorgeous, quirky things that no one wanted and that she, Rebecca, could buy – cheap – and have the pleasure of fixing up. It was like building a set, establishing herself in her apartment, the set where her new life would unfold. She let old copies of *Now* and *Theatre Crafts Magazine* accumulate beside the fold-out couch where she slept. She proudly watched the pile grow taller, a reflection of what she did with her time, what she did with her couch. But she washed her dishes lovingly and scrubbed the bathroom floor every day to keep the pristine whiteness that she had worked so long to achieve.

Rebecca took the Bathurst bus up to work every day, staring out the window so she could memorize this part of her new city. Back home in Quebec, an hour's ride would have taken her past fields and farmhouses, through towns where the buildings had wooden staircases clinging to their sides. Here, she watched downtown apartment buildings give way to the Tudor homes of Forest Hill, then to bungalows, strip malls and parking lots. In the midst of all the traffic and construction there were families walking together at a dignified pace, the women in long skirts, the men in coats and hats. Even the children were formally dressed. The city was pushing up and out, paving and tidying as it went. All summer, Rebecca felt light, borne along by possibilities.

Her younger sister Janice called every night or two to talk about the election, and the prospect that "Lyin' Brian" Mulroney would get in. "First Thatcher, then Reagan. Now the fascists are coming here. We're headed for the dark ages!" As if they had planned it in advance, Sarah, her older sister, would call immediately afterwards to tell her about the new era of prosperity they could look forward to with a Conservative landslide. Rebecca didn't care about any of this, and for once, her family's superior grasp of politics didn't make her feel like a fool. Rebecca Weir, Stage Manager had a show to put on.

To escape their calls, she ambled around her neighbourhood, inhaling the smells from the meat store and bakery (*Talho, Padaria*), studying the windows as if they were museum displays. Everything stayed open so late. Even as the dark was gathering, fruit was still laid out in baskets on the sidewalk. Sometimes she'd eat an apple as she walked, rolling the taste of smog and exhaust and the waxy residue of the box in which it had travelled – far from its orchard – around her mouth with every bite. There were furniture stores displaying bedroom sets with built-in night tables and headboards upholstered in coloured leather. The neighbourhood had several bridal shops, too, their windows crowded with mannequins. Rebecca stared at them with fascination but not longing. Marriage was not in her plans. Marriage, to Rebecca, meant one thing, sharing her apartment, her stuff. And right now, all she could think of was: *mine*.

But all that changes after Rebecca's first day at SenseInSound. She gets home from her first Journey wanting nothing more than to lie down. She doesn't even pull out the couch to make her bed but lies straight on the floor. Eventually, she gets up and nibbles some bread, walks vaguely around the apartment. She feels eagerness and anticipation all over her skin. She unfolds the couch, lies down, and sleeps fitfully, in her warm bath of desire, until the next day's Journey.

The second morning she reunites gratefully with the floor. Marlin tells them to first be still, then to make sounds that they associate with each of the elements: earth, air, fire and water. Rebecca is silent. She wants only to feel the floor, and her desire. As Marlin talks, she tries to anticipate what will happen. Marlin will come down her row, now. Marlin will touch her. Where will the touch come? On her head, on her hand? Maybe her thigh. Each part comes alive as she imagines Marlin's fingers on it.

Risk keeps us alive.

She has never been so alive.

Marlin passes her row. He doesn't touch her.

We all yearn for it. Even you, Rebecca.

Rebecca yearns. All her life she has been yearning to yearn.

On the way home that afternoon, she passes the Elections Canada sign outside the library, hears her sisters' voices arguing in her head. "Go away!" she answers aloud. It feels like *they* are the ones disturbing her stillness, making her into the person Marlin does not touch, keeping her apart and alone. She needs to lie down.

When the phone rings that afternoon, she rises so quickly from her bed that a harsh pain springs up behind her eyes. It's her sister Janice, of course.

"Did you vote yet?"

"I'm not voting."

"Do you realize how women have struggled for this? You're trampling on –"

"You are trampling on *me*!"

"What are you talking about?"

"Stop. Stop phoning me. I'm waiting for a call."

When the phone rings again a few minutes later, she picks it up and holds it in the air long enough to identify the voice of her other sister, Sarah, buzzing on the other end of the line. Then she quietly puts it down again.

Rebecca does not call the number Sylvia gave her. *There's a girl, Martie.* Does not call Martie. *Tuesday, Wednesday you'll call.* It's Thursday; it's Friday. Each morning Rebecca feels drawn back to the warehouse. Embarrassing, confusing though they might be, the Journeys give her back a part of herself.

What do you want to be when you grow up?

I don't know.

Her eyes went blurry when Dr. Delman in her cardigan and pearls started in on those questions. It was obvious to Rebecca: Dr. D. was looking for some connection between the death of their father when she was four, and her stupidity in school.

"Not stupidity, Rebecca. Don't put yourself down like that! You know you can be anything you want to be. Why don't you draw me a picture of something you want?"

"Nothing."

"Can you tell me what you're feeling right now?"

"I don't know."

That is all over now: that block between Rebecca and others, between Rebecca and her feelings. It is nothing she can put into words, but this thing that everyone at SenseInSound calls "The Work" is like a taproot reaching down to her essence: an unquenchable loneliness, a longing that will never be satisfied.

After a week of Journeys, Rebecca's period starts. She doesn't recognize the feeling at first, and stains her jeans before she realizes what is going on. Normally, her periods are scanty and irregular, as if she had never quite got up and running, as a woman. Her sisters always flowed together; she was out of phase, out of step. Now, a rich, full-blooded feeling suffuses her, and she is grateful. She rushes to the corner store and buys an assortment of supplies, arranges them around her on her bed.

Arriving at the warehouse the next day, Rebecca immediately finds her spot on the floor. She breathes deeply. Stillness. Yes, she is still. Her limbs feel heavy. She has surrendered: to gravity, to her body. To The Work. When Marlin calls for "earth sounds," she begins growling. The sound vibrates through her, softening her muscles so that she seems to merge with the floor and into the mass of others who voice with her. For a week, her sounds flow, her blood and tears flow. She is still.

The day the bleeding stops, Rebecca feels clear-headed. As the rest of the group fold their blankets, she remains sitting. Instead of enumerating what needs to be done she examines the wood floor around her. She runs her finger over one of the boards, exploring its surface like skin. The sharp points, she realizes, are the tips of sewing machine needles. This was once a garment factory, probably a sweatshop. The workers must have just left them on the ground when they broke. Over time, they embedded themselves in the wood. A magnet – that's what she needs – and a fine set of pliers. She will clear them all, one by one. Later, as the others make their way down the ladder she strides across to where Marlin is pacing. "I need –" she says. He stops and grins, as if delighted with some secret part of herself she were revealing, only to him.

"Yes, Rebecca. What do you need?"

"Pliers. Have you got some?"

Marlin makes a show of patting his thighs, even though there are no pockets in his drawstring pants. He shakes his head. "No. Have you?"

"At home, yes."

"Okay then. Let's go to your home."

Let's go to your home. The words are out, but Rebecca cannot believe she's heard them because Marlin is acting like he didn't say anything. He drops his gaze and frowns, scanning the floor in his usual way. He makes no move to go anywhere. With Marlin, there is a moment's pause before any word, any eye contact: a moment of decision. He bestows his attention, doesn't spill it all over the place. Not like Rebecca. For every bit of Marlin's stillness, Rebecca feels a corresponding amount of agitation within herself. He draws stillness over himself like a veil, destroying her own in the process. Did he really say he wanted to go home with her? Maybe she is just making it up, hearing what she wants to hear. Rebecca looks down at her feet while the others leave the building, knowing that each person who descends the ladder is glancing at them silhouetted against the windows. Though Marlin is not even looking at Rebecca, it must appear to everyone else that she's got his attention. Triumph surges within her as she thinks about this, then she clamps down and doesn't let herself enjoy it. Because she might not have the right to. She's already heard Marlin's warning many times: *assumptions and expectations violate The Now.*

When they are all gone, Rebecca takes a deep breath and makes for the hole in the floor. Marlin moves quietly. She has to glance over her shoulder to know if he is following her at all. Down the ladder, down the stairs, out of the building and up to the subway. There are eleven stops. Then two blocks up to her apartment building. Rebecca carries herself stiffly. Marlin trails a little behind, always at the edge of her vision. He wavers this way and that along the sidewalk, slowing his pace, sometimes, to look in a window. It seems that he might change his mind at any time, turn around and go back the way they came. There is trouble in his face as he looks over his glasses, his eyes roving over everything, sometimes taking in Rebecca. Sometimes he mutters a few words she cannot hear. She wants, more than anything else, for the muttering – and the trouble – to be about *her*. But she knows nothing, nothing about what Marlin thinks or feels or wants, nothing about anything, any more.

As soon as he gets to her apartment Marlin sits on the couch. Rebecca pours him a glass of juice, which he drinks thirstily. She refills the glass and he gulps it down. She watches his Adam's apple move in his throat, wishing she were the glass resting on his lip, wishing she were the juice he is taking into himself. He gets up, now, and walks around investigating the apartment, arms folded over his chest. Rebecca follows him – more or less. She is careful never to come too close. Now, the tiles of the parquet floor seem nothing but ways of measuring how far she is from Marlin. He examines the pictures on the walls, the carefully dusted books and scripts she's accumulated on the shelves. At last, he looks her way. "Is the bookshelf built in?"

"Yup! I made it myself." Encouraged by Marlin's nod, she tells him about the challenge of fitting the shelves to the odd measurements of the room. Marlin goes up close to examine them over the tops of his glasses. He walks away by himself, humming and pacing back and forth then turns to look at Rebecca, his arms folded across his chest. He grins at her, which brings some relief. Not much, though. She cannot depend on Marlin's smiles or anything else about him. There is always the chance he'll make for the door.

But he doesn't leave. He sits back down on the couch and nods at the space beside him. This is it. She takes a deep breath and sits down, not quite touching him but still feeling his heat, and crosses one knee over the other, both hands clamped between her thighs. He looks ahead, frowning. She wants nothing but to attract and keep his attention from one moment to the next. The best way to do this is to get him to touch her. But how to start? He seems so tentative about being there at all that if she made the first move it would ruin everything. She concentrates on making herself available. Or rather, *feeling* available and hoping he senses it, because she cannot not show it too much.

They sit forever on the couch, Rebecca's hands growing increasingly numb, Marlin staring off into the distance over his glasses. She is thirsty. Then thirstier. When she can't stand it anymore, Rebecca untangles her legs and gets up. After taking a few steps she feels hands grasping her around the waist from behind. Marlin has got up too. His hands are on either side of her, turning her toward him. The motion is quick and rough. She has to move into the turn so that her shirt does not chafe her skin. Then they are kissing, half way between the kitchen and the couch and four tiles from the wall. Marlin's hands are under Rebecca's arms, beside her breasts. Hers are on his shoulders. Rebecca barely feels the kiss.

Rebecca is kissing Marlin, she thinks. Not *Marlin is kissing Rebecca*. She must not make him the active party, even in her mind. Must not even think of herself as "I" doing these actions. It would scare him away. From moment to moment she wonders: *Will we go on or stop? Does he want me or doesn't he? What does he intend?* His tongue goes into her mouth. For as long as the kiss goes on, she is not asking herself those questions. Then Marlin pulls back, panting, covering his chest with his crossed arms, and hurries out the door.

Now Rebecca's apartment becomes the scene of her waiting. And the telephone – the sleek olive green Contempraphone she decided to splurge on – is in the spotlight. The phone is now the thing she *expects* from, expects a call that does not come. And the door – with its chains and bolts and the vintage poster for *South Pacific* she bought in a used bookstore – that door became the place where *he* does not knock. Where Marlin does not knock. Even though it is not reasonable or right or even possible that he will call – much less arrive at her door – Rebecca expects Marlin. And the expectation is bound up with disappointment. Each night, Rebecca falls, alone, into a fitful sleep.

And each morning, she flings herself into the Journey. Her flesh feels new and hot and singing with nerves. She howls, gurgles, screeches, groans, makes other sounds she cannot name. For the duration of the Journey, she does not even know her own name. One day, Marlin gives a talk she thinks might be for her, though she can never be sure. It is about something he calls "dis-ease." Dis-ease happens when you hold in your emotions. The Work purges them. Rebecca understands she has allowed herself to become polluted with unexpressed emotion. The Work is cleansing her, and Marlin's voice guides her through the process, through the mysterious world inside her that she cannot navigate herself.

After each day's Journey, she takes her pliers and a magnet from her knapsack and sits on the floor pulling out needle tips while everyone else puts away the blankets and leaves. Marlin paces up and down, talking to himself, and eventually sits on the floor, cross-legged with his eyes closed. With all her senses alert, she waits for him to stir. When he stands up, she descends the ladder. Every day, Marlin follows her home. He talks about his plans for SenseIn-Sound. "We have got to find our own space before the cold weather comes. We can't go through another winter like last year travelling from basement to basement like refugees." His voice catches. "I can't put them all through that again." Rebecca's hand tingles, longing to touch Marlin. He raises his arms as if silencing a crowd. "We *need* a space. Then we'll be a real company. We'll be building up to something instead of just trying to survive. I won't force anyone to be part of it. Only those who feel truly committed will move with me. And those who don't, well: too bad for them."

Marlin springs up as if forced from the couch by this thought. His words are percussive, a door banging shut. His hands knot into fists. He means Amanda. Too bad for Amanda. Rebecca will move with Marlin. Anywhere. Those fists must never, ever be for her. Marlin begins pacing up and down. "I long for a space. I *ache* for it. Do you understand?" He turns to Rebecca as he says this, tilting his crotch forward as if the ache were located there. Rebecca nods, trying by her gravity to show Marlin that the space is as important to her as it is to him. If she wants the space as much as he does, then some of the longing Marlin feels for it might land on her.

It does not. Even though they are alone together, Marlin's voice is the same as the one he uses to talk to the whole group. There is nothing particular, nothing for her. The talk is followed by touching. His touch feels different from what she felt at her first Journey. His hands don't listen; they dictate which way she should go. They push and pull and turn her abruptly, position her as if she were a mannequin.

But she always wants more. From the kiss on the mouth to the touch on the breasts, from the touch on the breasts to lifting the shirt, from lifting the shirt to pulling her down to the couch. It is a story Rebecca wants more than sex. She hopes that Marlin's following her home day after day, that his kissing and fondling will add up to something. Nothing adds up. Marlin disavows connection, not just with Rebecca, but even with the movements of his own mouth and hands. His face is blank, his eyes forever looking past her shoulder. And she never knows when he will leave: mid-kiss, mid-caress, mid-sentence. Each moment stands divided from the next.

Be still. She is everything but still.

Honour the Now. She lives in The Yesterday, The Tomorrow, The Never-Will- Be. Alone, she is haunted by the memory of his hands stroking the hair back from her forehead. In her imagination, she hears his sonorous voice say things that she would be embarrassed to admit wanting. *I love you. Come live with me. Marry me.* She feels anxious to get to the next time, to get back to being with Marlin so that she will have another chance to be the kind of person who could make him say these things. But the kind of person who could make him say these things would not be anxious to hear them in the first place. She can't ask anything of Marlin. It's an unspoken taboo. If she does, he'll get angry, and … she must make sure she can never finish that thought.

Then one night – for no reason she understands – the clothes are off. They lie on the floor, which is cooler than the air but still sticky with their sweat. Marlin enters her, his whole body jerks a few times, then he pulls out abruptly, pinning her down with his weight. She is hollow, full of longing, on the brink. She thinks for a moment of grabbing his butt and pushing his dwindling erection into her. Instead, she leaves her hands outstretched on the floor, the cool surface of the parquet absorbing the heat from her palms, feeling a cold trickle down her thigh.

And then he's with her every night. She stays on after rehearsals, doing chores on a list that grows by two items for every one she ticks off. At dusk, she goes home, alone, to grab a sandwich, an apple, a few leaves of lettuce as she paces the apartment. To wait. Marlin arrives when he arrives. Sometimes she is in bed, and the intercom buzzes long and repeatedly as if he were in danger. The more nights Marlin spends with Rebecca the more his hunger for her grows. Aroused once, twice, three times, but quick to spend himself he sleeps briefly, then wakes again, priapic.

Rebecca has had one other lover. It happened over a summer, the last summer before she left Quebec. There was no question Luc would lick and stroke her whole body. She figured out a few comparable things to do for him, but truthfully, she found them embarrassing and preferred to be on the receiving end. She slipped out of that relationship as easily as she slipped in. Marlin, on the other hand, doesn't do anything for Rebecca. He *makes* things happen. Her own desire comes to fill the gaps in his lovemaking, transforming her into a fearsome, ravenous creature. He splits her open, makes all her juices flow. Marlin is part of her. There would be no getting away, even if she wanted to.

Rebecca's desire grows each time Marlin does nothing to satisfy her. Next time. It just makes the next time more urgent. When they are apart she fantasizes about addressing himself to her, to all her needs. When they are together she whispers in his ear, telling him how he turns her on. She is shocked to hear herself speaking this way, but the words pour out of her. She loves to taste his sweaty chest, loves to brush her body over his. He takes it all, silently, and after a few quick thrusts, falls asleep, leaving Rebecca with her left-over desire.

What is he like with Amanda? In her mind, she plays over and over again the scene of them together at the cast party. She remembers his hand on Amanda's waist, their bodies conforming to one another as they turned to go. Does she remember, or is she just imagining that as he kissed Amanda on the top of the head, he breathed in the smell of her hair for a moment, leaned his cheek where he had planted the kiss? *Too bad for them.* Marlin is furious with Amanda for leaving, yet she occupies a central place for him. Rebecca is the one he spends every night with, yet she is still on the fringes of his life.

What is he like with Amanda? She can hardly bear to think about it, yet goes there in the moments after Marlin falls asleep, when she's left trying to calm her own ragged breath. Imagines a glimpse of flesh, the skin of two arms entwined, sometimes a breast, a dark flash of pubis. Can't go there, because – as far away as she is – Amanda infuses every daylight hour. Must go there, to tip herself over the brink as she rubs herself against a fold of sheet. Her tiny or-gasm is a bodily function. A siphoning off of the worst of the ache. So she can get to tomorrow. To next time.

They get up at six every morning. In silence, Marlin eats the breakfast she prepares, then leaves. And she goes back to bed and dozes for a while, arriving for the Journey at 10 a.m. Marlin and The Work have become fused, for Rebecca. Mornings are spent listening to his voice, exploring the longing at the core of herself. There are discoveries all the time, and no one day is like any other. Like any day she's ever known. Marlin's visits in the evenings are an exten-sion of this, each moment imbued with significance as she wonders what he is going to do next. Even the weather seems to have been affected by what Rebecca is going through. It is still unseasonably warm. Fall is being impossibly staved off.

Rebecca saved enough in the summer to last her for two months.

She thought it would be plenty, that she'd have a job by October. But she has not looked for a job, and soon her money is going to run out. She knows she should be going to shows and hanging around afterwards, getting to know more people in the city, but it would disturb the seamless routine that her days and nights have fallen into. She cannot look for a job any more than she can ask Marlin to buy groceries for breakfast, to clean up afterwards or even help fold the pullout couch. It would mean bringing attention to what they are doing, admitting that there is something going on. Even looking at want-ads means crossing a line. It is not just that she'd be trying to work somewhere other than SenseInSound. Thinking ahead at all is a kind of betrayal, a violation of The Now. She is worried about money – but only in the moments when she first wakes up, before the huge event of Marlin's arrival in her life comes into focus again. She loves him all the more for the way he banishes her practical nature, turns her into a woman willing to risk anything for love. One day she finds a scrap of paper in the back pocket of her jeans. First she wonders if it is a bus ticket, then decides it's a napkin before realizing it is Martie's business card, softened by many launderings. Martie. Le Coupe. *My husband likes to give people a chance.* It all belongs to a world she has outgrown, a world as flimsy and frayed as the card she rolls into ball before throwing it in the garbage bin.

Then it happens, the night when Marlin does not arrive. At first, she thinks he is just running late, then it is one a.m., later than he's ever shown up before. Rebecca paces the apartment. Eventually, she forces herself to go to bed. She lies awake, scouring the air for sounds that might indicate his arrival. By straining her ears she can make out a few cars going by on nearby streets. There's a siren in the distance. Footsteps approach, recede. Then there's silence.

Will he arrive now? Now? Now? Maybe it isn't too late.

But the blankness she hears comes more and more to signify that Marlin is not going to arrive, tonight, or ever again. She drifts into half-sleep and is awakened by thunder, a cold wind blowing over her body. The situation feels inevitable – and weirdly familiar – yet this does not stop it from being frightening. In Marlin's place in her bed there's a precipice. She clings to her own side to stop herself from falling into what she knows is a bottomless abyss.

No. She must not feel this way. She clenches her jaw to stop herself from shaking, gets up and closes the window. The sky is getting light. She makes herself a coffee, stares at what would be the sunrise if it weren't pouring with rain. She will go to the Journey this morning, as usual. She must not be the kind of person who would be stopped by this, the kind of person who lingers in the feeling that lay beside her last night. If she allows it in, it will never let her go. There are two people in this relationship. Marlin may be done with her, but she's not finished with him. If she keeps her side going, it does not have to end. The sadness and rage she feels can never be mentioned. She doesn't even have the right to feel them, anyway, because no agreement has been broken. The past few weeks may be everything to her but they are nothing in the outside world.

It works. The structure of the routine holds her up: going to the warehouse, climbing the stairs. And once she is there, everyone helps. Marlin stays by the windows, not opening the fresh wound she has barely covered up to come here. Amanda is back and greets her with a hug. Seeing Amanda, Rebecca is blindsided by relief – a relief she can't explain and doesn't want to analyze. After the Journey, Connie invites Rebecca to lunch. Before she has a chance to think about an answer Connie takes her by the arm, directing her toward the newly repaired ladder before she can look in Marlin's direction. Rebecca goes down the ladder first.

A few days later, as she lies on the floor breathing in synch with the others, Marlin approaches and kneels beside her. He places one hand on either side of her ribs and compresses as she exhales, releases as she inhales, making space for deeper and deeper breathing. It is nauseating; all he has to do is touch her in this expert way and she feels good. It is nothing but mechanics, having to do with the pumping of ribs, the capacity of lungs to take in breath. Is there tenderness in his touch? Yes. But it is a professional tenderness. For weeks she has craved this sensitivity, yet it is only present now because touching her is of no significance to him. Yet she is amazed by it, by the air flowing – free and cool – in and out of her body, and by Marlin's power to bestow this on her. It is clear to her; anyone with that kind of power must be followed, must be stayed with, no matter how bad it feels.

She is sitting on her couch a few nights later when the intercom rings. "Yes?" she answers. There is a fierce burst of static on the other end of the line. Tentatively, she goes back to the couch. A wild ringing calls her back. She presses the "listen" button: "Rebecca! It's me!" The voice is a reprimand. She lets Marlin in.

Rebecca stands in her nightgown, cardigan and work socks at the door of the apartment, holding it open as Marlin makes his way grimly toward her down the hall. He dips his head in greeting when he sees her. She opens the door and stands aside. Marlin entwines his fingers in his hair and paces. "Damn! God*damn* it!" he mutters. Rebecca stands back, feeling she must staunch his anger and not knowing how. Finally, she leads him gently to the couch where he collapses in the crook of the arm she extends over his shoulders. "She's pregnant!" he sobs.

Gesendet: 28/12/2011. 6:43 a.m.
An: Director@Graddrama.UToronto.ca
Von: AmAndAm@gmail.com

Betreff: The Truth

Dr. Charbonneau,

You say if I talked to you it would give some shape to my memories, make sense of them for the good of both of us. But first, the experience would have to be in the past.

There was a time … when was it? I was sitting across from Marlin at a table. It was early – frighteningly early – in our time together. I remember wondering: "Why do I feel so terrible right now?" And then telling myself I had no right to feel bad. And telling myself it was my problem in various ways. And feeling even more terrible. There was a web of glances and shades of meaning and tones of voice that added up to the message: "You're not important." I knew that web was there, but I could not see it. And I thought, as if bobbing up to the surface for just one gulp of air: "When I can understand what he's doing, it'll be over." And then I went under again. For years. And now it's too late to go back and dissect that conversation. Feelings linger when words are long gone.

It's over, I told myself. In a new bed, next to a new lover, in a new country, living a new story. It was good. Real. But in the supposedly safe hollow of the blankets, I heard accusations of betrayal like a fire alarm clanging in my head. As if Marlin were right there with us. In a way, he was. His words still shaped the way I saw my own life. *It's over.* In the blasting sun, an hour's drive north of the city, looking into a hole in the ground. I took the shovel and threw my weight into it, grunting and sweating as I tossed chunks of dirt on the pine box below. But the hole was so big. There was no way to cover it all in. I had just slipped away, never properly ended things. Now it was too late.

We don't have to finish it, my son said, leading me away.

He was a wise child. He became a wise man. It's still not over.

Yours truly,
Amanda M.

1975-1984

Falling behind.

Rebecca heard the phrase daily while she was in school. All that sitting had been torture for her, cramming her long legs under the desk, trying to keep still while she strained and twitched like a confined racehorse. With difficulty, she made it to high school, but was soon bringing home notes advising "extra help." She didn't so much fail her classes as fade from them. Inertia set in with the first homework assignment. She'd notice something around the house that needed doing – like touching up paint on the porch rail – and that led her to realize just how uneven the steps were. The unfolding series of tasks would shut out all else, especially the sound of voices, scolding, nagging, begging her to get her homework done.

That's your problem. There was a constant campaign to identify Rebecca's problem. Sarah, eight years Rebecca's senior, called her "obsessive-compulsive," "passive-aggressive," and sometimes "blocked." Janice – only eighteen months younger than Rebecca and dividing her attention between tormenting Rebecca and cozying up to Sarah – which often amounted to the same thing – clung to the trusty moniker of "space cadet." Their mother, Audrey, responded to Rebecca's problem with a single phrase: "Get on with it!" Yet there was nothing any of them could do because Rebecca herself was helpless in the face of her problem. School just didn't work. Rebecca didn't work.

There were tests: colours to match, blocks to put in holes. Later, there were reams of multiple-choice questionnaires. The result: she was normal. In other words, lazy. Then came the long drives to see Dr. Delman, who put on soft music, gave her picture books to look at. Rebecca wasn't fooled. Dr. D. was trying to soften her up for the questions.

What do you want, Rebecca?

Nothing.

Yet Dr. D. eventually pronounced that she was normal. This meant she was stubborn, and liked wasting people's time and money.

"That's your problem, Rebecca. Mom lets you off the hook!" Sarah said. Sarah was always making sacrifices for her. When she was articling, worked to the bone, she still flew in from Vancouver every few months to "help out" with the project of fixing Rebecca.

"You think you can stay here forever and live off her. You've got to get out."

Getting out was a big one, too. She heard time and time again that there were no opportunities in Quebec. Businesses were getting out. Professionals were getting out. Home was a sinking ship.

It's not that Rebecca ignored all these admonitions; they just fell into the background once she had a job to do. There was so much to organize around their house. Janice adored garage sales and flea markets. Being surrounded by old things, she said, fueled her imagination, and this was obviously paying off with the poetry prizes and essay contests she was winning. The house was also full of clothes and books deposited by Sarah, who – despite having gotten out – passed through the house every few months like a tidal wave, leaving a coating of junk on every surface. And there were her mother's seed catalogues and gardening supplies, which came inside the house for the winter for some reason instead of staying in the shed where they belonged. Rebecca needed to know where everything belonged. She built shelves and cubby holes and storage bins as if under a spell.

One night, her mother knocked on her bedroom door. Rebecca

loved the way Audrey always knocked before coming in to a room.
She wished people would knock on doors, everywhere she went.
She wished she *had* a door to close, everywhere she went.

Audrey walked over to the bed and arranged her long legs with
care as she sat. She looked down at her hands, clasped on top of her
knees and said, "Have you given any thought to where you might
want to live?"

"Here."

"I mean, when you grow up."

"I don't know."

"You've got to get on with things, Rebecca. You're almost twenty
years old. If school is not for you, then you have to get a job." She
paused between sentences. No doubt she had planned the whole
lecture with Sarah and was reassembling the exact phrases she was
supposed to use. Rebecca felt like her eyelids had weights on them.

"Can we talk about this tomorrow?"

"What do you want in life, Rebecca?"

"Nothing!"

Wrong answer. Sarah was in the room now too, lecturing her
about the importance of goals.

But it was true. There were so many things she was supposed to
want: clothes, makeup, shoes. A boyfriend. Mostly that. Boyfriends
were the main preoccupation for Sarah and her friends, who spent
hours in Sarah's room, planning whatever dates were on the horizon. Janice lingered in a corner for a few years, then eventually
joined in the discussion. Rebecca tried to take part but all she could
really do was listen, nonplussed, to the complex round of strate-
gizing and interpreting that kept them up late into the night, their
formidable minds applied to the task of understanding Guys, that
species so foreign in their household. Sometimes they dressed Rebecca up, consulting articles on how to mask a problem figure. But
they lost interest when she stood dolefully in place, never sharing in
their giggles, waiting for it to be over.

Now there was this career business. Really, all she wanted to do
was stay around The Property (as they called their house and the

five acres of land it stood on) and help her mother. There were fences to maintain, dry branches to trim from the trees. Snow to shovel six months of the year. Most of all, she loved being near Audrey with her husky voice and fresh-air-and bonfire smell. Her height. They literally saw eye-to-eye. Audrey didn't hug or kiss Rebecca like other mothers she had seen, didn't linger long enough anywhere to be cuddled up to; Rebecca's best hope for being close to her mother was to work beside her in the garden. She loved turning over the soil, planting, weeding, saying a few words here and there but mostly just working side-by-side. *Weeding vegetables is not a career.* She could hear Sarah's voice in her mind.

Now, all that was over.

"Tough love!" Sarah pronounced, the next day at breakfast. They were sending Rebecca away. She watched while they loaded her bedding and a suitcase full of clothes into the car. Then they drove the eight miles to Town, where everyone nearby did their shopping and churchgoing and banking, and where the kids were bused for school. They left her in a room in the attic of a musty smelling house, saying she could come home soon, but only for a visit. Rebecca accepted it silently, a lump in her throat.

For a month, she worked part-time at a *dépanneur* on the highway, but the cold lights of the store did something to Rebecca's eyes. Whenever she went to make change, her vision blurred. One day, facing a lineup of six people, she simply left the store, unlocked, and went back to the house to sleep. The next day she was home. Feeling alert for the first time all month she began replacing some rotten boards on the porch.

Then came the autobody shop. "There is nothing wrong with the trades!" said Sarah. "You've got to embrace this opportunity. It's your last chance." Within a week she was home. Home. There was a bakery, too, and even a hardware store, all ending more or less the same way. Month after month her family piled the same items in the car and tried to plant her elsewhere. Without success.

"It's like *The Incredible Journey*," said Janice. "You're just like that dog making its way home no matter what." But it was Janice, already

– at a precocious age – enrolled at nearby Bishop's University, who found Rebecca a job that stuck. A professor named Ian Hope had been brought in to teach a seminar course. He was a famous director from Toronto. "A complete weirdo," Janice said, tilting her head significantly in Rebecca's direction. "He makes us call him Professor Hope even though he doesn't have a degree in anything. School of Life, he keeps saying, as if he's pissed off at *us*! Even though we're paying his salary with our fees. He keeps talking about how he's such an urbanite and can't live anywhere but in a city. So what does he do? He buys an old rundown farmhouse an hour's drive from school.

"Thing is …" she said drawing the words out, "Thing *is* … He's afraid to drive!"

Rebecca could drive.

On Mondays, Wednesdays and Thursdays, she picked up Professor Hope, took him to campus and back in his station wagon, which she then drove home. It was hers to use between times; plus she made a hundred dollars a week! She was more or less on call when Professor Hope needed something, usually a bottle of what he called "Malt" from Vermont. He insisted she go over the border to buy it because they had zero appreciation of whisky in this godforsaken place.

Rebecca didn't mind. She liked Jan-O, as he instructed her to call him by the second week. "It's the name my friends have for me. And you're my friend. My only friend in this cultural wasteland." Jan-O told her about *real* theatre. Theatre Alive, which Jan-O had founded in Toronto, had made collective creations, plays that grew from nothing but an idea, where everyone played all the roles, had an equal share. They had made a show about the battle of Amiens, which led to another called *Home Fires Burning* about young women widowed by World War One. They had made a show about schoolyard bullying which had toured schools around the country. But Theatre Alive had closed after ten years, at the height of its success. Why? Greed. And now he found himself here in this backwater. Rebecca was the only one he could turn to.

Jan-O looked like he was steadily puffing up week by week. His eyes became cloudy and a web of veins appeared on his cheeks. Rebecca took to checking his fridge when she dropped him off, supplying him with leftovers, sitting at the table to make sure he ate. On Sunday evenings, she called him with the excuse of confirming the week's pickups, knowing he'd be lonely after the long, solitary weekend. As Jan-O became more and more troubled, Rebecca felt her own strength growing, as if the role she played in his life was working its way inside.

"Oh, my Amazon! My great-hearted warrior!" he declared, and told her theatre stories until late at night.

He took to offering her a "drinkie," after she dropped him off in the evenings. His voice jumped to a childlike treble to pronounce the word. He encouraged Rebecca to taste three malts in a row, blending them with teaspoonfuls of water and describing their qualities with the same passion with which he spoke of the collective creations. She had seen the shocking prices, and allowed herself only the barest sip of each. Still, it was enough to make her head fuzzy and she grinned and sang to herself all the way home on the dark roads.

The next September, she audited a course in technical theatre. At the first meeting, a few students, vastly younger than her and ridiculously well dressed, stared at a wall of tools (all labeled) while Gary Curtis, the school's technical director, pointed to each. She had to lean forward to hear his voice, so soft it was almost a whisper. An enormous, grey-bearded man, his shoulders filled the doorframe when he walked into a room. Somehow, he managed to move silently in his steel-toed boots. He was even taller than Rebecca. *Okay. This might be okay.*

In a few months she'd rented a room in The Bastion, a mansion on top of the hill overlooking town. It was carpeted everywhere – including its four bathrooms and two kitchens – in something that resembled worn-down Astroturf. Her teenage habit of sleeping all day flipped to its opposite the minute she left home. She was consumed with a deep-down restlessness that made her unable to settle. She ranged around her room, pacing barefoot on the carpet, which was impregnated with dust. The only antidote was work. She went in to the theatre at seven in the morning, stayed there until eleven at night. Even on the days where she drove Jan-O, she returned to the theatre for an hour or two before going home. The Bastion was home, now. Theatre was home. Work was home.

She bought a pair of painter paints, like Gary's, and furnished the pockets with various things she had seen him produce from his own. Band Aids had been known to appear from those pockets, nail-clippers. A box of raisins came out once when someone felt dizzy in class. There was a square of sandpaper wrapped in plastic, even a sewing kit. There was a wrench (secured to his belt loop with hitch knots). And most importantly, a Swiss Army knife with two blades, a screwdriver, a corkscrew and an awl. Soon, her own belt loop was weighed down with keys to all the doors in the theatre. She began getting paid for stage-managing the plays the department put on, as well as some of the productions that rented the theatre in the course of the year. Then she acquired keys to the student union building (including the laundry room, so she could wash her clothes in the middle of the night!). By the spring, Gary had given her a portion of his office and was leaving her to supervise the first-year students in the carpentry shop when he needed time off.

And she got to sit by Jan-O for his scene study class. Yes, she actually sat still, and it did not bother her. This process had got hold of her: body and mind. Once in a while, Jan-O touched her wrist and she knew to make a note. Eventually, she didn't need him to do that. As her pencil slid over the paper, she felt enfolded with Jan-O in a cocoon of attention, both of them focused on the imaginary world under construction before them. Her awkwardness and incompetence began to seem like a coat she could take off as soon as she entered a theatre. She could – she must – do this all her life.

But then it was May, and Jan-O hosted a year-end party at his farmhouse. Rebecca sat by him at the kitchen table. After – she was counting – four shots of whisky and two beers, he stood up. "Welcome to the theatre, you fools!" he called, in a voice that would fill a football stadium. He flailed one hand in the air, a gesture for people to gather. "This place has broken me," he announced. "Tomorrow I'll be gone. You can all come and visit me in Stratford. Not on stage: at my B and B. I'm done with this stinking business."

That night, Jan-O put away twice his usual astonishing amount of booze. No one could outlast him. Rebecca, who'd been drinking water, sat with him at the table while people fell asleep on the floor and couches. She was desperate. It felt so right working with Jan-O that she could not believe it would ever end. But it was ending, and it felt like her life was about to end with it. Finally, they were the only ones awake. "I'm finished," he told her. "Taking this job in the first place meant I had given up. But you: you're too big for this place, you majestic girl. Find real theatre. Go to Toronto as soon as you can!"

Soon there was no car and no Jan-O to drive around, and the campus was empty for the summer. Gary took her out for a drink. "You can't stay here forever," he said, and Rebecca felt her throat tighten.

"There's a guy name of Bart Johnston. In Toronto. My buddy for years. I'll give him a call. He'll fix you right up." And he did, again and again. Up until *South Pacific*. But Rebecca has not spoken to Bart in months. And she has to, because she's broke. She must find work, and work of a particular kind. A day or two here and there, half-days if possible. Nothing to interfere with her time at SenseInSound. After taking a walk, gobbling two bagels and reading the newspaper, she picks up the phone and dials. She knows Bart's voice. Still, she asks, "Could I speak to Bart, please?"

"You're talking to him."

"Rebecca Weir, remember me?"

"Rebecca who?"

It makes sense that he'd forget her. The last couple of months might as well have been years for Rebecca.

"You got me the Thespians gig in the summer?"

"Oh. Right."

In the long silence between those two words, she realizes what he means. "I'm sorry. I meant to stay in touch."

"Well there were other jobs I had you in mind for, good ones. You missed out on them all. You know Becky, Gary Curtis and I go back a long way. He asked me to look out for you and I'm a man of my word. But I don't stick out my neck like that for everyone."

"Sorry."

"Sorry will get you precisely nowhere in this profession."

"I've been working."

Silence.

"At SenseInSound." The name that rings so proudly in her mind sounds ridiculous when said aloud.

"Sensing *What?* Oh…. *Oh.* Marlin Low-ass. Fuck! I get it."

And she knows that he does. All of it.

Bart sighs. "Becky –"

She is angry, then. At his choosing a nickname for her and using it without her permission. At his self-assurance, his ability to shake her own. Everyone seems to know what's best for Rebecca. What about what *she* wants?

"Bart, I appreciate your help, but it's my career. I believe in SenseInSound and I've decided to make it my priority."

"Congratulations. And you're calling me to inquire about my hemorrhoids. Is that it?"

She thinks of Marlin's grin when he saw the bookshelves she created and feels stronger. "You know I'm a good worker, Bart. I'm asking you to keep your eyes open for jobs."

"So he doesn't pay you."

"Marlin believes …"

"Spare me. Despite my better judgement – and entirely for Gary – I'm going to give you one more chance. Serge Melançon is in Toronto this week with *Danse-Usine*. You give Serge a call and you take him to lunch. That's all. Eat. Lunch. With Serge. (Pay the bill, by the way, since we appear to need instructions on etiquette.) You give some serious thought to *your* career. And after that if you still want to drink the Kool-Aid, you do that. Drink it right up. Just don't come crawling back to me again. Deal?"

Rebecca is back to being an awkward, lanky kid who doesn't know what to do with her life. She answers, "Sorry."

Among the Hungarian restaurants around Bloor and Bathurst are a few newer businesses: cafés and a cheese store, as well as one selling a kind of Japanese mattress called a futon. (Rebecca feels a tug of regret whenever she passes it. Why did she go and buy that pullout couch?) In the midst of all this change, By the Way Café has left its roots exposed. It used to be called Lick'n Chicken, and they never got rid of the sign. Instead, they've posted another sign announcing: All Out of Chicken. Knowing the history of the café makes Rebecca feel like an expert on her city. This compensates for the brusqueness of the wait-staff. Also, they serve cinnamon-flavoured coffee, a treat Rebecca allows herself only on weekends. But today is a Wednesday, and she's on her third cup, finishing Serge's cheesecake, as evening falls. French words bubble up from a stream she is delighted to learn still flows inside her. She is high on caffeine and electric with enthusiasm.

Serge's face is gaunt, and pitted with long-ago acne. His hair is gathered in a braid down his back. As they talk, Rebecca notices that his prematurely lined face is softened by an expression of perpetual astonishment. His laugh echoes from the café's walls whenever he's excited by an idea. This happens often. "*Faisons un projet! Ecoute! C'est une super-bonne idée.*" Somehow, he manages to eat a three-course lunch and order several rounds of coffee without ever ceasing the flow of conversation.

There's just enough time between ideas for Rebecca to remind herself they can't possibly bring to completion all the performance pieces, installations, films and mixed media productions they are dreaming up, that he's a production manager, busy – like she is – with the practicalities of putting someone else's vision on stage. Except that Serge is no dreamer. He's been with *Danse-Usine* for almost a decade, has seen it grow from a group of students wanting to keep working together after they graduated to a company with its own studios and training program. And he wants her to move to Montreal.

She is not attracted to Serge – nothing like what she feels for Marlin – but his features please her. The whole afternoon pleases her. The burn of too-much coffee, the ache in her cheeks from the long-unused French syllables, the darkness and chill that passers-by are bracing their shoulders to resist. Serge claims the bill and opens the door for Rebecca with a bow. Outside on the street, he kisses her on both cheeks as a few specks of snow land on their shoulders. He brushes her hair out of her eyes. She feels the tickle of his striped, fingerless gloves. She finds herself taking his face in both her hands and smiling, just appreciating his features, strong, crooked and kind. He backs away at a skip for a few paces, still facing her way, and – with thumb and pinkie extended – mimes talking on the telephone. He mouths, *"Demain!"* blows her a kiss, and then turns away, shaking his head as if leaving were the last thing he wanted to do.

But all that is forgotten at the next day's Journey. Twenty-odd people sit in a circle on the floor. They wear sweaters and gloves against the wind that streams in through the windows. Amanda sits opposite Rebecca, catches her eye and smiles. Seemingly impervious to the cold, Marlin paces up and down in the middle of the circle, fingers twining and re-twining themselves in his hair. At last he stops, stretching his arms out to either side, including the whole group in his announcement. "I was dying!" He says. Everyone gasps.

"I need to tell you that I was dying! Eighteen years old, and my life was over." Rebecca lets out her breath, reassuring herself. He said, *was* dying. Not *is*. Yet his words have taken on a kind of death-bed significance. No one moves or makes a sound.

"I was being consumed by this malady for which doctors produced one useless label after another. I was told I would not see thirty." Marlin grasps at his belly, pinching a scant fold in his hand. "All the men in my family have the same trait. Our bodies rebel, from within. These complex coils inside us don't retain nourishment. You've all heard the expression, 'My bowels turned to water.' Ours turn to water. As if we were constantly afraid. Afraid of what?

Afraid to say no. Afraid to give offense. Afraid to stand up and be who we are … as men."

Rebecca experiences one of those moments – familiar, since meeting Marlin – where everything she thought she knew is in question. He has always seemed bold and confident, yet here he is, admitting to his fear of giving offense. She sits in the thrall of this man who has the ability to dash all her assumptions. The words "as men" were spoken in a deep voice, almost a growl. They frighten Rebecca, hinting at wildness about to be unleashed. Marlin is rejecting something. She doesn't know what it is, but knows she is part of it. *As men*: the force is women, women who want something from Marlin that he can't say no to. Women who get pregnant, for instance. There's a criticism of Amanda implied. Rebecca allows herself a tiny swell of hope.

Then hope collapses again. He's criticizing her too. For having hope. For attaching to him at all. Desire surges, overlaid with regret. Rebecca surveys the rapt faces around her. These people must all long to touch Marlin in the way she has touched him. She flashes back to his clumsy thrusting, the pinched eyes and gritted teeth, and knows she must be remembering it wrong. These people must be seeing, responding to, the real Marlin. She is flooded with shame, and a general crumbling, not only of her trust in her own memories but in any good feelings she may harbour about herself.

"Look at this." Marlin turns away from the assembled company and removes his shirt. His cotton pants are loose on his hips, barely held in place by the slight swelling of his buttocks. He puts a hand behind him. "The pelvis is where we get our support. When I was young, this did not hold me. I was collapsing with every step." Rebecca's breath catches with the intimacy of Marlin's revelation – not just of his body, but of his story. He is the one who teaches them The Work, this special way of living *in* their bodies. Most special of all must be his way of living in his own. He has access to a level of sensuality beyond what the rest of them possess.

If Marlin isn't with her any more, it is because she wanted him too much. He has already shown himself capable of reading her body, her truth. Her fantasies of Marlin declaring love for her, of doing things to please her in bed, these hopes must be what drove him away. She feels guilty panic, as if she had missed a cue. The most important cue of her life.

"Now, let me tell you a story. There was once a man by the name of Isaac Samuel. He was born in England at the turn of the century to a family of religious Jews. He seemed destined to become a scholar. He seldom played with other kids, and from an early age, spent hours every day hunched over sacred texts. By the time he was twenty, he wore thick glasses and his joints were as stiff as an old man's. The doctors pronounced he had a degenerative disease. It got to the point where he was using two canes to get around. Eventually he got the opportunity to study in Berlin, and ended up living there for several years. He set aside his books and went out into the world. He met all kinds of artists and thinkers, as well as psychologists and doctors. He experienced an awakening, emotional, creative ... sexual. And he was cured. He swam naked, he climbed mountains. He slept outdoors. He threw away his glasses and cane and his heavy, musty books. He came to believe that our whole society is as handicapped as he had been. He asked himself how we start out as expressive, loving, instinctual beings, and within a few years, manage to become crippled, not just physically but emotionally.

"He began to study children, from birth to the age of three. And he also studied what happens after that, when they start using language and the freedom stops. He discovered that when adults were experiencing restrictions – in any area of their lives – he could help them by taking them back to the very early stages before they could write or even speak. He encouraged them to vocalize freely, to move like babies exploring their environment for the first time. In other words, he brought them back to The Now.

"Berlin became a dangerous place for Isaac. He had to get out. He moved back to London in 1930 and worked in the poorest areas of the city. He worked with everyone: people who were blind, people whose bodies were affected by rickets and polio, people who were paralyzed by accidents and strokes. Then came the war. There were civilian casualties: amputations, brain injuries, traumas of all kinds. He treated everyone who needed help, charged only what they could afford. Eventually there were politicians consulting him, as well as actors, philosophers and – yes – even doctors.

"That man was my uncle, and his work came to me in a time of desperation. I was in England, just beginning my studies at the Royal Academy of Dramatic Art. Their most promising student in a century, the admissions committee said. I had full scholarship, including room and board. I was a poor actor from Canada and didn't feel comfortable having a whole apartment to myself. I invited a homeless teenager named Jack to live with me because I wanted nothing to do with their hierarchies. Talking to Jack every night kept me sane. But nonetheless, before the first term ended, I was sick. Holding nothing inside. Draining away.

"Jack found work as a servant for an old woman. She was wealthy, encrusted with privilege and entitlement. She had known my uncle. After he died, she started practicing his work out of a manor house in the West end of London. I dragged myself out of bed one day and went and knocked on her door. I told her who I was. I told her to give me back The Work. The struggle almost killed me, but in repossessing my birthright I became strong again. Isaac left papers, documentation of his work, but this tells us nothing. The work of the body must be taught through the body. There is no other way. Enough talk. Let me show you."

Marlin now crouches, and executes a slow headstand. Then he back-flips so that he comes to stand, perfectly balanced, on both feet. He bows down, somersaults twice, then does a headstand again. He tucks his head under one shoulder until he is balancing on it, then rolls over until he is on his back. He brings his thighs to his chest, swings his legs high in the air so that his whole body leaves the ground. He lands on his feet. All of the movements are executed with absolute control.

"You see this?" He indicates his belly. "You see this?" He indicates his back. "Power in the pelvis. Power in the spine. I found it. You will, too."

Rebecca has always known about Marlin's intellect, his ability to influence others, but so far she has not seen his physical agility. He is flexible, delicate, at the same time as he is strong. He is both masculine and feminine, needing no one to complete him. She feels hopeless and exhausted and shivers in the dampness of this neglected building. She feels ashamed of her outpouring of conversation with Serge, of how superficial it was. All that coffee-fueled enthusiasm yesterday: it was not the truth. It took Rebecca away from the profound well of feeling Marlin has opened up within her. The longing she howled out in the Journeys, her role as second best, the third member of a pair. That is the truth to which she must yield.

"In the work – the true, embodied work – of Isaac Samuel, my uncle, I saw the human drama playing itself out. The drama of life itself. And I knew that it must form the foundation of whatever is done on stage. I took The Work to the avant-garde practitioners in Europe. I went to Poland, France, wherever I heard there were innovations in theatre. I was rejected, vilified, and all the while, imitated. And finally, I realized that I had to go my own way. Our bodies are instruments of the truth, not someone's text. Because the truth is what we all hold within us. And the amazing thing is that we've all got access to it, not just people who are specially endowed. There's nothing I've done here that you – every one of you – didn't do when you were children, before you began to speak. You only need to rediscover it, to go back to the beginning. This is *our* work, yours as much as it is mine."

Stooped and holding himself around the midriff, Marlin moves apart from the group. He takes deep breaths. Telling a story – departing from The Now – was a sacrifice. It has depleted him. The others begin to chatter. Rebecca is silent, remembering everything Marlin said about the danger of words. Rebecca must contain hers. Just as her tears sit inside the rims of her eyes, her words remain unformed, unsaid. *Demain,* Serge said. There is no tomorrow, for SenseInSound, no promise of something better, but no disappointment, either. There is only The Now, imbued with the loneliness she has felt all her life, and can never leave behind.

Marlin returns and quiets the group with a raised hand. "The truth is hard. This is the truth I have to tell you today. There are divisions coming among us. Some will stay, some will go. I've watched you all grow, grow from amoebae into the beginnings of people and so when some of you separate from the company it will break my heart. But it needs to happen. We're going to form a company now, but not a commercial one. Those who stay will make it our lives. This is a deep commitment. No different than marriage."

Rebecca feels her stomach drop away; the wind cuts through her two sweaters. *When some of you separate* ... She will certainly be one of them ... *No different than marriage* ... An arrangement so permanent cannot possibly include her.

"I want to stress that no one will be turned away entirely. That's not The Work. We will continue to journey every morning from eight to ten a.m. Anyone who's interested can attend. But some of us will stay all day. The company will consist of twelve, including Amanda and myself. My friends, we are ready to speak. Gradually, haltingly, we are ready to form words from our base of inarticulate sounds. We're not ready to present anything to the public yet. We'll need dedication and focus before we can get there, but we are ready for words.

"I can see clearly now who's going to go with us into the next stage. Some of you may believe you're staying, but sadly, you won't. Some of you will feel you don't have it in you, but you do. Over the next few days I will meet with each and every one who is now in this space, and by Monday of next week, the SenseInSound theatre company will be formed. Alright. Let's gather on the floor for the last time in our wordless incarnation. And prepare to transform."

Rebecca rolls down to the floor along with the others. Marlin directs them to lie in a circle with arms out to their sides, touching the edges of their neighbours' fingers, breathing together. She feels more space inside her than she has ever known was there. She breathes into her fingers and toes and head. Her chest moves, where most of the time it feels like a rigid cage. All she has to do is breathe, in this moment. The next. This is all she really has to do, ever. Together with the others she inhales, feels the separation to come like something being excised from her body. Sobs are wrenched from her solar plexus. She hears the sobs of others and loses the distinction between herself and them. It's okay! She's okay! Joy breaks over her like sunrise. She laughs, and notices she's not the only one. They roll against one another, possessed by giggles and then belly laughs. Just as they start to calm down, another wave starts and is passed between them in delightful contagion. The laughter subsides, and they get up, embrace each other and go their separate ways.

Wikipedia

Isaac Samuel
From Wikipedia, the free encyclopedia
Isaac Samuel (Birth-date unknown –1954) was a teacher of body mechanics.

Life [edit]
Isaac Samuel is widely thought to have been born in Germany, though some claim he was British-born. He is credited with widespread influence in the performing arts, medicine and psychology.

External links [edit]
Marlin Lewis
Lewis Technique®
Kevin Purcell
Regressive Progression®
Dorothy Lewitsky Samuel
Sylvia Bloom (Leon Garten)
To End All Wars
Lady Amelia Quine
Rachel Foss (See Fossil Oil Inc., The Cousinhood)
Dame Robina (Bobbie) Lance.

1984

Rebecca lies weeping on her couch when the phone rings.

(She's bleeding. Bleeding again. It hasn't been a month – or has it? She has to start keeping track.)

It's Amanda. "We haven't had a real chance to talk since I've been back. And I have so much to tell you!" Rebecca pictures them resting their elbows on a marble café table, leaning in toward each other as they exchange confidences, imagines jealousy, guilt and the confusion about whether she's supposed to know about Amanda's pregnancy curdling in her gut as she strives to maintain a smile. Jealousy about Marlin – sure – but even more about Amanda's very optimism and confidence. For Rebecca "so much" means so much sadness, so much dread. She tries to formulate an excuse for not getting together – postponing it. Maybe in a few months …? No, never. They can never really be friends.

"Rebecca, I'm so sorry about Marlin."

Rebecca feels a surge of warmth. Maybe she knows! Maybe it's okay!

"He should have spoken to you by now. You know, that warehouse is ridiculous. I'm surprised no one has caught pneumonia. But we've got a space! A real space: ours! Daddy's going to support the company for a couple of years while we get on our feet." She giggles. "Literally. Anyway, you know Marlin and I are hopeless. We need you more than ever. You're the most important one."

"Thanks!"

"Thank *you*."

Rebecca vows to make it worth their while to have included her. But there will be no more losing control. From now on she will be upright and attentive and in charge.

Their new building started as a Vaudeville theatre, then it became a cinema, then a department store for a while, then it stood empty for years. There are apartments on the two upstairs floors. Rebecca and Amanda tour the hallways of what they immediately begin calling Gerrard Space. Rebecca picks at plaster, taps walls, squats down to look into the deepest recesses of cupboards. One door remains closed. Amanda points to it, says, "Marlin's" and they walk past it by mutual consent. Rebecca feels lighter. So Amanda is shut out of part of his life, too. So Amanda unquestioningly accepts *being* shut out. She and the baby will have an apartment of their own. On the third floor are four smaller apartments which will eventually be converted to studios or be used by visiting artists as SenseInSound builds its international reputation. Amanda did not mention details, but Rebecca has no doubt Leon Garten has bought the building for them.

There is so much to do in this cavernous space: stripping, painting, rewiring, hacking through old linoleum and carpet. And cleaning, cleaning, cleaning. Layers of history have to be peeled away. They aren't ready to use the stage. It will serve, for the time being, as a storage area. The proscenium and walls are decorated elaborately in plaster. It is falling away in patches yet so gorgeous that they just have to hope it stays in place until they can get it professionally restored. The actors will journey in the area that was once the house. The red velvet seats will have to be pulled out and stacked away until they can afford new upholstery. Rebecca cringes at the thought of touching their clumped, stained surfaces. She knows that she will be the one to handle those cushions, to probe all the filthy and neglected corners of this building. And that she will do it alone.

It will be worth it, though: she has trouble not whooping for joy when Amanda takes her up a flight of stairs to what was once the projection booth. There is no balcony in the theatre, but a room above the entranceway looks down on the stage. This will be her domain. From among the ancient lighting and sound equipment heaped there she will do her best to salvage a few items to rewire until they can afford a new system. *We need you more than ever.* Of this there can be no doubt.

Rebecca begins enjoying her Contempra-phone again. The ache of losing Marlin will always be with her, but the waiting is over. She has stopped expecting his calls; meantime, others have found their way to her. The loose collection of people who gather daily at the theatre now consult her on everything from schedules to what temperature to expect in the building on any given day. Sometimes they just call to say hi. During lunch breaks, they walk along Gerrard to the restaurants they discover lie just east of the theatre. There is Little Portugal, Little Italy, Chinatown. Now Rebecca learns about Little India, yet another area of Torónto that claims to be a mini-version of some other part of the world.

But it is the first part she discovers with others, and they brim over with excitement seeing windows full of gleaming jewelry and saris, which contrast vibrantly with Toronto's winter palette. Whiffs of spice travel on the wind smelling sweeter and more complex than what came from the curry tin that sat unused on their spice rack back home. Rebecca learns to order thali in the restaurants that line the strip. For just a few dollars, an assortment of dishes is presented to her on a tray by a waiter in a white shirt and apron. She loves eating with her fingers, soaking flatbread in eye-wateringly spicy gravy, finishing with tea that is milky yet so strong it makes her ears buzz.

And Amanda calls several times a week. "It's hard," she says one day, "caring so much about what no one understands. But this means so much to me. I'll never give up." She means The Work of course, but also Marlin. He belongs to her completely now she's carrying his child. Why should Rebecca devote herself to a man who is not really her boyfriend, to work that does not seem to be leading ·

anywhere? Because she and Amanda share conversations in which those kinds of decisions make sense.

"Marlin is so absorbed in The Now, he gives himself over to it and has nothing left at the end of the day. He can't publicize The Work. He's not built like that. But if only more people could *feel* it, feel the power of it, they'd understand. We just have to make sure more people do."

Rebecca remembers the parquet sticking to her skin, the smell of Marlin's breath, his sweaty chest and hands, the ardent nights and too-early mornings that followed. But the memories flee as quickly as they arrive. The Fall seems like a different lifetime. Amanda never asks Rebecca what happened while she was away. It is clear though that she trusts Rebecca, feels closer to her than ever. And it all makes sense, in the way something can when it is never fully brought to light.

It lasted a matter of weeks, her time of journeying with the actors, but she found treasures along the way. There are three scenes in her mind. Disjointed, but absolutely clear, they are part of the mass of memories and urges and emotions that The Work has taught her roil like lava beneath the crust of everyday awareness. They are from before: before her father died, before the great blankness that divides her from her past, from others and even from herself. She does not discuss them with her mother, her sisters, or even the people at SenseInSound, who have come – in such a short time – to feel like her real family. The memories are too precious, too essential to share. For all the insecurities and discomforts of her life at SenseIn-Sound, just having these memories gives her a kind of solidity she has never felt before.

A red plaid blanket. Held up by brittle grass, it seems to rest on a cushion of air. Some broken stalks poke through, and Rebecca brushes the wool surface over and over again, letting the grass tickle her palm. After a while it seems the prickles are not on the blanket, but on her hand.

The air smells of blossoms, and there's a warm breeze swishing the leaves above and the grass all around. Rebecca sees her father's blue-jeaned legs, her mother's white blouse, and the tangle of their arms on the plaid. Her mother is lying with her head on her father's stomach, and he's singing. His voice is deep, so deep it seems to be the force which moves everything around her, vibrating down into the earth, shaking the trees and the grass. Her mother is giggling, a sound which bounces on top of her father's singing like water over rocks. There's other laughter too, other water. Her sisters squeal and splash somewhere nearby.

And then the memory ends, like a dream interrupted by the ring of an alarm clock, leaving her wanting more.

Mom lies on a pilled blue couch, an orange afghan bunched around her waist and hips. She's tangled in it like a bug in a spider's web. Her arms are folded over her face, elbows to the ceiling. Only her chin can be seen. *This is wrong*. Rebecca should be able to see her mother's eyes.

There's a bad sound, a fast, low knocking. Mom's teeth are chattering. Something has taken over her body and is shaking it from within. Rebecca wants to pull at her mother's clothes, yell and hit: anything to bring her back. She does none of these things. Whatever is shaking her mother has got hold of Rebecca too. She is stuck there, watching.

Summer. They're driving full-speed with the top down. Rebecca's scalp burns in the sunshine. Light glints off passing fenders and windshields, cutting into her eyes. Her throat screams for a drink but she knows not to ask. Everything is different now.

Rebecca's stomach is growling, her throat hurts, but she sits still. Sarah is up front with Mom, and Janice is in the back with Rebecca. Janice occasionally punches or kicks her, then a wad of spit strikes Rebecca on the arm. Audrey's hair tangles in the wind as if clumps of it were fighting other clumps, struggling to be on top.

Rebecca knows she's going somewhere far from home. She

doesn't know where it is or when they'll get there. She knows she can't ask for water or a bathroom or anything to eat. She can't *need* anything. And she knows something is missing, something big, and that it will never come back.

Now installed in their new space, the group of regular followers who gather to journey every morning will go through all the stages of human development, starting with moving their eyes and mouths, then rolling, creeping, crawling, sitting and eventually standing, enacting the drama of the evolving organism. Marlin tells them that the development of a child echoes the evolution of the human species. Right now, they are reptiles. In the course of each morning they creep around the theatre, dragging their bellies on the floor. They don't speak; rather, they gurgle and howl and flub their lips as if exploring their voices for the first time.

The Work has to be available to everyone, so Marlin has an open door policy for these sessions, but not everyone is able to meet the Journey's demands. He regularly takes people aside as they leave for the day and invites them for private coaching in the vacant apartments upstairs. Rebecca hears shrieks, wails and sobs filtering through the walls. Sometimes, there's an eerie absence of sound.

The pay-cheques arrive weekly in a courier envelope and are placed on a table by the door. There are thirteen of them, twelve for actors, including Amanda and Marlin, and one for Rebecca. They are written on Leon's company, RxWorld. Rebecca discovers that she is making $50 a week more than everyone else. She vows to earn every extra penny. Now, she is at the theatre every day for twelve hours, at least. She begins with setup at eight a.m. followed by phone calls, errands. Journeys are from ten to four, with an hour for lunch. She doesn't go out but grabs a sandwich, reviews her notes as she chews a raw carrot and some cabbage leaves to fulfill her daily quotient of vegetables. Marlin needs her to keep track of everything. Decisions are made then changed. She must record each phase of the show's long, long development so that he is free to live in The Now.

"Stop!" he cries, time and again. "Slow down, all of you. You're building illusions! Look around. What's happening? The ceiling is literally dropping on your heads and you keep on with the story you think you should be living. Listen to yourselves. Listen to The Now."

If she stays quiet long enough he will sometimes ask her what she is up to, consult on what treasures she's found under the junk in the booth or what she thinks about insulating the apartments upstairs. After one of these conversations, he sighs and says, "I feel better now." It is as if he had turned on a light bulb in her heart. She *can* help him, by being as practical, as concrete as possible. And she carefully studies the ways that other people anger him, adding to her store of things to avoid saying or doing. It hurts, loving him and not being the one he returns to every night, but she treats the feelings Marlin sets off in her as if they were aches in her biceps or thighs after a good day's work. Well, they *are* part of her work, The Work. Whatever comes via Marlin is The Work, and it was never meant to be easy. She can handle her feelings. She can handle anything.

Except she's still bleeding. Bleeding so much. One cycle barely finishes before her body is caught up in preparation for the next. At first, she enjoyed surrendering to these powerful tides, but now they exhaust her. Her hair becomes slack and clings to her forehead, pimples erupt on her skin. She is freezing, always freezing. And she is always, always tired. Rebecca grew four inches the year she turned fifteen. She picked her way around, seeing the world from far above, not trusting her stilt-like legs. Her mother took her to see Dr. Reid, who prescribed vitamins and gave her a note excusing her from gym. And within a few months she was back. Back to gym class, back to fixing things on The Property. When she was fifteen, there had been a diagnosis: *anemia*, a problem that could be fixed, but this new drain on her strength was simply part of being a woman as far as Rebecca was concerned, and there was no taking action against that.

But Rebecca's job is to create an ordered space for everyone else's creative chaos. Her job is to be there, no matter what. She has to keep going. She buys a red skirt, which she wears over her jeans during her periods. Its function is to camouflage the spots that make their way through her jeans every month. It becomes threadbare but she doesn't care how it looks. Rebecca doesn't care how *she* looks. All she cares about is work. She bores into her tasks, always doing more things, better, putting one day after another efficiently behind her.

In April, the weather turns cold and stays that way, with the sky blue and cloudless, and frost on the ground every night. It is happening. Without discussing it, the actors have developed a way of organizing themselves into pairs or groups, using each other's bodies as support in order to stand. Then the standing ones offer their hands to help the ones who are left sitting. They go over and over these basic moves, progressing in increments. A form is establishing itself. Marlin grasps Rebecca's hand as they sit together in the seats, causing her face to flush and her pulse to quicken.

Amanda gets up from her stool and paces the perimeter of the room. Then she sits on the floor with her head leaning against the edge of the stage. She seems to be dozing. Rebecca's attention frays and scatters. She can barely hold her pencil. She writes the letter "L" backwards, writes "F" when she means "4." She does not have time to use the eraser but scribbles things out, then panics at the thought of how messy her page is getting.

"Oh!" Amanda cries, and sits up straight. Rebecca begins to rise from her chair but feels a hand on her thigh, directing her to stay. The warmth and authority of Marlin's touch take precedence, yet she feels a drive so powerful she is unable to concentrate. In the time it takes to blink, she envisions all the women vacating the rehearsal space and following Amanda upstairs. She feels this urge in her own body, yet resists it. She stares at the page, willing herself to make sense of the words, but they are just marks on paper.

Marlin continues. "Yes, we're getting it. Mary and Nick: let's see that again. The way you step in to each other as you transfer the weight to the front foot. Down to the floor please and let's try it again. Connie? Do you mind?" Connie stands, and leads Amanda upstairs. It hurts to see someone else chosen but Rebecca is not surprised. And she can concentrate again. Everything is in sharper focus than it has been in months.

It's a boy. From the shelter of his bassinette, Safra contributes his infant sounds to each day's Journey. Amanda sits leaning against the stage, cocooned in blankets with a pillow on her lap. Connie brings the baby to be nursed. This is something Rebecca can hardly bear to watch. It makes her cry. She goes often to the booth to be alone and feels her own breasts tingling as the tears flow.

The others pick up Safra, stroke his cheeks, croon songs they create with his name. They take turns walking him up and down if he is fussing – which he rarely does. He is a saint-baby, an old soul. Marlin calls his birth, "an ordinary miracle." Rebecca imagines him supporting Amanda from behind while she squirts out the miniature human as if it were a kitten. Easily. Naturally. For her own part, she has no idea what to do with this tiny person who cannot speak. And not knowing what to do with Safra seems just one more indication of a deficiency within herself, a lack of connection with her instincts, a lack of humanity, really. She must not let anyone know.

Gesendet: 8/1/2012. 4:30 a.m.
An: director.graddrama@UToronto.ca
Von: AmAndAm@gmail.com

Betreff: The Truth

Dr. Charbonneau,

Even the first time I met you, your hair was flecked with grey. By now you must be middle-aged, with mottled patches on your hands and creases in the skin around your collarbone. Maybe you have a scar somewhere that you don't see any more, even when you're staring right at it.

Natto is on tour, which means I'm on my own, which was okay until I hung up from a dutiful, Friday-night call from Safra. I felt desolate. Hours later I was lying awake staring at the ceiling. I went to the bathroom and caught a glimpse of myself, naked. There's barely any scar, just a ridge, a sort of lopsided grin at the base of my belly. I stretched the flesh upward, trying to see where the stitches had been. There was nothing there.

Twice, I was opened up. Yet all these years later the scar looks like the indentation from a tight pair of jeans. They say we forget the pain of giving birth. It's nature's way of making sure we do it again. For me, the experience was tucked into a pocket in my mind. And it was easy to stash a few extra items in that pocket.

Marlin: "She can do it!"

Connie: "Get the fuck out of my way!"

And then the big hands of the ambulance men, the first hint of safety in an eternity of knowing something was wrong and no one believing me. Of screaming: *Help!* and being condemned to more pain.

I heard: "Hang on. Almost there." Soon, there was the anesthetic. I felt my insides rearranged, the baby lifted free.

"Okay: sutures," a voice said, and I was sealed up again. Just like new.

No amount of labouring would have made a difference. I was relieved when the doctor told me that – relieved to know I hadn't failed Marlin and The Work.

Marlin didn't have sex with me for a long time after the baby. Fine. It had always been, let's face it, something I did for him. As a lover – well, he just didn't get it. I lived for the time right afterwards, the way he pressed against me like a puppy. He was grateful – even thanked me. It seemed like he'd never be angry again.

But the way he looked after Safra! That utter focus he was capable of giving was tailor-made for an infant. Safra belonged to Marlin and he to Safra. Night and day, night and day. And I got to be included in that bond. Marlin's voice was like velvet, asking me if I wanted anything. His touch was so sensitive, helping me to sit. Hot milk! Soup! Toast! Seeing him silhouetted in the window, his head bent over Safra night after night I fell in love all over again. I traded sex for tenderness, a more than fair exchange. At least for a while. All of it was for a while. The safety of those months seemed like it would last forever. That was the nature of Marlin's attentiveness. The opposite was true. Soon enough I wondered if I had ever experienced it at all.

Is it true that you've never given birth, Dr. Charbonneau? Still, you must know something about memory. It's a matter of giving yourself permission. To trim and tailor and tuck away, in order to keep going. Most of the time, you don't even notice you're doing it. It helps if others believe the story. Sometimes they create it for you. I was Eve and Woman and She. And part of that was being Mother. Everyone knew some version of the Mother story. No one asked what really happened. Now, I look for evidence and see only fiction. Even my skin has forgotten the details.

Just like the city forgot SenseInSound. Forgot Marlin. *To End All Wars* came thundering in, overshadowing the long, long gestation it had taken to bring it to birth.

Maybe you don't live like this. Maybe your memories are arranged in a clean line: the before, the after, the highs and lows, the causes and effects, all visible in the bright sunshine. Maybe you trust what you know is the truth, since you didn't spend twenty years performing it.

With apologies for not being more helpful,
Amanda M.

1985

Safra is a month old when an old woman shows up for a Journey. Rebecca hates her – actively hates her – though she argues with herself that she should be more compassionate. But the woman irks Rebecca from the very first glance: her late arrival, the self-conscious, almost defiant way she struggles putting ballet slippers over her gnarled feet, shuffling her limbs as she gets settled, disturbing the momentum of the Journey. Yet Marlin does nothing, speaks as if the company – and not the visitor – were in the wrong.

"Breathing, please, everyone. Stop judging your experience. Honour The Now!"

The words might as well be meant for Rebecca. Her thoughts are raging. *How long is Marlin going to allow drop-ins while we're supposedly working on a play?*

As long as necessary. It is up to her to adapt.

Every Saturday Rebecca takes a ruler and draws squares on sheets of graph paper. Each square represents the floor, and each page, an hour of work. The notes go all around the square, and within it, she uses dots to represent people. She knows that the personnel will keep changing, so there's no point in recording names – except Amanda's. Amanda is her lodestar. Rebecca always knows where she is. But this morning she can't even count how many people are in the room. The lady is tangling her perceptions.

Marlin says: *When we believe something is ugly, it's showing us the way to what we are unable to accept in ourselves.* Rebecca tries to figure out what the visitor represents for her, but can only come up with superficial observations. The woman's curiously flattened nose makes her look like she has slept on her face. Her spindly legs are grotesque in their cream-coloured tights. The twisted toes distort the tops of her slippers. She wears a poorly fitted wig with synthetic hairs radiating out from a single point in the centre of her forehead.

Welcoming everyone is an unspoken rule at SenseInSound, people of all backgrounds, levels of training, gay people and straight. But they've always had one thing in common: youth. If this lady stays and becomes part of the ongoing group they'll have to change their process to accommodate her. She will be slow to move, frail in the joints, maybe hard of hearing. What she represents is more work.

These thoughts must stop.

Commitment to The Work means being a good person, and that means having a generous, accepting attitude, the attitude that made them welcome Rebecca herself into their midst, even though she can't – or won't – express herself. The Work means looking for some good-hearted – healthy – part of themselves they had left behind when they grew up. Yet Rebecca cannot help feeling that the arrival of this lady has spoiled something, a cohesiveness and certainty they previously shared. She dislikes her even more as she forcibly converts anger to pity, only to have it revert back again. The lady is singing in a penetrating, nasal voice. Off-key.

Marlin says: *There is no off-key here. Every sound is right and welcome.*

The lady is off-key. And Rebecca is off-human for hearing her that way.

"Connie?" Marlin asks, loudly at the end of the Journey. "Can you explain to this *newcomer* the way we work here? That arriving late is not acceptable? Thank you, love."

After having a terrible time sitting up, the lady looks straight at Marlin, her head bobbling with a tremor. There is determination in her stare. He does not return her gaze, and she directs it to Rebecca instead. Rebecca looks away.

"Rebecca!" Marlin says sharply. "I'm wondering if you can come upstairs have a look at Amanda's sink." He puts an arm around her waist, guiding her. She loves the forcefulness of his touch. He will sort everything out.

The next day, the stranger arrives forty minutes early. She settles herself on the floor and places a cushion behind her back. From a large handbag she draws a book and positions it so the title can be prominently seen: *Thicker than Water – Healing Your Embattled Family.* She puts on a pair of glasses and begins, intently, to read, one tic wobbling her head side to side and another darting her eyebrows up until they disappear into her wig. As unwilling to talk to the woman as she is to leave her alone in the room, Rebecca starts to clean the glass doors of the theatre with vinegar. Amanda arrives with Connie, who's carrying Safra. Connie settles on the floor beside the stranger and hands her the baby.

"You darling! Let me look at you!" the stranger coos.

The others start to arrive. The lady replaces Safra in the bassinette. Amanda takes her place, propped up against the edge of the stage. Marlin's voice is strong and steady. It crosses Rebecca's mind he is struggling to keep it that way. At the end of the Journey he gestures to the lady as if to direct her upstairs.

"What you have to say to me you can say in front of everyone."

"Alright then. You're not welcome here."

"Marlin!" Amanda touches his arm and he shakes her roughly away.

Rebecca calls, "That's it for today, everyone. Sunday at ten, please."

Marlin turns and goes upstairs. Amanda links her arm with the lady's and they walk toward the door, speaking quietly. Amanda pats her shoulder as she leaves.

The following morning a call comes early on Rebecca's home phone: "Hi-dear," says the caller as if the two words were one. Rebecca has no doubt of who is on the other end of the line. It is the stranger, bringing the feeling that everything is rapidly being spoiled into Rebecca's own apartment.

"Good *morning*," she answers pointedly. "It's very early."

"I'm calling you-dear, because I can see that you're in charge around that place."

"Marlin is."

"What do you do, then?"

"I'm the stage manager."

"Like I said. You're in charge. Well-dear, I'm Doctor Dorothy Samuel Lewitsky Goldman. And in case he hasn't mentioned it, I'm the mother of Marlin Lewis who used to be Menachem Lewitsky before self-hatred got the better of him. And I'd like to give you my number because I've moved to the city to be near my grandson."

"Mrs. Lewis, I'm sorry. I can't."

"Samuel. I go by Samuel, and I go by Doctor. I just want you to have my number. I'm not asking you to use it."

"I'm sorry, Mrs. Samuel."

"*Doctor.*"

"I'm really sorry, but I can't get in the middle of anything."

"I'm not asking you to get in the middle-dear. I understand my son has his boundaries but I want you to be able to reach me. Don't you get an emergency contact number when someone joins your … classes, or whatever they are?"

Rebecca's mouth goes dry. They do not. Infuriatingly, the lady now articulates what just raced through her own mind: "What if someone gets hurt?"

Rebecca is silent.

"So get your pen."

"Okay. What's the number?" Rebecca does not have a pen anywhere near the bed. She rolls her eyes while Dorothy recites her phone number with infuriating slowness.

"You may not be aware of this, but I am a prominent child psychologist. Twenty years ago I received my Ph.D. from McGill University, the only mature student in my class, and one of a handful of women. The degree took eight years and for that whole time I cleaned a five-bedroom house, cooked dinner every night for my second husband and his three sons. And Marlin, before he decided he was too good for us. Now I added it up; an average of twelve weeks out of every year Marlin was in hospital for colitis and who was with him? Not his father, let me tell you, and not his step-father either. Every Friday I made Shabbat for my second husband's family: fifteen people. Religious. I kept that dish away from that spoon. I blessed this I blessed that. Five Kosher lunches I packed every day. Put up with Moe's complaints. He resented me: my intelligence, my ambitions. But I got that degree. *That* is what a determined woman I am. I'm clearly not welcome in your 'institution.' But I love my grandson and I want you to know-dear that I'm not going to go away."

"I'm sorry."

"Sorry again? You must be a middle child! You should learn not to apologize for yourself-dear."

"I'm sorry. I mean, goodbye."

Rebecca sits among her rumpled bedclothes, listening to the street waking up. She is sweating, yet has a strong desire to cover herself up to her chin. Marlin's mother is like the shadow of Amanda's mother, as unattractive as Sylvia is beautiful, as outspoken as Sylvia is tactful. She feels it; she must feel it. Rebecca wishes she could be more like Amanda, who was so kind to Dorothy yesterday. In this way as in all others, she is better than Rebecca, who is treating Marlin's anger as permission to bathe in her dislike of the newcomer. Rebecca wants to keep Dorothy away from SenseInSound but knows it won't work.

And then there's someone else. All of a sudden, she's there. Between the new baby and Dorothy's intrusive presence, the crumbling ceiling and the uninsulated, heat-sucking apartments upstairs, Rebecca did not notice the arrival of Victoria (or Vic, as she calls herself). But she noticed her when Marlin noticed her. His attention made her visible. More: it placed a spotlight on her. Now Vic is everywhere.

Vic is full of contradictions. Her freckled arms and legs seem packed with muscle, yet her face is delicate, with a turned-up nose and soft lips. Rebecca notices her grubby, bitten-down fingernails. Yet after their work on the floor each day she stands up to reapply lipstick and frosted eye-shadow before putting on her bicycle gear. It's winter, but she rides her bike to the theatre in shorts. Vic is bold. She interrupts the wordless sanctity of the Journeys with a barrage of questions in her husky, tomboy voice. Marlin does not tell her to stop. Rebecca notices the sense of utter concentration that Vic gives each moment, and thinks of how her own attention is split. Part of is it always with Marlin, no matter what else is going on.

Vic brushes against Marlin whenever she passes him. After each day's Journey they talk, standing inches apart, looking intently into one another's eyes. Rebecca argues with herself: *it doesn't mean anything.* Vic shows that same intensity with everyone. Yet Rebecca feels a pain in her gut around Vic, something akin to hunger, but deeper. She feels guilty – or at least, shamed – as if she were being punished for something. For Amanda to come back from New York and claim Marlin made sense. Vic, on the other hand, is a threat. The very idea of her is a threat. The whole world is full of women who might draw Marlin in, occupy that place by his side that Rebecca is so carefully creating for herself. On the subway, in the grocery store, Rebecca looks at the way one woman tosses her hair back over her shoulder, at the way another counts out change. She tries to see them through Marlin's eyes, as if by doing so she could intercept their claims on his attention. But there are too many women. Always more.

Rebecca looks to Amanda for how to handle this. She seems impervious, wrapped up in looking after the baby. Yet – is it possible? – yes, it's true. Thinner.

A glimmer – no – forbidden. But there, anyway. A glimmer of satisfaction. Maybe Vic is getting attention because Amanda was friendly to Dorothy. And was Amanda trying to irk Marlin by being friendly to his mother? No. Of course not. They are both above such underhanded tactics.

The following week a letter arrives, the envelope made out to Amanda Lewitsky. Rebecca waits for a moment when she is alone in the theatre with Amanda, who opens it and shows Rebecca the contents: a cheque for a thousand dollars from Doctor Dorothy Samuel. They look at it together for a long moment, then Amanda shakes her head.

"This is a lot of money for her, but she'll be insulted if we don't take it. Marlin will say she's manipulating us. He has a good reason to be angry but your mother is your mother, you know? What are we going to do?"

Rebecca says, "I don't think you should take the money. The truth is so important to Marlin. Think what he'd do if he found out."

"You're right. You're so right, Rebecca, but what am I going to say to her?"

Marlin calls out from the back of the theatre: "When you finish your armchair analysis of my character, tell her she can never give back what she stole."

Dorothy is gone, after that. And for no reason Rebecca can see or understand, Vic arrives twenty minutes late one morning. She has a pimple on her chin and her eyes are red. Marlin studies her as she comes in.

"Sorry!"

Marlin raises an eyebrow. "I don't think you are."

"Okay, you're right. I'm not sorry. I'm pissed off."

He just watches her.

"I woke up feeling pissed off."

Again, no answer.

"And I can't lie down. I can't lie down here."

"What *can* you do?"

"Run."

"So run."

The Journey resumes, an agitated Vic doing laps around the perimeter of the room. Rebecca is livid at her getting away with this. Hectically, Vic continues to run. Now she begins to jump over the prone bodies. If anything, the potential distraction serves to deepen everyone's concentration. The actors begin rolling toward one another, forming a solid mass like a carpet in the middle of the room. Amanda stands up. "Excuse me," she whispers. She picks up Safra and goes upstairs.

When the actors make contact, they make sounds. They roll away from each other, then come close again, and touch. The sounds grow louder. They have a fit of laughing as they pile in a heap, unable to distinguish one person's limbs from another's. On and on Vic runs, in an ever-tightening circle around the pile of bodies. Anyone else would be exhausted. Vic runs for an hour, then leaves.

But she's back the next day. And she's quiet. The whole room is quiet. "Let's just go back to breathing today. Back to stillness." Some of the people roll onto their sides to sleep. Marlin walks over to Vic where she lies and asks if she knows a lullaby. She hums at first, then sings in a language Rebecca does not understand. "That's right." Marlin's tone is solicitous. "Keep climbing." Vic sounds uncomfortable, trying to force her normally husky voice up high.

"Okay. Feel the earth beneath you. Trust that you can take your notes up even higher." Rebecca has the impulse to walk away from this intimate scene but doesn't want to do anything to disturb the sense of concentration. She glances around at the others. Many have quietly sat up and are watching Marlin and Vic. Vic's notes have becomes piercing. She breaks into giggles, a girlish sound. "Okay," says Marlin. "That's it for today."

Whatever was going on, it's over. It shows in Vic's whole body. She looks unattractive in some indefinable way. All the charm has drained from her tom-boyishness and she is left awkward and grubby and gruff. Rebecca feels a mixture of compassion and relief, noticing that Vic's fingernails are bitten to their bloody quicks, that her normally lustrous hair hangs on her shoulders in clumps. Her connection with Marlin is gone. There are no casual touches, no face-to-face intensity, that day or in the days that follow.

Rebecca wonders if Vic will leave, but she continues to arrive every morning, even though she has lost, lost Marlin's attention, lost out to Amanda. Lost out – Rebecca dares think – to "them" – the unit the three of them have become. Vic's shoulders take on a stooped appearance, clamped down in a wrestler's determined stance. One day, Marlin approaches her and kneels down where she lies, whispers, "That's it! That's it! You can't lose what was yours to begin with. Let it go!" Rebecca has no idea what he is responding to. Victoria's voice has blended with the others' and can't be separately heard. Rebecca remembers Connie's encouraging touch on her elbow, her first day after Amanda's return. Catching up with Vic at lunch time she smiles and does the same thing.

"Want to get thali?" she asks, and doesn't wait for an answer before guiding Vic out the door.

The Homestarter
The Online Newsletter for Staff of Homestarters Corp.

September 2011

Last week, our new President, Victoria Fodor addressed all staff across the country by Webinar. Here's the text of her speech.

Good morning, everyone. You know, when I was a little girl, it was a big treat to come to work with Magda. That's what I called your past president, who also happened to be my mother. It was a treat because I didn't think people worked in this place! I had the impression everyone just ate chocolate cookies and played hide and seek between the desks. The biggest treat of all was to sit in Magda's big chair. A treat for her, that is. I think it's the only time she could get me to sit still. Sort of! I have vivid memories of spinning it around and around, bouncing up and down on the squeaky leather. I wonder if she could have imagined this day would come, that I'd take over her role at Homestarters. Maybe she did. Maybe that's why she bought a chair it was impossible to break!

This should be the part where you laugh and I tell you how I plan to occupy that seat proudly. But I'm going to change that script right now. Instead, I'm going to talk about the elephant in the room. Magda – my mom – died two weeks ago. She was an alcoholic, a chain smoker, a binge eater, and one of her feet had been amputated due to complications of diabetes. She was seventy years old.

The Magda I watched fade away in that hospital bed is not the tough-talking lady who ran a company, raised a daughter on her own and looked after her parents on the weekends. That woman was long gone. It was right around the time this company went digital that my mother's health started to decline. I remember coming home for Christmas – it was about twenty-five years ago. I was involved in theatre in those days. I worked my body hard. I was dead tired and looking forward to spending some precious time with my mom. I expected a holiday breakfast, just the two of us, and instead I woke up on Christmas day in a big, anonymous condo, alone. She was at work.

People say you never feel as alone as when your mom dies. But that feeling started a long time ago, for me. My mom was stolen from me. And my intention as your president is to make sure no one ever says this on account of Homestarters. Ever again. Every one of our branch offices will have a floor given over to wellness, including a meditation room and – get this – a space for naps. Everyone will clock out at 5 p.m. and the phones will be turned off at that time. No weekend work.

My mom was very encouraging of my creative work. She poured tens of thousands of dollars into the theatre company I was part of. Who knows, without her support, the company might not have eventually made it so big. Back then, she just saw it as an outlet for my energy, and she was right. What she didn't know was that it helped me find the little girl I had never been. I found my receptive side. Learned to be a human being not a human doing. And so, as my first act as president, I'll be getting rid of Magda's big leather chair and walnut desk, replacing it with a standing desk and a treadmill. I hope you'll join me in moving into the future.

1985

"Depuis quand, mademoiselle?"
   How long has it been?
   "Six mois."
   But she's been bleeding this way for a year.
   "Environ six."

The doctor is busy with Rebeca's lower half. She's grateful he won't see her blush as she tells this lie. She plucks at the sheet covering her body and stares up at the ceiling. The doctor, who seems little more than a teenager with his downy blond beard, runs water in the sink and returns to sit beside the examining table. Instead of finding a doctor in Toronto or visiting Dr. Reid, she has chosen to come here, to a clinic miles from her mother's house. She does not think about why she chose this place but the answer is there in the neutral tone of the doctor, the stranger, who now faces her. He does not know her or her family and won't ask if there's anything else bothering her. And it's a French-speaking clinic. In this anonymous place, in this, her second language, her body feels less her*self*. It could be, the doctor says, that she's had a miscarriage. He'll book her for a D and C in a few days. The doctor's confident tone renders this explanation plausible. To him, the mysteries of her body have been reduced to a manageable task. As long as she's in the room with him she feels the same way.

Rebecca wakes from her drugged sleep. Groggy and freezing in the bluish light of the recovery room she dresses, takes a few sips of water then pushes her way out to the reception desk, choking back the desire to puke.

"*Mademoiselle! Tu n'dois pas!*"

It was difficult to convince the staff to start the procedure this morning but Rebecca pacified them with assurances that Audrey was on her way. She had not said anything to Audrey, though, hadn't told her that she was going to have an anesthetic, that she would need a lift home. She left before her mother got up, scribbled a note: "See you this afternoon."

Over the nurse's protestations, Rebecca turns and walks out the sliding doors, leaving the prescription for painkillers on the desk. She walks out of sight and sits on a low, stone wall a block from the hospital. Blood drips into the pad the instruction sheet told her to bring along. What if something is wrong? She feels the ground buck and dip under her but holds herself steady until the wave of dizziness passes. Steady. Steady, and she is okay again. She must do this alone. She takes the bus home: the jolting, sick-making milk run. The familiar landscape wavers. She drops her head against the seatback in a near faint.

"*Ça va?*" Someone is jiggling her knee. Rebecca's eyelids flutter open and she glimpses a wrinkled face, brilliant orange hair and a shelf-like bosom decked in magenta flowers.

"*Oui-oui.*" She does not face the lady, certain her breath must smell sour.

"*J'crois pas, ma p'tite.*"

Tears come to Rebecca's eyes. Never in her life has she been referred to as small, even as a joke. She straightens up, shaking her head, assures the lady it is just her period. The woman pats her hand as Rebecca dozes off in her seat. Her kindly tone of voice penetrates Rebecca's waxing and waning consciousness. For this woman, periods are just a memory. Maybe desire and jealousy and guilt and longing are, too. Maybe Rebecca can fast-forward her emotions a couple of decades, put all that behind her. She resolves to become cool and dry and wise, like this lady. She'll smile and nod sympathetically while others recount their upheavals, never losing her own steadiness. She sleeps for a while. Then it's time to get off. Insisting that her mother will be meeting her, she gets off the bus at the gas station, waits for it to drive away, and calls a taxi from the booth inside.

"Rebecca!" Audrey calls as Rebecca lurches in the door. "What happened?" Rebecca discerns fear in her mother's gruff tone. She answers: "I'm okay!" and goes straight up to bed. She wakes in the dark. Her mid-section seems to be folding in on itself from hunger. She walks downstairs, gripping the banister. She drinks one, two, three glasses of water to slake her massive thirst. Standing at the kitchen counter she eats leftover chicken and potatoes, smearing them in congealed fat. When she's full, she begins walking through the sleeping house.

She took to doing this when she was a child. She would lie awake in bed, listening to her sisters and mother brushing their teeth and flushing the toilet one by one. Within a few minutes they'd surrender to sleep and she'd have the house to herself. Rebecca learned how to move silently, spreading the bones of each foot so that she did not produce any creaks in the floorboards. Tonight, she walks from the kitchen (as always, a chaotic mess) through the dining room – where her mother's newspapers and seed catalogues have replaced piles of homework on the table – and into the front hall. She stands in the doorway of the living room, looking in.

High-pitched snores emerge from behind the couch where Buster the dog has succeeded in creating a bed. The room has always felt out of bounds, but she takes a deep breath and steps over the threshold. The mantelpiece is the source of the forbidden feeling. It holds an array of small, framed photos, all off-centre or out of focus. The Weirs are not a picture-taking family. These were snapped by people trying to immortalize someone else's birthday party or graduation, and who happened to catch one of the Weir girls in the frame. There is only one big one, her parents' wedding picture. Rebecca carries it to the window to look at it in the glow from the full moon.

She has studied this picture before. They all have. She remembers Sarah sighing that it was a half-assed job, like everything else in this house, with one unknown person's leg and another's arm visible at the edges. In this light, Rebecca can only see the two white blotches of her parents' wedding outfits. Audrey's blotch is cinched in the middle, her skirt flaring wide and finishing at the knee. She is taller than Stephen, Rebecca's father, and their two blotches are connected. They are holding hands. Rebecca used to gaze at Stephen's earnest face in the picture when she was a child. She concluded that he looked serious because he was dead.

She replaces the picture on the mantle and makes her way towards the stairs, being extra careful as she passes the room that was once the verandah. Last year she enclosed it to make a bedroom for their mother, allowing her to live downstairs in the winter and save power. Rebecca hears her mother's breathing, regular and self-contained. Audrey has slept alone for many years.

Upstairs, Rebecca passes Sarah's room, now a guest bedroom decorated in beige and pink. It has a queen-sized bed, with a doll Janice bought in a local rummage sale propped up between the pillows. The room was redecorated two years ago, the year of the weddings, though nobody actually slept in it. Rebecca's sisters got married the way they used to fall on the basket of fresh bread that Audrey placed on the table at Sunday breakfast: ravenously, and both at once. First, Sarah met a corporate lawyer and relocated to Edmonton so that they could have custody of his twin toddlers. They planned to get married that August, in the garden, as Sarah started calling their yard. But in the spring, Janice announced her pregnancy by a guitar player named Freddie Phoenix. He would spend most of his time in L.A., but they did a quick, city-hall wedding before he left. Sarah's wedding was then relocated to Malibu, and she was soon pregnant, herself. The sisters were effusively happy for each other, but Rebecca wondered if they were each trying to get there first. For Rebecca, love has been all about melting and yielding and loss of control. This race to the finish line of marriage seems yet another competition she is destined to lose.

Rebecca's sisters stay up late at night when they come home for holidays. In short order, their relationships with their husbands, in-laws and children have developed problems that require painstaking analysis. They go away for weekends together, visit each other's cities to catch up. Presumably, they talk on the phone as well. Rebecca has given up trying to participate; it only makes her feel more alone.

She ventures into Janice's old room with its toy box and shelf of dolls. It is a room for a little girl and it never changed over the years. When Sarah moved out, Janice took over her room, leaving this one as an ongoing junk repository. Now it stands waiting for grandchildren. Audrey doesn't say she's happy to be a grandmother but her constant subject of conversation is the changes they will need to make in this room before the kids come to stay. So far, it's yet to happen. Rebecca backs out of the room, closing the door behind her.

What do you want, Rebecca?

Nothing.

That was never true. It was children she didn't want. She would not have been able to formulate this thought, back in the days of Dr. Delman, but knew that there was something down the path of *wanting* that she must avoid. On that path, lipstick led to boyfriend, led to marriage in one unstoppable slide, fueled by everyone else's expectations of what adult life should look like. The next step after that would have been children. It was best to shrug and say she wanted nothing at all, best not to start.

I don't want children. The words are as clear as if she had said them out loud.

Now: her own room. In this rambling house, there were plenty of rooms for Rebecca but – like Buster – she enjoyed jamming herself into narrow spaces. Once a closet, the room has one, round window high up on the wall. She lies on her back, feeling an ache through the whole bottom half of her body, with occasional, mysterious twinges that make her fear once again that something has gone wrong. She breathes deeply to quell the images of raw meat that crowd in on her. Miscarriage. It's not possible. The heavy bleeding started before she and Marlin were lovers, and there's been no one since. Yet today's procedure seemed part of the relationship with Marlin. The dip into unconsciousness, the purging of her insides were a necessary ritual, ushering in a new, quiet-hearted, clear-eyed phase of her life.

Rebecca has lasted a year, has lived through Amanda's return, the birth of the baby. Through Victoria – though it's clear she will not be the last one to attract Marlin's attention. Most of all, Rebecca has lived through a move and change of personnel which saw some people shunted to the periphery, or out the door entirely. She, on the other hand, has retained her place by Marlin's side. The three images from before her father died glow in Rebecca's memory, more solid and precious than any diamond. There will be no wedding, but this will do. Rebecca has found her place.

Harvest time. The buzzing of cicadas and the drop, drop, drop of beans in the pail. Rebecca and Audrey stand in the fenced-in plot that takes so much work in the spring and fall, but for a short time in summer does nothing but yield. Rebecca loves fresh beans, hot from the sun. When she is alone she eats as many as she takes in the house. But today she is disciplined and ordered in her picking. She has something to ask.

I will say it.

I won't say it.

Audrey doesn't like questions. She has a way of snapping back in a tone that means the answer is obvious and you are foolish if you don't know it. She has her opening words planned, "I was wondering …" but they do not come out as she wanted. Instead there is a burst: "I need to know!" Now she's started wrong. She should begin again, go back to the script she created in her mind, but her own words have drawn confidence from her. After all, she is no longer a stranger to need. She takes a breath.

"I need to know about my father."

Audrey stops picking.

"Yes." Audrey says. "It's only natural that you do."

Rebecca's eyes prickle with tears of relief, but then Audrey goes back to her work with no hint that she's going to say more.

"So, what was he – at least – can you tell me what he was like?"

Audrey drops a handful of beans in the pail and looks at her daughter. She takes a breath before saying, "He was a good man. He would not hurt a living soul. Not me, not you kids."

"And what else? I mean, tell me about him."

Audrey goes on working as she talks. "Organized. There were lists for the groceries, the chores, for everyone's birthdays and anniversaries. Everything in the house had to have its place or get thrown away. And it never seemed to bother me even though I'm the total opposite, as you know. I was under a kind of spell, the whole time I was with him. He was there and he was my husband and he had a certain effect on me and that's the way it was.

"We were young when we got married. I was eighteen, just out of school, and he was nineteen and it was just – assumed – somehow. We grew up together and it went on day to day. There was a progression. From being friends to being boyfriend and girlfriend to getting married and having a family. (I was not pregnant when we got married, in case you're wondering. All that came afterwards.) We were together for a long time, when you think of it. I mean, compared to you kids."

"And what happened when he died?"

"I told you."

"I mean how did you *feel*?"

"He fell off a ladder at work."

"I know, mom, but …"

"You get on with it." Audrey barks, as if Rebecca has failed to get on with something, herself. She has to remind herself that she is a woman of twenty-five and that a little change in her mother's tone of voice should not make her run away. She is trying so hard to control herself that it takes a moment to register Audrey's next words.

"Now listen. It's different."

"Different ... ?"

"For you girls. You need to understand that. These days the girls want everything and get nothing. And the boys want only one thing and they get it. Free." She glares at Rebecca, who watches her own hands snapping off clusters of beans.

"It wasn't an abortion," Rebecca says at last. "I needed a – procedure – but not ... I'm not ... well, I'm more or less married to my work these days."

"Well then." Audrey takes a deep breath, pours our more words than Rebecca has ever heard from her at one time. "Having kids was the big idea in the fifties. Everyone wanted kids. Not just the girls. I mean the men still want kids – of course they do – but they like to put everything on the girls, for some reason. Back then, you both wanted a family and you were happy when you started one. And when your father died he couldn't help it. He didn't *intend* to hurt us. Wasn't running away, God knows. And when he was gone, he was gone. I saw him in his coffin. I knew he was dead. Not like he was going to show up in the bar the next day with my best friend. And that made it easier to get on with life. Maybe I should have explained that better."

It is comforting to hear Audrey soften, express doubt about any of the choices she's made. But the words "should have" linger in the humid air.

"What do you mean?"

"I mean you've all settled, in your own ways."

I'll say it: "For less than we should?"

Audrey shrugs. "Low thyroid," she says. "I got it when I was your age. Makes you bleed. Get yourself a prescription before you let anyone go scraping around in there again."

PART II

Gesendet: 4/2/2012 5:07 a.m.
An: director.graddrama@UToronto.ca
Von: AmAndAm@gmail.com

Betreff: The Truth

And then, Dr. Charbonneau, there are my journals.

Natto never asked why I needed to bring them to Berlin, why I needed to keep them in my own room. Why I needed a room of my own. Why I *needed* anything. No wonder I could not take him seriously at first. How could it be love if I didn't walk around feeling dissected, flayed?

I wrote the date but not the year. I have no idea when any of this happened. Days were years and years were days. This morning I am transcribing. And rushing back and forth to the bathroom, a spasm in my gut pushing everything inside me up, down, out. The past is poisonous.

Last night Marlin said "I don't have time, Amanda. I don't have energy to supply the positive feelings for both of us." I feel sick to my stomach and I want to cry. I hate myself. Is it true, what he says? I dreamed he held me to his chest and read a book at the same time. I dreamed he turned on me the way Othello turned on Desdemona. I had better let it go because the next time I talk to him, it will be next week. By that time the bad feelings will have turned rotten inside me. Why can't I just let things go? I am bad. I am hateful. I should be everything I'm not.

I close that notebook, flip to the middle of another one.

All that acquiescence. Trapped in being nice. Trapped in the family pattern of not "rocking the boat," breaking the ice. Trapped in the family pattern of answering everybody's needs. I just want to give up. At times, the routine is unbearable. And I feel as if I am somehow failing.

I turn the pages in clumps, looking for – I know this is crazy – but I'm looking for my body, my voice.

Pleasure as I watch my body dwindle, feeling my body grow numb, stiff. Pleasure at my standard, controlled meals. Pleasure at eating little. Feeling no hunger. But I'm not thin any more and am never going to be.

Distortion: you look in the mirror and see your body larger than it really is. You perceive one thing, believe another.

Couldn't sleep. I was twitchy. My heart beat loudly. I didn't eat well yesterday. Or not enough. I enjoyed that. This morning I felt my jeans were a little loser. [!] I enjoyed that. Will I ever be rid of this wanting to be thinner. The familiar things, the familiar ways are gone. I feel a sense of dread.

Page after page. Notebook after notebook. I articulated hurt, anger, even recorded verbatim what Marlin said. And then it would be the next day: the Journey. All that shrieking and writhing served as a safety valve. The emotions were siphoned off. I stayed.

The Work was the anti-technique, it was The Truth. It was our Selves. Yet there were skills I learned to execute with scientific precision: to appear open while protecting myself, to emote while keeping a central part locked away. Reigning my feelings in while giving the performance of letting go.

Who was I writing for? Me, as I am now, with my new home and new name, living a life so safe and happy I need to be reminded why I still feel an undertow of fear?

You, even though I'd never met you?

Or someone else? The public that I spilled my guts for? Letting them know there was someone in here all along?

Sick again.
Enough.

1988

Darkness.

When the lights go down there is a hush, followed by chatter. Marlin slips out of a front-row seat to tap the hand of Jimmie Johns, who squats at the front of the stage. Jimmie sends forth a series of cackles and wails.

"Let there be light!" Margo – playing God – wears a pinstriped suit, the fabric straining over her chest. Her hair is tucked under a fedora. There's a lightning flash as she strikes a match and brings it to her cigarette, then all the lights come up, a merciless blue wash, revealing the company scattered on the floor. The only set is a box-like scaffold made of iron pipes, something like a play structure from a park.

Rebecca stands in the booth with two Strand Junior 8 dimmer boards she has managed to salvage. They must date from the fifties, judging from the brittle wires she has had to replace. One is mounted on the wall and one laid on a table in front of her. Both emit an alarming amount of heat. She has to unplug one or the other at moments when they're not in use. Between the two boards, she is able to execute her rudimentary lighting design. She flips a switch on the left-hand machine. Gingerly, to avoid sparks, she plugs in the right-hand board, whose switches are already set to fade position, and cheats the dimmers up together, using a piece of wood. It's a matter of holding as steady as she can and praying nothing shorts out. Then, with a shoulder-wrenching heave, she unplugs the board on the left.

Now that they're putting on an actual show, she's been forced to recruit actors to help her. Two newcomers, Gail and Katie, were supposed to play Cain and Abel and – when that section was cut – were assigned to help Rebecca. They have no experience, aptitude or – for that matter – interest in helping her. It's pretty clear they're only doing this to please Marlin, who for some reason has seen fit to string them along. "The girls" – as she privately calls them – arrive and leave at the same time and eat all their lunches together. One smooth, flaxen head, one curly black one incline toward one another, then turn away as she approaches. Gail's brown arm circles Katie's white shoulders; Katie's rests on Gail's waist. They always seem to be sharing a private joke, quite possibly at Rebecca's expense. Now she has them keeping track of a few props and helping with one cue at the end. She has written up painstaking instructions for each of the girls, rehearses them to the point where her own mind is numb.

There was never any question Margo would play God. She was the one most willing to make untamed sounds: wails and grunts, ragged orgasmic sighs, bleats and rasps, screams of rage. "Never again," Margo announced frequently while they were creating the show. "No one will ever shut me up again." Margo makes it no secret that she is in menopause and strips down to a functional, graying bra whenever the hot flashes come.

"God separates: light from darkness. Waters above. Waters below."

Margo barks her orders. Dressed in rags, the members of the company roll around on their backs and bellies. Sometimes they glide over each other. They make sounds like babies squalling for attention. Margo/God struts this way and that. She kicks at the creatures under her feet every so often, demanding obedience, at which they cry out in unison: "It is good!"

Lights go on and off abruptly (thank God no sparks). It is day, then night, then day again. All the while the members of the company gradually make their way to crawling on hands and knees. Some come to their feet and others swoop around the stage squeaking and squawking as they flap their arms. The sounds are anxious, distressed. Margo grabs one actor, Kevin, restraining him in his "flight." She positions him under a glaring light and as she paces around him, strips off his clothing until he is naked. She poses his beautifully muscled body like Da Vinci's ideal man. Then Margo fishes among the prone bodies for Amanda. Lasciviously stroking her and whispering in her ear Margo strips off Amanda's clothing, down to a flesh-coloured body-stocking, and positions her in front of Kevin.

Margo grabs a couple of other actors, tossing them at the feet of Kevin and Amanda, sometimes wiping her fingers over their mouths. "Everything on earth is yours," she says, "subjugate it, consume it! Do with it what you will!" Then she settles on the ground to sleep. The light softens. Kevin and Amanda tumble to the floor in an embrace. The others frolic around them, chuckling and babbling until Margo gets up again. She breaks the aura of playfulness with a single word: "Man!" She knocks Kevin to the ground, then takes a jack-knife out of her pocket and makes as if to hack away at his side. She kicks at Amanda who rises, seemingly drugged, from the ground. Margo arranges the pair together in an attitude of copulation.

At first, the serpent is portrayed by seven people following one after another in a human chain as they drag themselves along the ground, hissing. Jimmie separates himself from the group. He is small in stature, quick to move, quick to speak – which he can do in several languages. He amazes them all during lunch breaks by performing complex calculations almost instantly in his head. But he cannot dress according to the seasons, cannot cook a meal or count his change or find his way around the city without help. He had been employed in a sheltered workshop for years when one of the staff brought him to a Journey at SenseInSound. Soon afterwards, Connie and Bill invited him to live with them.

In some combination of languages only he can produce, Jimmie mutters a running commentary as he climbs the scaffold and hangs an apple in a plastic bag on one of its joints. He climbs down and takes a sash out of his pocket, which he waves in the air, eventually wrapping it seductively around Amanda. For Jimmie to learn all this has taken two years. Rebecca made a routine of Xeroxing her daily notes at the shop down the street, handing them to Connie and Bill, who took them home to help Jimmie study at night. Despite all their work, he often forgot what he was supposed to do next. But Marlin did not give up on Jimmie, and increasingly, the part has become tailored to his particular style of moving and speaking. He points to the apple, muttering and enticing Amanda to climb the scaffold, pressing himself against her. Then he binds her to the scaffold using the sash. She turns her head away from him.

"You want it, you want it you want it," he chants. Hanging on to the scaffold he whispers in her ear. Gradually, she turns to face him. He rips the plastic, takes down the apple and holds it to her lips. She continues resisting for a while then takes a bite, the juice running down her chin and chest, as he unwinds the sash. She slips down to the ground. Rubbing herself against Kevin, then withdrawing, Amanda seduces him as he tries to resist. When he breaks down and reaches for her, she hands him the apple instead. He bites. They kiss, then mount the scaffold.

"Let there be light!" they say in unison, and here's another difficult cue. Rebecca has to kill everything on the left-hand board at the same time as she turns on the right. She watches the reflection of her hands in the booth's window, and beyond them, the play, that miniature world for which she is responsible. With Marlin. Their work is a dance, and their collaboration connects them more intimately than any embrace.

Then it's on, off, on, off as the actors chant, "Light, dark, light, dark!"

Amanda and Kevin rest their heads together. Margo roars, shaking the scaffold, cursing the snake, then Amanda and Kevin, in Hebrew. They cry out, cover themselves with their hands and descend to stage level. The others tear off bits of their own costumes and wrap them around Amanda and Kevin, who run between the audience members to the back of the house. At the end of the play the company climbs the scaffold in formation. They present themselves like acrobats in a tableau.

In a rage, Margo tries shaking the scaffold, but the group remains solid. She tries tearing one or the other down. They don't move. Finally she whispers in the ear of one, who says the word "Truth," and another, who says *"la verité."* Then another: *"veritas,"* and so on, until they are all shouting the word for truth in different languages. They lose their balance and fall. They begin crawling on their bellies again. Gail and Katie loosen the knots on the frayed, hemp lines and bring the curtain down.

The play is an hour long, cut – just a few months before – from four hours. It was originally meant to include the stories of Cain and Abel, Noah and the flood. They had laboured painstakingly on the killing of Abel, yet the scene never quite worked. First, the two brothers killed each other, then Cain was a pure villain, murdering Abel in his sleep. Then a suicidal Abel begged Cain to kill him, putting the knife in his hand and lunging toward it. At times Cain was played by a woman, then Abel was, then they both were.

When it came to staging Noah's ark they fought about who was going to pair up with whom. One day Marlin announced that the play was falling into malignant narrative traps: the dualism of hero and villain, the exclusive matching of heterosexual partners. Radical surgery was needed. Whole sections were excised and three people cut out of the company entirely. Gail and Katie would stay, but with no roles. And there would be three newcomers.

Kevin was one of these. A doctoral student, he attended rehearsals at SenseInSound, but took time out for school when he needed to. Kevin had something special about him that no one questioned, not even Marlin. Keven was gorgeous. He was tall and strong, his face, classical with a wide brow and long chin, his manner, direct but polite. He managed to party good-naturedly with everyone on Friday nights, yet never seemed to get drunk. And he stayed faithful to his girlfriend, Samantha, who was waiting for him "home" in Prince Edward Island. He didn't say *at* home, or *back* home, just "home," and he said it often. The others teased Kevin about the challenges of being nude on stage with Amanda. Kevin shrugged and said, "A man's gotta have self-control!"

Marlin's way of working amazes Rebecca: his kindness, his brutality, his ability to flip from one to the other. Most of all, she admires his willingness to keep changing the play. He attaches to nothing. Scrupulously, he intercepts any facile story that might emerge. It reminds her of the way her mother constructs their woodpile every year at the back of the house. In the midst of building, Audrey shakes the reinforcing ends to make sure they hold steady. If it falls, so be it. She begins again.

Genesis runs for ten days. There is a single review with the headline: "Promising SenseInSound could use few laughs." Still, it is given four out of four stars by the critic, who interprets the show as scathing critique of the Free Trade Agreement with the United States. The review ends with the words: "A company to watch."

After *Genesis*, Rebecca spends two weeks on her biggest project: the basement. She has set up a rudimentary workshop down here, in the driest and brightest part of what resembles a medieval crypt. Even now, when she goes downstairs to appease the temperamental furnace she gets lost in the warren of rooms with their uneven floors and crumbling brick walls. When she first explored it, flashlight in hand and bowing her head to avoid banging it on the ceiling, she was convinced she would come across a skeleton. Instead she found furniture, appliances, lawnmowers, rotting carpets, old girlie magazines, lumber crawling with bugs. She knows she must reclaim all this space, but for the time being, encloses the mess behind whatever fire doors have been installed over the years. Someone has dug out a section at the back where she can stand to her full height. The floor there is covered in linoleum. A drain carries away the water that seeps in during wet weather. In this section, she has painted the walls a battleship grey, installed hanging lights, and created a raised platform for the power tools she found in the building or purchased second-hand.

Rebecca loves using her table saw, the intense focus of guiding the wood through the blade, the satisfaction of stacking up a series of uniformly sized boards when she's done. She positions the first for cutting and is about to switch on the machine when a movement catches the corner of her eye. It's Safra. Rebecca leaps away from the saw and places herself in front of it, holding the piece of wood like a barricade. The very presence of the three-year-old in the room with this lethal tool has brought an instinctive reaction, even though the machine is off. She puts the board to one side and strides over to Safra. They stand looking at each other, facing off. He wears his usual, grave expression but seems unconcerned about wandering so far.

Then his face crumples. Tears fall in a sheet and he emits hiccupping sobs. He raises his arms above his head, and – surprising herself – Rebecca picks him up. The child of two miniscule parents, he is small-boned and light. He wraps his legs around her waist and his arms around her neck. He fits there. She belongs to him. Everything is precluded now, other than making sure he is okay. She transfers him to one hip and walks him around, telling him the names of various pieces of equipment, grinning when at last his crying subsides and he begins to point to the tools and echo her words. Finally, he points to a counter-top she has salvaged and balanced between two filing cabinets. "There's nothing there," she says, then she understands. Transferring Safra to one hip she sweeps sawdust off the surface and puts him on the counter. She goes back to cutting boards while he sits and watches her. She thinks from time to time that she should go and tell someone, that they might worry, but it does not surprise her that no one comes looking for him.

Sam's House of Dreams

About

You're looking at a woman who never thought she'd own a guest house. Twenty years ago, I was teaching high school in Charlotte-town. My fiancé went to Toronto for university and we planned to move to wherever he got a job, and raise our family there. Well the family started a little sooner than we expected, and I found myself in a pawn shop trying to get a few dollars for my ring because my boyfriend's inner self was telling him to become an actor and commit himself to the present moment instead of to the future he had promised me. And I had twins on the way.

I moped around my parents' house watching this alien balloon growing on the front of my body, telling myself it would be over in a few months when I'd sign the kids over to a good, wholesome woman whose husband kept his inner self in his pants where it belonged. Then my grand-dad passed.

My grandparents' farm was always a magical place: the hill out back for tobogganing, the pond for skating and catching frogs in the spring, the wild berries, the rabbits, the tree house. Modern life being what it is, I didn't get out there as often as I'd like, but when I started making up a description to give real estate agents, looking through old photos and maps I realized how attached I was to the old place. It was like abandoning a person, not knowing who would care for them and how. And then my babies started moving inside me, and I knew what I had to do. I said *Mom, Dad: I'm going to do it. All of it. The kids, the farm, the whole thing*.

Well, my boys are grown up now, though I'm happy to say they live close by and still work with me. We have a simple and good life here. We work hard, and we're happy to have visitors from all over the world come and share it for a few days or sometimes even longer. Meals are plain and plentiful, and there's good talk and laughter and music around the big old kitchen table every night. To try it for yourself, click <u>here</u>.

1991

"You're it!" Connie sings, punching Rebecca on the arm as she whips by her in the front entranceway. Rebecca winces and reminds herself this is just a game. She doesn't chase Connie; instead she laughs and calls out, "Have fun!"

Connie pretends to be outraged until Bill scoops her up and runs away, carrying her over his shoulder as she shrieks with laughter. These days, there's lots of wrestling and chasing and giggling in the theatre. Their play, *Memorysong,* opens next week. It will take place in a schoolyard, under rented Klieg lights, in what is predicted to be sweltering weather. Based on children's rhymes and games, it calls for all of them to tumble, throw balls, cartwheel, jump rope and ride bicycles. For different segments they will gather and then disburse the way children do with their groups of friends. Sometimes they'll part ways sadly, sometimes angrily, sometimes they'll get distracted and simply drift away.

The play started out with improvisations on a series of nursery rhymes, and touched on the threats that children have faced throughout history: disease, starvation, natural disasters – but most of all, war. Then the United States began amassing troops in the Persian Gulf and a present-day war loomed. Operation Desert Shield became Operation Desert Storm, and one morning in January, a fighter pilot was interviewed on the radio. "Baghdad was lit up like a Christmas tree," were his enthusiastic words. Marlin gave them a day off, a day of mourning – not just for the people killed in Baghdad, but for the truth, the first casualty of war. When they came back to work the next day, he said they had to get more serious about aggression. They had to truly fight for each skipping rope or ball as if their lives depended on it. He said, "We have to get back to that time before the full range of emotions was prohibited. What we do in our Journeys, we don't need to do on the battle field."

Along with the aggression, a flood of playfulness was also unleashed. Rebecca thought of the actors as puppies wrestling together in the grass, completely without malice, fighting one moment and embracing the next.

All the roles are done interchangeably, with no identifiable characters except for one: Amanda, who is dressed all in white while the others wear canvas flour-bags, decorated with colourful patterns which they painted themselves. During their games, Amanda remains separate, hovering on the margins, trying in vain to get invited in. At last she is brought into a skipping game but when it comes her turn she gets tangled in the rope. She crouches on the pavement, holding herself around the middle while the others try to coax her to get up. She resists. At last six-year-old Safra, also dressed in white, joins them. He has shoulder-length hair, always a little matted on the right side where he sleeps. He draws close to Amanda, touches her hand and leads her away from the others. She flails – violently at first – then less and less until she settles into immobility. Eventually the others see her lying there and carry her away on their shoulders, humming the now-ominous nursery tunes.

Marlin has taught the group all the acrobatic moves he demonstrated years before. For several weeks he worked on the moves in the evenings, in a vacant apartment on the building's top floor. Sometimes he arrived bruised, once with his arm in a sling. He said, "You people are risking everything when you go on stage. I have to take that journey too."

But not everyone has taken the journey of *Memorysong*. One

day, Margo stopped partway through a session and retreated to one side, her face an almost florescent pink. She took deep breaths, cradling her arm. Then she fainted. *"Don't you get an emergency contact number when someone joins your … classes, or whatever they are?"* Guiltily remembering a long-ago conversation with Dorothy, Rebecca rifled through Margo's wallet and found a card listing her husband as emergency contact. Margo would be furious – she had left him – yet she did keep his name in her wallet. He drove over immediately to take Margo to the hospital. Rebecca tried calling a week later to check on her, and he said to leave his family alone.

Then Jimmie started having trouble. He managed the running and skipping, but when it came to throwing a ball he could never coordinate his movements. Learning to ride a bike was impossible. No matter how hard he tried, no matter how much extra attention was given to him, he could not do it. One morning he refused to get up, and the next and the next. He refused to walk around his room to stretch his legs, refused to bathe, eat or even get off his futon to use the bathroom. Connie and Bill were in tears when they told the group about it; neighbours had started complaining about the smell coming from their apartment. "He can come to live with me," Marlin volunteered without hesitation, but the next day Connie and Bill said they had gone home to find Jimmie gone. They called around to the hospitals and learned he had admitted himself to a psychiatric ward.

The review describes *Memorysong* as "a searing meditation on AIDS and the arts community" and says it is their breakout show. It is accompanied by a feature on Amanda in the "Living" section of the newspaper. The photo has her looking out from behind a theatre curtain. Her long hair falls over one naked shoulder. The headline reads, "Mother courage."

The theatre is full, and the Journeys are full, too. Full of people wanting to be part of SenseInSound.

Secrets from a Beautiful Marriage: Neuro-Typs from Sophie Johns

About

It all started when I met a man who told me I stank. The year was 1993, and I was thirty years old. Pretty hot if I do say so myself. I wasn't accustomed to hearing anything but propositions, but at least he got my attention.

I was an office temp, doing a placement at a psychiatric hospital, and this particular day I had a hangover, and was trying to sneak into one of the unused rooms and close my eyes for half an hour. But instead of quiet and darkness I found a strange, pipsqueak of a guy sitting at a computer terminal, chatting away to himself in another language. He shrieked and I shrieked, and he yelled "You stink!" And I said something in the order of "Effing Sicko!"

But Jimmie was right. I smoked a pack a day, back then, and told myself that if I loaded on the perfume no one would notice. And I was still reeking of beer from the night before. Long story short, Jimmie's infamous pickup line was the wakeup call I needed to change my life. That was the last time I drank, or smoked. And after a whirlwind seven-year courtship, we were married.

If you found this website, it's probably because you're dating, or considering dating someone on the <u>autism spectrum</u>. That's great! And there are lots of sites out there that will help you. *I'm* here to tell you about how our neuro-diverse relationship is a recipe for marital bliss. For anyone. Here's the secret: know yourself. Yourself? That's right. To be close to someone on the spectrum you have to know how you feel, what you want, and be able to say it in simple words. If that's not the recipe for a happy marriage, I don't know what is.

I should mention that Jimmie was already married when we met, and still is, and I have nothing but thanks for the one who came before me. It wasn't a woman, it was The Computer. Not one single computer, but the whole idea of computers, the whole invention. Just like any good first wife, The Computer transformed Jimmie from a Project into a Catch. I'll talk about the importance of fulfilling work here.

The right work was not easy to find, and for a very long time, Jimmie suffered because a whole lot of people had their own ideas about who he was, without ever asking him. As just one horrible example, he spent a few years with a theatre company where they created a kind of freak-show around his aptitude for languages and put him on display for the public. When he — not surprisingly — had a psychotic break — the couple he was living with left him on the steps of that fateful hospital in the middle of winter in the middle of the night and took off. But after lots of treatment a very, very smart resident sat Jimmie in front of one of those clunking, huffing machines they used back then. And he was home.

Jimmie went on to invent Operation Polyglot, a special translation app for doctors, and I have the five-bedroom house and SUV my mother always wanted for me. Except that's never been important. What's important is the worlds Jimmie opens up for me when we look at a painting or listen to a piece of music together. And the way I can count on him to be honest, loyal and funny. And the way I can still go out for a (dry) girls' weekend, and know exactly where I'll find him when I get home.

1993

"The Ballad of Lucy Jordan," hisses and buzzes over the new – to them – sound system. Rebecca sits cross-legged on the floor, sorting at last through the flour-bags that served as costumes for *Memorysong*. Some can be re-used. She puts them in one pile. The others will be torn up for rags. The song is an old favourite but doesn't energize her. Nothing does. She works in an exhausted trance.

"Here we are! The lady who keeps you all in order. Do you ever take her out for a treat to thank her?" Sylvia has snuck up on her. Amanda follows now, a flushed and coughing Safra in tow.

"No! We're terrible."

"We shall have to put a stop to that. I'll say goodbye now, dear. Rebecca and I will enjoy a boozy lunch and leave you on handkerchief duty. Up you get!"

Rebecca straightens herself unsteadily, one leg prickling. Reaching out a hand to shake Sylvia's, she hastily draws it back when she notices how dirty it is. She tells herself to smile graciously but can only manage a twisted expression that she decides must look like she is about to cry. She *is* about to cry, all of a sudden, but stops herself by jiggling the leg that has fallen asleep.

When the alarm rang this morning, Rebecca felt glued to her bed. She burrowed deeper under the covers, attributing her listlessness to a hangover. No. Admit it: the evening she had spent with her sisters had deflated her. She had come away feeling everything she was working on was meaningless, everything she felt proud of, trivial. Sarah was in town for a conference and Janice had come in from Montreal to join them. Rebecca wanted to show them all the work she'd done on the theatre, take them to one of the local buffet restaurants for dinner. Finally, they were visiting her city and she had a chance to spend time with them as adults, not revert to her childhood role as family fuckup. But Sarah had other plans. First, a show of expressionist paintings at the Art Gallery of Ontario, then dinner and drinks on a new strip of fashionable bars that had opened on College Street. It was, her sisters told her, a celebration for Rebecca's thirtieth birthday, which had come and gone three years ago because she refused to celebrate.

Rebecca leaned against a wall at the back of the gallery's lobby, looking out for her sisters and mentally composing reasons why they should cancel dinner reservations and see her workplace instead. Sarah arrived first. In spike heels, she looked as if her inflated bust might tip her forward at any moment. She had – as she put it – *invested* in breast implants last year. Sure enough, she had "made partner" immediately after returning to work. Sarah's heels resounded over the noise of the lobby as she strode forward, bangs and glossy ponytail undisturbed by the jostling crowd. Janice followed soon after, glancing down from time to time at her own body as if to make sure it was still there. Her eyes were ringed with black, hair bleached and arranged in spikes. She wore cowboy boots and tight jeans, a ripped T-shirt barely covering her chest beneath her leather jacket. *Who are these women?* Rebecca thought at the same time as she rushed forward to hold first one, then the other against her. *My sisters. My kin.* And she felt something return, not any particular memory but just familiarity: the way they were – in childhood – the *main* people for each other.

For better or for worse.

"How about some lipstick?" Sarah whispered, and left a smudge of her own on Rebecca's cheek.

"Sorry," Rebecca said, feeling her shoulders stoop of their own accord.

They walked from room to room, never able to get near the canvasses because of the crowds. There were couples all around her walking hand-in-hand, well-rested, well-dressed people, people with mates. Rebecca felt more and more alone, and – as she realized over dinner – people her age owned houses, too. Even if they didn't have money they took out loans. Even Janice, who went from one waitressing job to another to support her writing, had somehow found the means to buy a condo in Montreal. Immediately, there had been a contract for a novel, with what she called, in hushed tones, "a six-figure advance."

"It's a sign you made the right decision!" Sarah declared, and then they both turned to face Rebecca. She had clearly not made the right decision about anything. So this birthday celebration was nothing more than yet another discussion of Rebecca's "problem." Janice said there was someone meeting them later, someone from the film industry who could help Rebecca find work. *I don't need help! have a job! I have a life!* Rebecca protested in her mind.

They set out along College Street in the rain. What had once been a strip of dry-goods stores and men's-only coffee shops was now decorated with twinkling lights and flower boxes. They stopped in a bar to hear soul music, surrounded by wood paneling and mirrors. Despite the pounding rain, all the women in the room seemed to be wearing high heels. When had that become a requirement? Rebecca tucked her work boots into the rungs of her stool. And Janice's friend, Hi-Hat Slominsky, joined them. "The nick-name is from his drumming days," she explained. Now, he worked in film and had way too much work. Hi-Hat couldn't stay long – his girlfriend had been alone with the baby all week – but he gave Rebecca his card.

She watched Janice tuck herself under his arm as she hugged him, watched him stand back a little too quickly. "Baby!" he said, backing towards the door. Rebecca put the card in her knapsack, let it sink to the bottom, said she had an early call the next day and needed to get home.

Rebecca got out of bed this morning because she always did.

Standing in the shower, she noticed a black speck between the tiles. She picked away at the calking with her nail, saw a bloom of mold spreading underneath. Too much to do. There was not enough of her to go around. She wanted to go back to bed. But she went to work. She always did. She was the one who always went to work, anyway.

"The music!"

Rebecca points in the direction of the booth as if asking permission to go and turn it off. Sylvia nods and Rebecca bangs clumsily upstairs. *You'll call Martie.* Another business card, another phone call she never made. Over the years, guilt has shaded into resentment and Martie, a woman she has never met, has joined the ranks of her lecturing sisters in her imagination.

And everything she was doing instead of calling Martie. Those weeks when Marlin showed up at her apartment every night. She lives as if they never happened, yet the mere presence of Sylvia strips away the thin curtain of the present, leaving her memories exposed. Now Rebecca is going to be trapped for what might be the whole afternoon with yet another person who makes her feel like an oversized underachiever. She plods downstairs and waits by the theatre doors while the older woman strides confidently toward a red Alfa Romeo parked outside.

"This is it!" she calls, gesturing with her keys in the air. Not that there can be any doubt. The car fairly gleams among the low-slung, dusty and rust-eaten wrecks that line Gerrard Street. And yet those cars – not Sylvia's – manage to look out of place. Rebecca addresses herself to the task of folding her legs, pulling her knapsack in after her and trying to find room to stash it between her feet. Sylvia puts on a pair of red gloves before taking the wheel.

"First, home to change, I think. Which way?"

"Um. West. I'm on Shaw Street."

"Shaw Street!" Sylvia laughs, slipping deftly out of her parking spot. "Leon's old stomping ground. Some lovely houses 'round there. In those days it was all families bringing in one relative after another from Europe. So many people packed under one roof. Not us, of course. For his new English bride Leon bought a house in Forest Hill. My dear, the appliances! They were so bright I needed sunglasses to make a cuppa tea. Am I driving too quickly?"

"No," says Rebecca, gripping her own thigh as they round a corner. She feels like throwing up. What to do once they get there? Should she invite Sylvia up to her one-room apartment while she changes her clothes? Will she lock herself in the bathroom like a teenager or will some horrible, womanly intimacy open up between them, and she'll be expected to doff her clothes while Sylvia watches? And she has nothing but jeans and T-shirts to wear.

"Up here." She points up Shaw Street, thinking of the stained yellow bricks on the façade she once proudly greeted as home.

"I'll wait in the car," Sylvia says. "Dunno if I want to attempt those stairs with my creaky knees!"

"Oh, thank you! I mean … see you in a minute."

"Basic black is good anywhere!"

Sylvia is reading *NOW Magazine* when she returns. A keen expression puckers the corners of her mouth and Rebecca notices the bright pink accent that is the signature of Leon's company, Theatre in Bloom. They have taken out a full-page ad for their remount of *Oliver*. As Rebecca gets in, Sylvia continues to scrutinize the paper for a moment. "Very good," she says, "this little paper. Very contemporary. Marlin should take out an ad. When he gets around to putting on a proper play!"

Sylvia takes off in the direction of Bloor Street. "Oh, the city is changing!" she declares, exchanging her caustic tone for a cheery one with the same adroitness as she turned the car. "I often tell Leon that pretty soon we won't have to go to New York anymore! And speaking of new things, have you been to a sushi bar?"

"Never."

"They're cropping up all over these days. It's a new world!"

The restaurant is in a low, windowless building on Dupont Street. In the entrance-way Rebecca ducks under a curtain that seems to have no function other than to make her feel even more awkward.

A woman in a kimono greets them with a small nod. Sylvia nods at the hostess, who nods in return. Sylvia replies with the same sort of nod. She jokes with the waitress as Rebecca tries to fold her knees under a low table.

"That warm wine will have me on the *tatami* in a minute, but this young lady will try some." She meets Rebecca's eyes, nodding, and Rebecca produces a tiny, abashed nod of her own.

"I'll have a gin and tonic, thank you very much."

There are hot towels for their hands, and snacks in tiny dishes. Sylvia refills her thimble-sized cup from a carafe, then another one appears. By the time the dainty patties of rice arrive, adorned with strips of fish, Rebecca wants to scoop up these morsels five at a time and get on to the main course, preferably a steak. Sylvia picks up her chopsticks and expertly conveys a piece of food to her mouth. "Let me show you." She demonstrates with her tiny hands. As if hypnotized, Rebecca maneuvers the sushi into her mouth. Delicious! It is if someone has put together everything that is normally relegated to the side of the meal: the sweet, the salty, the sour, and packaged it in with the things that are good for you. Perhaps this miniature world is not designed to torment her after all. But after a couple of bites, the spell of Sylvia's instructions wears off and Rebecca's chopsticks clamp together. The rice goes on the floor and the fish lands in Rebecca's water glass. She is horrified, then looks up at Sylvia, whose eyes meet hers steadily. Rebecca takes a deep breath: "This fish is very fresh!"

Sylvia gives the trace of an approving nod before letting loose a tinkling series of giggles. Rebecca joins in the laugh. No sooner does it settle down than it bubbles up again.

"I've certainly seen a lot of the world since I've met Leon." Sylvia makes this comment as though responding to a remark of Rebecca's. It all flows effortlessly, yet Rebecca has the feeling that the whole meeting has been scripted, including the shared laugh, including her own role, though she hasn't even seen – let alone rehearsed it – in advance. Rebecca wishes that she could stay in this perfectly choreographed world forever. At the same time, she longs to get back to her familiar, sloping couch and mismatched dishes. Now she understands why fairy godmothers make rare appearances in stories. They wear you out.

"I always tell people Leon plucked me from the chorus," Sylvia declares. As the gin gets lower in her glass she embellishes her speech with accents as if they were colourful scarves. "Well, I'm afraid it was all a bit more tame than that."

Rebecca takes her cue. "I bet it's a good story all the same."

"Well it's got a happy ending, I can say that much. Do you want to hear it?"

"Please!"

"I'm from London, as I guess you can tell. It was a hard city to live in back in the fifties, a dark place, bomb damage everywhere. But I was young and didn't know anything else. I'd been working – on the stage, I mean – since I was six years old. When the war started a couple of years later, I struck a chord, somehow. Lifted people's spirits. That was my job and it was all I knew. I played love scenes, of course, but I had no experience with real boys. And when I met Leon it was in temple. It was a fluke. We weren't religious and only went twice a year for the anniversary of my grandparents' deaths, to say the prayers, the way we do. And it so happened that we went to *shul* on January 11, 1956. It was a terrible day, I remember. Icy rain. You're supposed to walk everywhere on *shabbos* – don't know if you're aware. We got a cab to drop us two streets away so no one would see. Now it so happened there was a group of boys who came from the YMHA in Toronto. (Dunno who convinced them to go to England in January, but he must have been a brilliant salesman.) Leon was twenty-six. He was doing well! Owned his first drug store, and like me, he'd worked since he was small.

"Anyway, after years of work Leon finally went on holiday. Now, he was much more religious than me at that point. So on Saturday he went to temple, and it so happened I was there too. Leon calls it *bashert* and I call it chance, but after the service we went downstairs to a dreadful sort of meeting hall in the basement, and there was the group of them down the end like a bunch of undertakers. But across a crowded room as they say … Here was Mrs. Mandelbaum of blessed memory making her way over to us with one of the boys in tow. Grinning, he was.

"Now Leon is the love of my life but he's not what you'd call a matinee idol and at twenty-six, he was not at his best. Thick glasses. Horrendous suit! He did the right thing asking a respectable widow to introduce him but once he got to our side of the room he barely let Mrs. M. get a word in. 'Hello, I'm Leon Garten.' Just like that. He stood there with those gargantuan teeth on display. I thought he must be odd, but, oh, he knew what he was doing! 'What a lovely city you have, Mrs. Bloom!' Before you knew it, mummy was chatting away. Thought he'd slipped something in the tea.

"And he winnowed out the information that I was in a show at the Comedy, a revival of *Annie Get Your Gun*, if you can believe it. I had the part of a boy! *Still we're happy as can be doin' a-what comes naturally!* It was hardly what you'd call a sex-pot role. But Leon went to see me every single night. And he always had a present for me. It started with one rose, then two. Three. And then there were chocolates, and next it was a lovely scarf. And each night Leon would come backstage and invite Mummy and me out for a treat after the show.

"Mummy's reaction was strange. As soon as Leon came along, she became distant. Whenever he visited the dressing room she just left! And I stood there trying to make conversation and refusing his invitations because I didn't know what else to do. I wanted advice but Mummy said nothing. She was trying not to interfere, I suppose, but at the time I felt very much – very much alone."

Sylvia pauses and sighs, and looks at a point beyond Rebecca's shoulder.

"But …" Rebecca begins, wanting the rest of the story.

"The course of true love never did run smooth."

"But you *did* marry him …"

"Eventually, the gifts were in smaller boxes. A bracelet and a necklace, one each night, then one earring, then the other, which gave them all a good laugh." Sylvia turns her head this way and that to display sapphires, framed in diamond chips.

"And finally, the last night – a ring. Three diamonds, it had." Rebecca glances at Sylvia's finger but finds only a plain gold band.

"I was alone in the room and I put it on. I held it up by the window and looked at it. I thought, 'This ring will light my way through the fog.' I looked at it for a long time. Don't like to say how long. And then all of a sudden I imagined it burning into my finger, going right through to the bone. And I wrenched it off and put it back in the box. When I think back, I understand. He sent a card with the ring: 'The girl that I marry will have to be ... you!' As if I had no choice in the matter. It was really too much for me. Because you see, the very same week there was a director, Bobbie Lance was her name."

There's a hint of contempt in Sylvia's voice. Rebecca asks, "Lintz?

"Laaaahnce." Sylvia draws out the syllable mockingly. "Not surprised you never 'eard of 'er. She had a little flourish, back in the fifties and then went back to obscurity. Where she belonged, as far as I'm concerned. *Annie Get Your Gun* was not to her taste, but Lance saw it anyway for some reason, and after that she sort of seized upon me and wouldn't let go. It had to do with the way I played the boy's part. She wanted me for the lead in a new production of hers. *Antigone*. A very serious play, a new translation from French. Bobbie's star was rising, but I didn't like this style of hers. It was all so negative. But Mummy was all for it, and I couldn't very well say no. Our livelihood rested on my career."

"But you *did* marry Leon."

"I sent back the ring. It's terrible to say now, but I *enjoyed* it a little bit, imagining what he'd feel when he got it back. It fascinated me, just that I had that power over someone. Well I never found out because he didn't give up. When he got back to Canada he wrote to me every week. He described Toronto, said everything was clean and they had lots of food and the sun shone and the houses had central heating and enormous refrigerators. Still not sure why he thought that detail would interest me. Anyway, I just put the letters away."

Rebecca feels relief without knowing its source. Then she remembers – she isn't the only one who's ignored a good offer. Sylvia has done it too. Was the reference planned? If Sylvia notices a reaction she doesn't show it.

"Bobbie's methods were a sort of brain-washing. She was forever trying to get inside you – right under your skin. I just wanted to get on to the next play. But we finally did it on a bare black stage, and I didn't get to wear anything but a little toga."

"I kept wondering what use it was, to make everyone miserable? I was in a cage that was lifted up in the air, and this was supposed to represent burying me alive. Bobbie had some reason for that. Confusing up and down. I was supposed to act like I was suffocating. I had to make sounds like a person really dying. We'd been through the Blitz. We'd heard voices of people in distress. We'd seen the rubble and 'orrible things poking out. Why would you want to go out and remind people of what they were trying to put behind them?"

She might as well be describing The Work. And she is making it seem pointless.

"Oh the caterwauling we made! Bobbie used me as an example for the rest of the cast. 'You must all be like Sylvia, drawing from the depths of herself.' But I was drawing from the singing and speech lessons I'd had since I was five! It's the only reason I had a voice, after all that scraping and screeching. It was held over. Seemed to go on for years. And then came *Oedipus*. No script at all this time, just a lot of scurrying about, flinging red paint and braying like donkeys. The rehearsal period went on and on. But it had a kind of momentum, all this nastiness. I would never have left, I think, if it hadn't been for –"

Sylvia closes her eyes for a moment before resuming. "We were alone in the world, Mummy and I. She was all I had. And then one day she went to the doctor, just for a check-up – at least as far as I knew and … within three weeks she was gone. She drifted away, quietly and quickly, may her memory be for a blessing. But sitting by her bedside I had time to think for the first time in my life.

"And I saw what was stopping me from marrying Leon. Of

course, he said that Mummy could come to Canada and live with us. But I could not imagine Mummy outside of London. Or myself without her, or us, together, without our work. When she died, Leon and his proposal just flooded into the space she left. I was terrified. Leon was so deliberate. Working away at me like I was a sum of figures he was adding up. And so confident it *would* add up. But I was exhausted. I thought, I've never had a holiday in my life. It's finally time. And so I went to Toronto. It was spring. Lovely. I stayed with Leon's parents for a month, and I saw him every day."

"And you got married."

"Not yet. You see, here's the reason I'm telling you this story. When I went back to England I went back to my old life. That's all. Bobbie wanted me again and we started a new play (about a man's liver being pecked out by birds if you must know) but you see, it was different. Because I owned a house. We lived in a flat, but Mummy owned a house, a beautiful house in Holland Park. And I inherited it.

"And *that's* when things changed. I'd seen my name on the marquee of theatres, but it was different, seeing it on the deed of a house. I was a full person who could make a big decision. And if things didn't work out in Canada I could come back. I wasn't completely giving myself over." She looks piercingly at Rebecca, who can only return the gaze with frankness.

"I thought: this Leon is a good man. He's not given up. He's good to his mum. He was good to my mum. Maybe he'll be good to me. I decided to take the plunge, and I've never regretted it. I've been the leading lady for him, and my life has been better than any play because it's gone on. So far. So far …Puh! Puh!" Sylvia makes a spitting motion to either side. "But you see, I waited too long to have a family. There were … disappointments. And when Amanda finally came along …" Sylvia finds a tissue in her purse and dabs her eyes. Rebecca's eyes fill, in response.

The waitress brings tea and some balls of rice with sweet, red-brown filling. "Now," Sylvia folds her napkin and places it deliberately beside her. The scene has changed again. "My husband likes to give people a chance."

"Yes," says Rebecca. She stares at the tablecloth with its bits of leftover rice and blots of soy sauce.

"And you have made a mistake."

"I didn't want to – I mean. I didn't know what to do so I just let it slide. But I didn't mean to seem … At least I – I just didn't know what to do."

Now it is no longer a fairy godmother sitting across from her, but one of Rebecca's own tribe, with the ability to switch from merriment to gravity in an instant, to make a criticism like a clean incision: in and out.

"What if you'd left a door unlocked at the theatre? What if you realized it in the middle of the night? What would you do?"

"It's never happened. But I'd go and fix it."

"Right away?"

Rebecca looks up. "Of course!"

"It's been almost ten years."

"Time just …"

"There are some mistakes you can't fix, Rebecca. You can't get the years back."

Rebecca is speechless with remorse and dread. Years pass. They wear you down. Slow diminishment is all she has to look forward to. And fighting the fatigue that is stronger with every early morning, every late night, every Journey. She should be doing something about this, living differently, but she's forgotten how.

"Rebecca, that man … He'll take and take. It's obvious to us. We need to …"

Reflexively, she is on guard, ready to defend Marlin – defend The Work, but she's wrapped up in politeness, unable to say a word. Sylvia's graciousness is more penetrating than her sisters' criticisms, though they all give the same message: she's doing everything wrong.

"What I'm saying is that you may not always have a salary. And you need to make provisions." A business card appears on the table. *Harvey Fox, Realtor.* It advances toward Rebecca, propelled by Sylvia's tastefully lacquered nail. "You'll call Harvey next week. You'll get in his car, and you'll travel around with him, and you'll find a place. We'll cover the down-payment. The rest will be up to you. You need to do this while you can still get a mortgage. Do you understand?"

Rebecca says, "Thank you," and takes a panicked breath. This is a gift, an overwhelmingly generous one yet it feels anything but good. To reach for the card means –what? Sylvia and Leon are so clearly against Marlin. She does not want to be in their debt. But there's more. *I was a full person who could make big decisions.* The very idea of owning a home – of making any big decision separate from Marlin and SenseInSound – feels like a cold, piercing blade that could destroy everything she lives for. Sylvia taps the card commandingly. Rebecca reaches for her knapsack but it's at home. She puts the card in her pocket instead. Sylvia raises an eyebrow, but rather than mentioning the card, she asks, "Can you keep a secret?"

Rebecca nods. Now what is she up to?

"Many years ago – Amanda was ten – I went back to England for what I thought would be two weeks. But word got around and I was offered a part – just a small one – and I said yes to it, and before I knew it the time stretched to three months. I was happy. So happy. Can you believe it, I had no lines! All I had to do was laugh at the end of the play. But I was *in it* again. The dust and smog, the broken Tube service, the short days, the cold. That food! It's not as if there was another man – Leon is the love of my life – but I was there again where I belonged and going on day to day, and I sort of – drifted. You didn't talk as much, long distance, as you do now. There was more of a separation. Leon – honestly, I don't think he noticed. It wasn't in his plans for me to leave." (She shakes her head and looks down.) "It didn't make sense, so it didn't exist. But Amanda knew something was wrong. I didn't answer her letters, and just gave her a quick call every now and again. That summer she was in a dance competition and she didn't … *do* terribly well. It was hard for me to understand. By ten years of age I was up in front of thousands of men every week. They were risking their lives for the country and I was there to lift their spirits. I danced when I had blisters. I sang with a fever of a hundred and two. If I was feeling – disappointed – that was nothing! Nothing! But Amanda … She had to go to a special sort of school for a while. And ever since … anything to do with … being abandoned or left. She takes it all so personally. Thinks she's not measuring up."

Rebecca feels as if there were a rope tightening around her chest. Amanda is smaller, prettier, richer, more talented, but most of all she appears to have a mysterious, self-regulating climate inside her that makes her able to deal with Marlin's wavering attention. Deal with it even better than Rebecca, with her carefully constrained waves of hope and despair. She comes before Rebecca in his life because she is the best at managing – not him – but herself. It is a quality, like Marlin's stillness, that people come to SenseInSound to learn. But it also made it possible for Rebecca to sleep with her boyfriend for two months without worrying about hurting her.

"We've tried to arrange things for her, thinking she'd grow out of it, but she never really has. And we are … comfortable … so … She's decided on her career, and the best way to keep her safe is to stay involved. You are part of this whole business that she's chosen, and we've supported you all along. We need you there, for her."

"I really appreciate –"

"I know it, Rebecca. This work. I've done it. Confusing up and down. Light and Dark. You confuse right and wrong, eventually. You get carried away with it all, and then you pass a certain point and you don't know which is which, anymore." Sylvia looks at Rebecca fixedly. "I think you understand what I mean."

Rebecca nods. She retrieves her wallet and puts the card carefully inside.

IMDB

Dame Sylvia Bloom

With a dancing and singing career that began before she could read, Sylvia Bloom was a rare visitor to the screen until her recent five-season run as the titular detective in the BBC's *Duck Undercover*. Bloom plays Sophie Duckworth, the unprepossessing wife of an impresario who knows nothing of Sophie's secret life in international espionage. In addition to her popularity on stage, Bloom was known for her dedication and fearlessness in entertaining enlisted men during World War Two. Accompanied by her mother, retired actress Lily Bloom, she travelled throughout Europe performing a grueling series of solo concerts for the troops. Bloom has been married to television and theatre magnet Leon Garten since 1956. She was made a Dame Commander of the Order of the British Empire in 2009 after dedicating her entire earnings from *Duck Undercover* to found The Bounty Centre for girls' mental health.

Actress (10 credits)

2006 – present (five seasons) Sophie Duckworth: *Duck Undercover*
2003/4 (2 seasons) – Nanna: *As We Go Along*
1954 – Mrs. Laidlaw: *New Horizon*
1950 – Secretary: *Bracken*
1945 – Susan: *Susan at the Seaside*
1940 – Wendy: *In the Trenches*
1937 – Mary Newcombe: *Newcombe Place*
1935 – Child: *Up Up and Away*

1994

Rebecca sets her alarm for six, layers on long-johns, a T-shirt and two sweaters. On the radio, there is news of ice on the roads. Fine. Nothing can stop her from getting to work. She sets out into the dark streets, walking with a confident, relaxed stride while others mince around, afraid to touch the ground. She looks forward to being the first one at work after Christmas break. She'll open the mail, check the plumbing and electricity, get the heating going in time for everyone's arrival the next day. And there is something else. The inside pocket of her parka is weighed down with a package: a small hammer, wrench and screwdriver for Safra. She imagines him coming toward her, standing close the way he does after he hasn't seen her for a while. He will wait there soberly until she holds out her arms. He'll squeeze her in a surprisingly strong grip, and she'll stroke the long, curly hair which he now combs out scrupulously many times a day. He will let go suddenly, stand back and put his hands in his pockets. That's when she'll crouch down and hand him the tools. He'll say nothing, just examine them. She'll clear an area of the basement floor and give him a piece of wood and some nails, teach him to stabilize them and hammer them in straight.

Rebecca is not the first one in the theatre, though. She finds all the lights on and the front door unlocked. A man greets her in the entranceway, dressed in a mauve cashmere sweater and crisp jeans. Light glints off his bald head. He is shorter than her, and solidly built, with a sculpted look to his chest that can only have been achieved by spending hours in the gym.

"You must be Rebecca," he says, stepping forward and taking her hand in a painfully strong grip. He's wearing a bracelet and smells like cookie dough. "Deverell O'Neill. I work for Leon, but for the foreseeable future, I'm here as your business consultant."

Rebecca loosens her ice-encrusted muffler and unzips her parka. She imagines Deverell sizing up its dirty sleeves, the fur coming out in clumps from around its hood. *It works*, she imagines telling him. *That's what counts for me.*

With a smile, Deverell turns, walks straight into Rebecca's office and sits behind her desk! Well, it isn't really her office. A candy counter during the building's movie-theatre days, sometimes it acts as a change room or box office. It is certainly not Deverell's office, though, and he appears to have staked a claim there. He has piled her papers on a table in the corner and Rebecca finds herself shoving them under her arm and heading for the door as if they held something shameful.

"I'll let you get settled," he says. (He'll *let* me *get settled?*) "We can meet later."

"I'm busy."

"Okay then. Next week."

"We'll see."

Leon and Sylvia are behind this. Deverell works for Theatre in Bloom. He's been seconded, he tells Rebecca, and will stay until SenseInSound is "financially viable." This will mean getting them their status as a registered charity, applying for grants and donations and bringing the theatre into the computer age. He has begun what he called a Needs Assessment, interviewing everyone associated with the company.

She ignores the schedule he has posted. In the end, he leaves her a note suggesting one Friday after work. She delays for an hour after everyone else has left, thinking he might give up on her, but no such luck. He is lying in wait when she walks past the office and puts an overly-familiar hand on her waist to steer her in. "Hard working lady!" he remarks, and flips the switch on the espresso machine he's installed, never asking her if she wants a coffee or how she likes it. He sweetens the coffee heavily before handing it to her, and settles behind the desk.

"Could you describe your role, Rebecca?"

"I run a theatre company."

"Take me through a typical day."

He poises his hands over the keyboard, awaiting her answer. Flushed, Rebecca stares down at her lap. He leans around the monitor which occupies the top of the desk. "I'm listening!"

"I find out what needs to be done and I do it." For the rest of the interview, she keeps her answers equally short.

On the following pay-cheque, she finds she's been given a raise. Deverell also tells her that she'd better advertise for an assistant in the coming months, because she will be visiting the other theatres in town to look at their lighting and sound boards before purchasing a system of their own. And he wants her to speak at the college where he teaches a course. She doesn't trust him or anything he offers. The more time she can spend in the control booth, the better. Deverell is not part of this company and never will be; she'll wait him out. Rebecca puts a couch in the booth and stashes all her files in a plastic bin beside it. This will be her domain.

But he has infiltrated the place. He leaves his scent everywhere. First, it's the vanilla cologne, then the coffee aroma that wafts from the office. In Rebecca's mind these smells become associated with his deep voice and the pop music he plays all day. *How many Lionel Ritchie CDs can a person own?* His careful grooming seems an insult to Marlin, to how hard life is for him, trying to convince everyone to see beyond the surface. And an insult to The Work itself, which demands a rigorous approach to every aspect of life. No feel-good music in the background. Rebecca continues to brew an urn of acrid, supermarket-bought coffee each morning and sets out sugar and powdered creamer for herself and the rest of the company. If anyone comments on the lovely smell from Deverell's office, Rebecca feels personally offended. He is an interloper, ignoring rules she never noticed she was following until now.

He always brings lunch, which he warms up in his own microwave. Sometimes he makes forays to the grocery stores in the neighbourhood and shows off the spices he has bought. He will take them home to his mother in Windsor when he visits at Christmas. "Won't she be thrilled!" After a few months, the cooking smells begin to emanate not from Deverell's office, but from upstairs. He is cooking in Amanda's apartment, first lunches, then dinners. Then the smell of coffee is there in the mornings when Rebecca arrives. She wants to be angry at Amanda but finds her so pale and thin it is hard not to feel sorry for her. Rebecca looks to Marlin as a guide to how to react. He is showing consternation. Sometimes she notices Amanda leaning against him, frail and pained. Each day, Deverell's voice gets louder, more confident. Proprietary. Here insinuates himself where no one is supposed to go.

Soon there is another newcomer, Davis. The names of the two men become instantly combined: DeverellandDavis. No one can talk about one without mentioning the other, though linking them is probably the last thing anyone should do. Davis is Marlin's choice – a kind of counter-move to the hiring of Deverell.

Marlin introduces Davis (Alan Davis is his full name) as a Renaissance man. He is a choreographer who also designs sets. He is also a movement coach, trained in something called Experiential Somatics. Whatever that is, it keeps him very spry. At seventy years of age, he still performs regularly as a dancer. He is going to be working with them for the next few years, on a show they tentatively call *Parturition*, about the violence of birth. Marlin says they are ready to work with more substantial props and sets. Davis will give up all his other work and join SenseInSound. He'll design the set, co-direct what are now increasingly being called "rehearsals" – and give private lessons in Experiential Somatics to everyone in the company.

Rebecca constructs a series of wooden blocks, which they'll move around the stage as the piece is created. There will be a heap of fabric available too, and some objects collected in a trunk. Rather than working with designs on paper, Davis will watch the actors improvise with these items for as long as needed; nothing has to be decided yet. Davis speaks quietly and his movements have an elegance that strips away distractions. He always dresses in black: a turtleneck and dance pants, with a scarf in some bright colour around his neck and soft, lace-up shoes on his slender feet. After each rehearsal he spends two hours with a different company member for an Experiential Somatics lesson. This means clearing the rehearsal area, leaving only a mat on the floor and a single, straight-backed chair. From the booth Rebecca sees him doing something resembling massage at times, with his student lying prone on the mat or sitting upright in the chair. Sometimes, the two figures seem to be dancing, standing a short distance from one another, swaying gently as Davis holds his student around the ribs or by the hands.

One day, Davis touches Rebecca's shoulder. "You're in pain," he says.

Well, now that you mention it … A dull throbbing comes to her attention and she thinks of the way the heating pad has taken up permanent residence on the end of her couch, of how many mornings she has swallowed a couple of painkillers with her coffee. Somehow, she forgets it all as the work-day starts. "How can you tell?"

Davis smiles. "Why don't you come and see me on Friday?"

Davis begins the session facing Rebecca. He places a hand on either side of her face, with his palms on her cheeks and fingertips on the back of her skull. He is a small man, yet he seems to take all of her weight in his hands. The feeling is disconcerting.

"Got the world on your shoulders!"

Rebecca sighs. Davis beckons her to sit, then walks around her chair, lightly touching her every so often in ways that make her effortlessly sit up straight with her hands resting comfortably on her thighs. He takes the wrist of the non-painful side and lifts her arm gently in front of her. Her arm begins to move almost of its own accord, waving gracefully in the air as if choreographed. She can't tell which of them is initiating it. A sense of lightness travels up her arm, across her shoulders and down the opposite arm. Her shoulder twitches.

"Aha!" Davis says, "There!" He touches a spot at the base of her neck.

Yes.

She feels a rush of admiration for Davis, for Marlin, for The Work. This is what it can do. Touch who you really are. Teach who you really are. Davis picks up her left arm. It moves stiffly, reluctantly.

"Okay. Okay." Davis chuckles and puts it down again. "Not so easy to lay that burden down. Let's go back here." He takes the non-painful arm again and it moves rhythmically in the air, as if it had a will of its own. It feels so good she wishes she could go on forever. Eventually, he sets her hand on her thigh again and takes her head in his hands, firmly holding her around the back of the skull. She has the feeling that he is taking all her worries and dilemmas into his hands. He guides her to stand, then guides her to sit down on the chair again, then to stand, then to sit. She feels weightless.

"Now on your own."

She does the movement herself, still imagining Davis's hands guiding her, taking a new pathway through the familiar movement, a pathway that doesn't hurt. Davis touches various points along her spine. A question gathers, but not a question in words. It is a question that bones and muscles and viscera might ask, something about a different way of living, a way that does not entail being exhausted all the time.

What if ...?

Davis steps back, nodding to encourage her to speak.

"Wow. I feel like a giant."

"An exquisite spine." Davis runs his hands down her back. "Remember this ..." (holding her around the back of the ribs) "... do you feel it?"

"Sure. Wow. I really do!" Davis beams at her. His neat and gracious manner has a kind of detachment to it, but for the duration of the session he is there purely for Rebecca. "I feel great. I feel great."

She meets Deverell on their way out of the building. "You've got a spring in your step," he says, and for a change she walks through the door he is holding instead of making a show of opening the one beside it.

"Davis is amazing."

"Any thoughts on when you'd like to come in to the college?"

She laughs. "Get me when my defenses are down! Okay. Sometime this month. One hour at the most."

Davis touches Marlin between the shoulders, rocking him back and forward on his chair until he sits up straight, straighter than he has in a long time. How long has he been slouching? Rebecca has not noticed the change in him until now. Davis says, "May I?" He takes off Marlin's glasses, puts them on a small table and continues adjusting his position in subtle ways. Rebecca blushes to see Marlin's face naked; she feels like a voyeur, yet stares, transfixed.

She's in the back row, hunched in one of the corner seats, feeling trapped. It took her longer than usual to clean up her notes tonight, and when she looked up from her place in the booth, Marlin's Experiential Somatics session was starting. Now what? Witnessing any of it seemed forbidden, yet trying to slip out of the building unnoticed would somehow make it worse.

Alright: she wants to watch. Wants to know Marlin as no one else can.

After leaving him seated for a while. Davis places a hand on either side of Marlin's head and helps him stand. He directs him to sit, then stand, sit, then stand again, just as he did with Rebecca. The next time Marlin is standing, Davis touches his rib-cage lightly, moving it a little, side-to-side.

"That's nice."

"Yes. Isn't it? And your voice is gorgeous. Now walk for me a bit, will you?"

Marlin does not move.

"Show me how you transfer your weight."

Marlin reaches in the direction of his glasses.

"A few steps without them."

Marlin snaps his fingers and points. "Glasses!" he commands. Davis shakes his head and hands the glasses to him. "Okay – I won't argue. But walk."

Marlin takes a few steps.

"What's going on?"

"Nothing."

What does Davis mean? Then it becomes apparent. Marlin steps forward with the right foot, then hesitates as if the left has not got the message yet. The pause lasts only a moment. Then he picks up the left, which flops forward as if a hinge had broken in his ankle. With the next, careful step he resumes his normal gait.

"How long have you had the drop foot?"

Marlin says. "We're done here." He continues walking away with slow, controlled steps, lifting each knee high. He hesitates at the top of the stairs, takes a breath, and then makes his way down them at the same deliberate pace, clinging to the railing Rebecca is glad to have installed.

"You need to see a doctor," Davis calls, but Marlin does not stop walking. Davis holds up his palms, looks into them as if reading a solemn message there. At last he sighs and packs away the chair and the mat. Rebecca slips out the door, a pain in her gut. The pain gets worse the next day when she takes the business card out of a kitchen drawer. But she calls Harvey Fox anyway.

Marlin flops down on the couch, hunched over with his head in his hands. Rebecca leaves him in peace and senses his gratitude for her silence. The next day he joins her in the booth again, and the day after that. At rehearsal the following afternoon she feels emboldened to approached Marlin, positioning herself beside him in their familiar way, surveying the room. Can it be? At first, she is not sure, then the sensation is undeniable. He is coming closer to her, pressing his side against hers. Then she feels an arm around her back, draping over her hip.

They look out into the room, pressed together. She feels ecstatic, yet takes care to show nothing in her face. Guilt mixes with desire. This is forbidden, fascinating. He rubs her back lightly, deliciously respecting its contours. Nothing else matters but this connection. Rebecca fears it will be a one-time thing, but from then on Marlin approaches daily and puts his arm around her or takes her hand. That touch! His touch is that of a man who knows bodies in a special way, who has opened up – still can open up – experiences for her that she did not know were possible. Days are filled with the warm haze of their closeness. At nights, she imagines him turning her toward him so that they're face-to-face, imagines the start of a kiss. But the fantasy is one of pure potential. It only goes so far before looping back on itself. This is fine; it keeps desire brewing, never boiling over, and it keeps at bay the memory of what she witnessed during Marlin's session with Davis. She's worried about Marlin, of course – but there's something else, too. Something wrong with Marlin means that there is something wrong with her, with all of them, with their reason for being there, which is to prevent disease. She feels inexplicably, yet inescapably, ashamed.

And on Saturdays, she puts all that behind a wall and drives around with Harvey Fox in his car. His first offerings are lofts converted from old factories on Queen Street West. "Ideal for artsy types," he says. Harvey shows her six, insisting that when she finds the right one she will snap it up. Rebecca keeps on saying no. Next, he tries to interest her in one of the houses in rapidly gentrifying Little Italy. She can divide it into apartments and eventually make a fortune on resale. No again. And again. When she asks to look at houses in the less trendy area around St. Clair West, he rolls his eyes, but concedes, "The customer's always right."

Harvey apologizes for the house. It has frosted glass and gold trim everywhere. All the wood is stained an orangey colour. The owner, a builder, has clearly lavished the most expensive – and least fashionable – materials on this house, which he designed for his mother. The tiles and cupboards have been installed with such thoroughness that the whole house would have to be pulled down in order to replace them. Resisting Harvey's attempts to herd her out the door, Rebecca examines everything. This is it. The house is solid, though not at all bright. There is also a miniature but dry basement apartment which Rebecca can rent out; still, she finds herself awake many nights trying to think of things she could do without, in order to meet the mortgage payments. The anxiety, she concludes, will be good for her, an energizing force.

Do people lie from weariness, or does lying make them weary? Rebecca is too weary to tell. And yet she enjoys her sliver of detachment, the way she manages to bathe in desire then walk away from it and do her house-hunting without mentioning it to Marlin. It reminds her of the way her sisters keep secrets from their husbands, and she's proud of it. Her relationship with Marlin has all the ingredients of marriage, even this.

Marlin does not like the way Amanda is being asked to move. The idea is for the whole company to form a vast womb in which she will "gestate." First she will be curled into a ball, then she will unfold her body and begin to move around. Eventually she will throw herself against the human "walls" of the womb and they will toss her back. Marlin directs her to imagine she is a prisoner, flinging herself against the unforgiving bars. In the end she will be projected, in a way that has not yet been decided, out into the audience. The actors will rush forward and scatter, representing the flowing of bloody afterbirth.

They experiment with different holds and turns. She is picked up and dropped to the ground, yet she gets up, ready to try again. Marlin addresses Amanda in a soft and yet very public voice: "Be careful, love. We don't want you getting injured."

"Listen," Davis says, "I've been a choreographer for forty years, with no injuries to any of my dancers to date. Do you think I'd let your wife get hurt?"

"She's not my wife and stop trying to pigeonhole her. She's an artist in her own right. And this is SenseInSound you're talking about. These people are not 'your' dancers. Remember that."

Then there is the sound. Marlin encourages the group to try clucking and sussing, invoking amniotic fluid. He likes it, Davis doesn't. They try shouts and echoes emulating the sounds of a prison. Davis likes it, Marlin doesn't. Finally, Davis suggests silence. The silence will be disconcertingly long, brought to an end with a howl of pain and triumph. That's it! Yes, that's the way it should go! The company applauds Davis's suggestion enthusiastically. Marlin says nothing. No one has ever questioned his judgment before.

The next day he announces he is shortening the Journeys. Kevin will lead daily meditation practice after each one. He and Marlin have recently become vegans and many of the others have done the same. Marlin says he has never felt better in his life. They have installed a juicer beside the coffee machine. Rebecca notices it does not reduce the demand for her supermarket coffee, and she replenishes the sugar and powdered creamer just as often as usual.

Marlin wolfs down the tempeh sandwich Rebecca has brought for him. For the next hour he sits on the couch, frowning into the distance and making the odd, dark pronouncement. "I saw Susan and Howard leave together Friday." And, "Anna and Rose have been going out to lunch every day this week."

Rebecca feels pulled in two directions. This conversation cuts into her work time. Though Marlin has limited the actors' hours, there is more than ever for *her* to do. Yet she loves it when Marlin talks about this stuff. He is the only one who shares her dislike of the recent, romantic trend within the company. In her years with SenseInSound she has come to know the actors' cycles of attraction and loss. First, the atmosphere is charged with arousal, then heavy with bitterness. And there are stories. All the stories eventually come home to Rebecca. She keeps a box of tissues in the booth for when people visit her, pouring out what for weeks has been a poorly concealed secret. They tell her she is wise and compassionate. She clucks her tongue, shakes her head, feels secret pleasure at hearing versions of the same, dependable story again and again: expectation is followed by disappointment, union by loneliness.

But something has changed. People have become more modest. No one is groping and necking in corners. There are couples, though, and – as far as Rebecca is concerned – this bends the company out of shape. The theatre feels desperately vacant when people leave hand-in-hand at the end of the day. And there is that feeling of isolation she remembers from when her sisters went on dates: all the preening beforehand, the near-manic hopefulness that Rebecca could never bring herself to share.

"Don't do this unless you need to. I mean, there's nothing in it. No money. No security. No recognition. You do it because you have no other choice. There needs to be a drive inside you that you can't argue with. You feel it one day, and there's no turning back."

Silence.

Now what?

Rebecca wishes she could merge with the whiteboard behind her. Did her lecture make sense to anyone at all? Rows of solemn faces stare back.

Deverell steps forward, applauding, beckoning to the students to do the same. "Now maybe you'd like to ask this seasoned stage manager for a few career tips?"

She cuts him off. "Live for your work. How's that for career advice?"

Surely they won't ask her back.

Walking her to the door with that infuriating touch on her waist, Deverell asks, "Any progress on the project description?" Again.

"How many times have I told you ... That's not the way we do things."

"Just put something on paper. The Canada Council deadline is next week."

Rebecca sighs and shakes her head. Marlin calls grants "drinking at the trough." But she knows the money has to come from some-where, and without Leon's support (which provides Deverell's su-pervision) there would be no SenseInSound. Surely, Marlin knows this too. But grant applications feel beside the point; she has work to do. Real work. *Parturition* has been going through the cycle of building, breaking down and building up again. At nights, Rebec-ca's sleepless mind ranges between two polarities: on the one side, the ever-changing details of the show as it evolves, and on the oth-er, the end product, which is forever being plotted out. Deverell is pushing them to describe the story, the set, come up with a date when they'll be finished. How does the show get there from here?

It doesn't. One day Marlin tells her to gather everyone into a circle. He paces in front of them. Davis has not come in today, and Deverell has reluctantly agreed to join them. He does not sit on the floor though. He has pulled up a chair at the edge of the group, arms folded over his cream-coloured shirt, not looking at anyone. Rebec-ca has noticed there's been no coffee smell from upstairs this week.

"This company has been afflicted with possessiveness. Poison-ous attachment, which amounts to a kind of greed. Alan Davis had a plan for us, which he adhered to without respecting our process. He was determined to cling to his plan, and all of us – including myself – have lost our reason for being, our centre, which is pro-cess. Ever-shifting process. Davis has destroyed our unity as a com-pany and done violence to The Now. We need to let go. Of the plan, of each other. We are a chain of individual links which must work separately for the whole to function. If any links fail to move inde-pendently, the chain will break.

"I'm afraid our chain is breaking –" Marlin's voice cracks. Con-nie sobs. Again. She's been doing that a lot, lately. Rather than chal-lenging her – as he usually does – on her tears, Marlin goes to sit beside her. He draws her head down to his shoulder and strokes her hair as he talks.

"We need to open up." This brings a fresh wave of sobs from Connie. Marlin nods at Vic, who takes his place comforting her. Marlin continues. "The only-twelve rule is finished. I'm going to announce in our public classes that anyone who wants to work with us will be part of this show. Even up to the day of the performance, we'll continue to shift our personnel, welcome new members into our midst." Rebecca feels nauseous, wondering how she'll deal with an influx of new people while tracking the evolution of the show. Yet she is also exhilarated. The lights in the room seem to brighten as Marlin gains momentum in his speech.

"And another thing. Our personal lives and our artistic lives are one. There is no distinction here. Personal possessiveness is creative death. You choose the company, or you choose your robotic comfort. You choose your stultifying habits or you choose The Now."

Howard stands up, gives his hand to Susan and helps her to her feet. They leave the circle. So do Anna and Rose.

"Think this over if you need to. We'll take the day off and start again tomorrow at ten." He leads the weeping Connie towards the stairs. Deverell returns to his office. Rebecca goes down to the basement to continue her ongoing project of cleaning up. She feels the place at her side where Marlin stood these past few weeks like a wound. She knows that part of the message about chains was directed at her: no more shared lunches in the booth. Yet the clutch of anxiety that has haunted her since witnessing Marlin's session with Davis has dissipated. Marlin is back in charge. And she is willing to give up anything to see that happen.

They cannot get it right.

Amanda keeps saying, "Sorry. Let me take that again," but she does not look like she can handle much more jostling. They linger in the section of the show where Amanda flings herself against the walls of the "womb." It is intended to look like she is bouncing and sometimes sliding off the bodies of the rest of the group, falling violently to the ground, but this is only an illusion. In fact, she is to be caught and laid carefully down. Amanda's final birth cry is supposed to be enormous, shattering, but her voice has a strangled quality and she cannot muster any volume. Marlin asks Connie to make the sound on her behalf. Connie starts to cry.

Rebecca calls for a break, even though Marlin has not. Amanda curls into a ball on her side with her arms around her knees. It is unmistakable now: she is pregnant. Beneath her gaunt ribs, her belly is expanding by the week, but no one says anything about it. *The father. Who is the father?*

The next morning there is another meeting. Marlin announces that they will all be taking the summer off. "Amanda has taken the anger surrounding this show into her body. The pressure inside her is dangerously high. This show is toxic. It has to stop."

Deverell interrupts the shocked silence. "Well, my time with your fascinating company is over. I'm going back to Theatre In Bloom. We have an actual play to put on. But in the meantime, I – and not your Guru here – have been thinking about how you're going to pay your rent. I've set things up so you can all go on Unemployment Insurance. The Records of Employment will be coming to you in the mail."

Rebecca sleeps for twelve hours that night and in the morning feels the day stretch out before her, oppressive. She feels restless and wants to get out of the house, yet she is also exhausted. She lies down to sleep again. Then it is two in the afternoon. Two in the afternoon with half the day gone. Only two in the afternoon. She curses her decision to move into a house that didn't need any work. She tries taking a brisk walk but the humidity fights her. After a few blocks she passes a window displaying chickens on a rotisserie. Feeling ravenous, she buys one, goes home and eats half of it. An hour later the hunger is back. And it isn't even dark.

Rebecca is maddeningly aware of all her inner sensations: every hunger pang, every digestive sound, her breath and heartbeat, the movement of her eyelids when she blinks. They all seem threatening. She imagines she can feel cavities forming in her teeth, polluted air poisoning her lungs. She sinks into the act of loading food into her mouth, never satisfied. Days pass; then weeks. She can't seem to look for work. And there is no word from anyone at SenseInSound.

The phone rings, early. Too early. "Hi-dear."

Rebecca feels grateful to have a call, any call, and grateful for a connection with Marlin, any connection, even if it happens to be through his mother. Too eagerly, she responds, "Hi!"

"I've heard about your *situation*. And I just want you to know that I'm willing to help in any way I can. If you need someone to talk to, feel free to call."

What situation? The cancellation of the show? Amanda's pregnancy? Or is there something she does not know about? Dorothy might be fishing for information. Best to remain silent.

"By the way, I don't know whether you read the *Toronto Star*-dear? Have you been reading my *Wee Ones* column on Saturdays? You might like to have a look this week. It's about my book, *Grandparenting Through Your Tears: Surviving Life as a Banished Elder.* It's a hidden epidemic, the secret shame that strikes late in life. Our kids grow up, have kids of their own. Maybe the toddler is getting on their nerves, maybe the school-child is not living up to their expectations. They see a family counselor. Suddenly they recall some trauma from their childhoods – or think they do. They decide their parents are dangerous. No more visits with the grandchildren. Parents get blamed for everything these days. Mothers especially, of course. There are a lot of us out there, you know, grandmothers who've been forbidden contact with their own flesh and blood. I expect a lot of press attention. It's launching next week at the North York library. Just thought you might like to know."

"Thanks." Rebecca is rampantly curious about the book, though to read it would be impossible: too disloyal. But to what?

"The main thing I want you to know-dear, is that I'm not going to give up. I'm sure *you* understand that."

Struggling to find a non-committal answer, Rebecca mutters, "Okay."

"You know, Marlin thinks I've taken something from him. He's been harping on that for years. But those papers were the work of my half-brother. It made sense for them to come to me. So I happened to become a child psychologist! It's nothing to do with those precious papers."

Curiosity is stronger than loyalty at this moment. "What papers?"

"Isaac Samuel, the founder of Postural Analysis-dear. That's what he called the hocus-pocus he performed on people. There are tons of things like that around. Health and fitness is all the rage. Everyone wants the perfect body. It's a denial of death if you ask me, but never mind. Postural Analysis never took off because Isaac was a megalomaniac. Paranoid, to boot. He never explained his work to anyone. When he died his followers couldn't agree on what it was, let alone keep going without him. They fought. And eventually they all created their own methods based on their own neuroses and it got called various things depending on which of his disciples was claiming the direct line to God.

"But Isaac had some documentation of his early work: drawings. They showed the whole process of development, from raising the head and crawling to sitting and standing. There were notebooks, too, and some ledgers for Samuel's business. And they ended up with me, and Marlin doesn't like it. He wants to believe his own story of how The Work started. He's got to be in control as I guess you've observed."

By asking a question, Rebecca created an opening. Now, she is being implicated, pulled over to Dorothy's side. There are always sides. It's clear; the driving force beneath all Marlin's words and actions is an ongoing argument with his mother, even when she isn't there. Rebecca is on Marlin's side with all of her ability to *have* a side. She sits up in bed and puts her feet on the floor.

"I have to go."

"You do realize your attachment to my son is pathological-dear. There is help available."

"I'm hanging up now."

Dorothy gets her final words out in a rush. "It's his father he was looking for, a father figure. That's what he believes I took from him. But he has no idea what I went through, the frustration of being married to that *prostak* when I wanted an education. Every day, the religion: this you shouldn't do, that you shouldn't do. Rules. Rules. I was at the breaking point. But Marlin was not interested in his mother's emotional state. He just wanted what he wanted and he wasn't getting it. The mother in the kitchen, the father in the office. Bringing home the brisket, you might say. All this business about the papers is displaced anger. It has nothing to do with Isaac."

"I'm sorry. I don't know anything about this."

"Well, you do now. And you're apologizing for yourself again-dear."

"Sorry."

"One day you'll stop. We all do."

After her conversation with Dorothy, Rebecca gets going. She sees the doctor and gets a higher dose of her thyroid medication, institutes a routine. Staring at the orange-carpeted wall of a carrel in the central reference library she listens, through headphones, to the recorded versions of plays. This helps. She works her way through a few Shakespeare plays before settling on the Greek tragedies. The endless afternoons become manageable when measured by the records' twenty-minute sides. And – she reasons – when else would she have a chance to study the classics?

Six weeks later, thyroid balanced and the library's classics collection surveyed, Rebecca goes back to the empty theatre. She does not walk through the dark area that used to be filled with activity. Instead, she takes the side entrance straight upstairs. Marlin's door is closed, as always, but Amanda's is open. She finds Marlin there, sitting by the bed where Amanda is sleeping, one hand resting on her forearm. He puts a finger to his lips and indicated a bundle which lies beside Amanda on the bed.

New life! Rebecca feels a surge of excitement, a sharpness of vision as if a veil of dread had been lifted from her eyes. The feeling grows even stronger as Marlin carefully stands up, passes a hand around her waist and guides her downstairs. Together they sit on the stage looking out at the darkened theatre. It seems not deserted, but calm.

"What have you been up to?"

"Studying," she says, tentatively at first, then gaining certainty with his respectful nod. "I'm getting to know some plays. Pretty much memorizing them."

"Which ones?" he asks.

"Greeks, mostly."

"Good!" One word from Marlin transforms her routine from an arbitrary make-work project to an important use of her time. Important to The Work. "Not long now. We're almost ready. I'll be in touch in a few weeks."

There are seven of them left: Marlin, Amanda, Rebecca, Victoria and Kevin, Connie and Bill. Sitting on the floor in this circle of people, Rebecca is home again.

Marlin says, "All of us have had the equivalent of an abortion, performed clumsily and with violence. We've been violated by deadlines and management and the ubiquitous bottom line. We must grieve the loss of our creative child." Connie starts crying. Again. He announces that they will start Journeys next week. They'll be fully open to the public. They're separating from Leon's company. He, Marlin, will be taking over business management. He has dates lined up already for their first production, which will tour to schools. "We're going to rent a bus, and take art to the children of this province. And as for material, we will start interpreting the plays of classical Greece."

He nods to Kevin, who stands and begins to speak. "Tragedy is clean, it is restful, it is flawless. It has nothing to do with melodrama – with wicked villains, persecuted maidens, avengers, sudden revelations, and eleventh-hour repentances. Death, in a melodrama, is really horrible because it is never inevitable. The dear old father might so easily have been saved; the honest young man might so easily have brought in the police five minutes before."

So Kevin knew about this meeting, was involved in planning it. Rebecca was not. She thinks of the empty, anxious weeks that have just passed, waiting for Marlin's call. She actually turned down the offer of a regular course to teach, though it meant her entire savings had gone on the mortgage. Hurt makes her listen critically. Kevin is trying to make his speech look spontaneous, but Rebecca knows it is memorized. "In a tragedy, nothing is in doubt and everyone's destiny is known. That makes for tranquility. There's a sort of fellow-feeling among the characters in a tragedy: he who kills is as innocent as he who gets killed; it's all a matter of what part you are playing. Tragedy is restful; and the reason is that hope, that foul, deceitful thing, has no part in it. There isn't any hope. You're trapped. The whole sky has fallen on you, and all you can do about it is shout."

"Thank you Kevin. That speech is from *Antigone* by the French-Algerian author, Jean Anouilh."

At least he acknowledged it. Yet Rebecca feels insulted. Lied to. "We will not be using this version of the play, though. We will perform the *Antigone* of Sophocles, and why?"

Royalties, Rebecca thinks. Connie calls out, "Why, Marlin?"

"Because Monsieur Sophocles' work is no longer covered under copyright, while the estate of Monsieur Anouilh would require compensation. But Anouilh's notion of tragedy is what will animate our exploration of the Greek theatre. This author did not invent the idea, of course, he just stated it in a particularly beautiful way. Tragedy belongs to all of us. All the tragedians did – ever – was to honour The Now. We'll call our venture Classics in Motion."

Something is gone. Her unquestioning belief in Marlin and The Work. Yet her system automatically responds to the challenge, and it's a relief: from the fears and doubts that have lurked during the group's hiatus, from the dissatisfaction that has threatened to engulf her during this meeting.

Investigate bus rentals.

Build crates for set.

Learn to drive bus.

She revs her internal engine with these thoughts. And soon she's up and running again. She can't stop now.

Gesendet: 4/2/2012. 11:30 p.m.
An: director.graddrama@UToronto.ca
Von: AmAndAm@gmail.com

Betreff: The Truth

Well, I've put the journals away, Dr. Charbonneau. I'm sipping ginger ale and thinking about hunger. You know, there's a smell from a woman who's starving herself: cloying yet gritty, as if she literally had one foot in the grave. Deverell must have smelled it when I clung, trying to get a rise out of him all those weeks that he showed up in my apartment in the mornings. The things people will do for my parents! He enticed me with bowls of oatmeal, croissants and *café au lait*. That coffee was the first food I let myself look forward to in – who knows how long? It opened a cavern inside me. I nibbled the edges of his meals, channeling all my hunger into a need for skin. He was professional. Detached. I was just part of his job. Ow. Okay. I just shook my head, trying to rid myself of the memory. Say it: Bill and Connie were technically separated. She was living at Gerrard Space, trying to adhere to that couple-embargo that Marlin imposed in the nineties. First he sulked, then he raged, then he came up with the idea of analyzing the couples out of existence. He planted doubts, nourished conflicts, pried people apart. Bill continued to eat dinner with Connie, let himself out quietly every night. Once, I intercepted him on the stairs. *No, please, Amanda. I can't.* Okay, it's out now. Breathe.

What do I mean, "out"? I'm a coward.

It was Kevin, finally, who read my signals. And it was alright. Tuesdays, Thursdays and Sundays he visited my apartment. Then I missed a period. Then I was sick. So sick. Kevin made himself scarce. At least for a while. Whatever it cost him, I didn't notice. Marlin was back. In father mode. Asking no questions, requiring no lies.

So you see it's not just *my* story you're asking for. We're interwoven. Still.

Yours truly,
Amanda M.

1997

"Stage managers are born, not made," Rebecca tells her class at their first meeting. The words come out like a rebuke. For what?

For signing up for a course in the first place, as if this whole process were a straight line when the proper way to become a stage manager is to know it is your only option, to drive yourself past shyness, fatigue, feelings of utter incompetence, swing perilously from one job to another, convinced a deadly chasm lies beneath. Someday, if you try desperately enough, you might find a place where you belong. And then you stay, no matter what.

And for looking so damned happy! They shouldn't even be looking *at* her in the first place. Their eyes should be lowered, their foreheads puckered, questioning whether they really have what it takes. They don't. After a month or two in this business they'll go running home to their parents, who'll of course take them in.

She begins pacing back and forth, listing her requirements. She doesn't use blackboards, doesn't do handouts. They need to become good note-takers and might as well start now. And nor will she repeat herself: "Get it right the first time! First incident of lateness loses you twenty-five percent. Second gets you kicked out of the class." One or all of these kids will certainly complain. Look at them in their coordinated outfits – do they consult each other every morning or are they just singularly unimaginative? They look like a magazine ad, not a group of people wanting to learn. They'll go home and tell their mothers, and she'll get called up on the carpet.

She is not.

Rebecca eventually concludes she can say pretty much anything and they'll just sit there taking notes. Her class, The Stage Manager as Co-Creator, is scheduled for Friday mornings, the only part of her week she is willing to sacrifice, and every week she doubts her decision to take the course on. Christine DaSilva, the new department head, was the one to suggest it. Described variously as "a punk genius," "a wunderkind," and "a thorn concealing a rose," Christine was the subject of a feature in *NOW* magazine when she moved back to her native Toronto. The article outlined her studies in London and California, her post-doc in Berlin. Christine is, in other words, an academic through and through; the rest is just window dressing.

She bustles along the halls in her crinoline and Doc Martin boots with two muzzled pit-bulls on a lead, her legs tattooed to resemble a trellis blooming with roses. Flashing a lipstick smile, she moves like a film star on a red carpet, flanked by students all trying to ask her questions. Rebecca nods politely to Christine when she passes, but someone always takes her attention away before they can have much of a conversation. Just as well. She did not call to thank Christine when she received an email offer to start a course of her own, she just replied laying out her terms. Her main loyalty, she declared, was to SenseInSound.

She's got work to do. So much work. That class on Friday mornings throws the whole week off. And she doesn't need to worry about money. SenseInSound is doing fine, now they have begun touring. Marlin – who signs all the cheques now – is close-mouthed about the specifics but it's clear they're thriving. The company is secure, can afford to pay her. Why can't she just trust that and commit herself?

After an endless streetcar ride back to the theatre, she rushes into the lobby and collides with a crowd of people. She forces her-

self to smile pleasantly as they chatter and hug and weep and eat
and do whatever else they need – so very urgently – to do. A number of them slurp beans from mason jars, others exchange recommendations for hair stylists and masseurs. The people who are free
in the mornings seem to be either poverty-stricken or very wealthy.
During his tenure, Deverell managed to get charitable status for
SenseInSound. Rebecca suspects that some of them are making
large donations.

Antigone, and the next play, *Electra*, were vindications of Marlin's decision to strike out on their own. With their tours around
the province, followed by sold-out runs in Toronto, more and more
people have been drawn to Gerrard Space, for a public Journey
which is offered every morning. Afternoons are for rehearsals. Over
the past few years, psychologists have found their way to SenseIn-
Sound, and referred their clients. So have one or two doctors. Last
year, a bank executive tried one class, then showed up the following
week with a deeply embarrassed management team in tow. That
gave rise to Marlin's first of many offers to do corporate trainings:
"to foster creativity, team-work and unleash hidden potential."

Amanda has started a class called WorldSound, which meets on
Sunday afternoons. It was designed for people with no singing experience, but in short order the group began giving recitals, selling
high-priced tickets to their friends and family who fill the theatre
for several nights. There has been media attention, too. World-
Sound is greeted as an example of Toronto's multiculturalism at
its best. Lately, there's been a waiting list for the class. Rebecca has
noticed, though, that even though the songs may be from Nigeria
and Georgia, even though the theatre may be situated between "Little India" and "Chinatown East," even though the children in the
schools they visit are from all over the world, the faces which greet
her every morning in the Journey, and in the audiences for their
plays are mostly white. A scrap of memory now: Marlin's voice, angry: *you people … you people …* what? And a strangled sob from
someone. Gail. He was shouting at Gail, the only black actor ever
to have worked with the company. That was the day she ran out in

tears, to be replaced by her white friend. *Black and white, we're all the same.* Are we, though? Memories are truncated. Thoughts fragmented. All she knows is that if this is a problem she's got no time to fix it. Along with the squeaky front door and the leaking tap in the bathroom, it will go to the bottom of her list.

Rebecca pushes through the inner doors. This is just too late to get to work. She needs to be there to keep an eye on the core members, who will stay for the afternoon. To keep an eye – let's face it – on Portia. Portia appeared in a Journey a couple of months ago. Her face was round and doughy, but she was striking immediately for her long hair, so blond it was almost white. Marlin started giving her attention the very first day. By her second week she was included in rehearsals. At the same time, she started losing weight. She got her hair cut short and dark rings formed under her eyes. Her once-solid body became more and more angular by the day. At lunch breaks, when others shared salads and sandwiches and stews from a long table they set up in the rehearsal area, Portia did stretches or went outside for a run. Yesterday, she just curled up on one of the seats and slept through lunch. As the afternoon's rehearsal began, Rebecca asked if she was feeling okay.

"Perfect! I'm just doing a cleanse."

"You can't get much cleaner than this food, Portia."

"I need to give my digestive system a rest."

There she is, in a seat again, her knees curled up and a hand folded inward under her chin. Another inch and her thumb would be in her mouth. Rebecca catches Connie's eye and looks in Portia's direction. Connie mouths the words "All morning," and shrugs.

The show is *Medea*. Everyone has learned all the parts, said the lines in unison, divided the roles up between two or three people, played them interchangeably. Men play women, women, men. Young people play older people and vice versa. Sometimes they mime the play, sometimes sing it. Sometimes they say the words in the original Greek, which they memorize phonetically. Sometimes they mix the languages up.

Soon, maybe even today, they will narrow down the myriad possibilities they have generated and find out who will play the roles. Rebecca knows there will be no surprises. Amanda will play Medea, Kevin will play her faithless husband, Jason. Connie will take the role of the nurse. Victoria will be Creon, the king. The rest: chorus. Somewhere in there, Portia will be given a major role, only to have it snatched away. Rebecca has seen all the variations of that scenario. There is an endless parade of rants to listen to, tears to dry.

Anyone who attends Journeys regularly has the chance to stay on for rehearsals. They are not overrun with candidates. Rehearsals are so demanding that few people stick with them for more than a month. And then there are what Marlin initially calls "talking circles," a term later shortened to "Circles," every Friday afternoon. Marlin leads them. He says little, but looks at whomever is speaking with that exclusive quality of attention only he is able to bestow. Eventually, the words come. People talk about their longings, their feuds, their fears. They narrate dreams and memories. Rebecca keeps her notebook handy for the inevitable moment when a Circle will become an improvisation. She likes having her notebook on her lap even when she isn't using it. It is something to focus on when the discussion becomes too intense, when a trapdoor of memory opens to disclose a teenaged habit of cutting or purging, a drunken father's slaps and curses. The notebook is a reminder of her role, which is to hold on so everyone else can let go.

Circles mean words, stories. The thing she had longed for when she and Marlin first met, years ago, was finally being provided. To someone else. To *everyone* else. Marlin had always seemed better than Rebecca because he was *still*, living in one moment, then the next, with no need for a coherent story. Rebecca berated herself for wanting things to be put into words at all. Now, Marlin wants every story articulated, and is showing others how to do it, seemingly without fear of violating The Now. Yet the Circles are good for The Work. Each week, the company works together more and more seamlessly, moving their bodies and entwining their voices as if by mutual consent, generating ideas as if with one mind.

This is what matters, Rebecca tells herself, trying to escape the version of a circle which plays out daily in her own mind. She has no right to feel betrayed. Yet she does. It adds to the general sense of wrong-ness she carries with her at all times. Guilt, anger and doubt spiral dizzyingly whenever she stops work long enough to think. Into this mix comes the occasional surge of desire for Marlin. Her entire system is geared to getting and maintaining his attention. She can't change it. It started with handing him her own beer more than ten years ago and has never gone away. Whatever doubts arise within her are combatted by an equally powerful determination not to give up. She's too busy to unravel this. Every day she gets up and simply returns to work.

Like today.

Rebecca fishes a banana out of her bag, puts it down on the seat beside the sleeping Portia. Then she runs upstairs to the booth and retrieves her notebook, ready for the Circle to begin.

Amanda is the first to speak. "I have some concerns," she says tentatively, "about the children."

"What concerns?" Marlin asks.

She takes a deep breath. "Exposing them to such a violent play." No one has mentioned it but it has always been assumed that Amanda and Marlin's children – Meira and Safra – will play the sons who are murdered at the end of the play. Meira, at four, is still breastfeeding. Safra is twelve. Rebecca's mind has often strayed to this topic and she's buried herself in work because she finds it so disturbing. If their parents are going on tour it makes sense for the kids to go along. But what if they don't want to be part of the show?

"The children are killed offstage." Marlin says. "Both they and the audience are protected from the scene. It's much less violent than anything on TV."

"Our kids don't watch TV." Amanda replies in a tiny voice. "And it's a horribly violent play." Kevin puts his arm around Amanda.

"What do you mean by violence?" Marlin asks.

Amanda nods. She pauses before delivering a measured answer. "The idea of a mother killing her children is horrific to me."

"Of course it's horrific. But maybe there's something else bothering you. What's going on?"

She takes a deep breath. "There's the fighting. Between Jason and Medea. She's appealing to his emotions and he gives her only reason."

"But Medea wins, doesn't she? She gets revenge and ends up marrying a king."

"She doesn't win."

"Why do you say that?"

"Well, no one wins. The children are killed!"

"Let's get back to the fighting. It reminds you of your own home?"

"Of course not. My parents were … are … You all know Mummy and Daddy. That never happened. I heard my friend's parents fighting once and ran home. I was six years old. I had never been exposed …"

"Conflict is healthy. What makes you think it's not alright?"

"My parents get along with each other."

"So you believe."

"It's a peaceful household."

"There is always anger. Maybe they do violence to themselves in holding it back."

"My parents are … just happy. They're in love." Amanda looks at the floor.

"Can someone help us out?" asks Marlin, with a gesture that takes in the whole group. One by one now, the members begin to talk about their memories: creeping into their brothers' and sisters' beds late at night when they heard shouting from downstairs, quietly filling cereal bowls in the morning while the adults sulked behind newspapers, too lost in their private battles to notice it was breakfast time, slipping away to school, returning to houses where there was no order, or too much. They speak in the voices of children, using the words of children, but Rebecca notices that, unlike in many other Circles, no one starts to cry. They *are* children at that moment, holding back their tears because they know they will not do any good. They are slow to disband, remain in the Circle even after they have stopped talking, leaning on each other's shoulders, resting heads on each other's laps.

Marlin goes to Portia, who has stayed in her seat, presumably asleep this whole time. He begins gently stroking her hair. She starts awake and he shushes her, continues stroking. "You looked like an angel when you slept," he says, in a voice that is low, but not too low for the others to hear. "You are a pure, pure soul."

Rebecca looks around to locate Amanda. Connie has her arms around her. Amanda is shivering and cannot stop.

Rebecca wishes that *Medea* would just go away, that they'd stop working on it the way they'd stopped working on *Parturition*. Yet something about the discussion touched everybody. The group's conversation felt inevitable, and needed. At the next Circle, Amanda raises the idea of starting a discussion with the high school audiences after the play. They can talk about family conflict. They can talk about betrayal. They will create Circles everywhere.

But Safra. Rebecca does not want Safra to take part in this play. His parents are deciding for him. As Dorothy pointed out in an early-morning call, he should be studying for his Bar Mitzvah instead of hanging around at rehearsals. *And Meira,* Rebecca reminds herself. *What about Meira? If you think about Safra, you have to think about her too.* A few months after Meira's birth the company went back to work. Meira took her place in the bassinette beside the rehearsal area. Things were different when Safra was in that spot. He seemed from the start to harmonize with what was going on. The cast often spoke of what a blessing it was to have a real baby beside them while they revisited an earlier time in their own development. It was as if he had showed them a past they couldn't consciously remember.

Meira's voice was grating. *She's just a baby,* Rebecca argued with herself in her own mental Circle. She did not like Meira. *She's a baby. You can't dislike a baby.* But she did. All the child's movements seemed aggressive: tight fists pushing out of the blanket, punching the air as if she were fighting. Her voice burst through at all the wrong moments – almost as if she intended to be disruptive. If Meira had a gun instead of just her vocal cords, she would shoot everyone in the place. *Maybe she's just bad.* This thought occurred to Rebecca more than once, but she closed her mind to it. *No child is bad.*

She offered to baby-sit one Saturday night, an interminable five hours. *Just because Meira doesn't cuddle up and smile, you dislike her.* The feeling was stronger than simple dislike, though, and it seemed to be mutual. *She's a baby. Babies don't have feelings like that.* Meira cried. Rebecca got up from where she was reading a book with Safra, gave Meira a bottle and rocked her for a while. Meira closed her eyes and drank, never making eye contact, never acknowledging Rebecca was there, as if to say, "I have what I want. You don't exist."

She's a baby. That's what they do.

Safra took himself to bed. Rebecca continued to walk and walk and walk the baby up and down. After a while, she felt something of herself go out to the child. It was a feeling from deep inside, beneath will, beneath control. *If she is okay, that's all that counts.* Rebecca felt better about herself, yet also empty and angry. This child could form a hold over her. And no matter how much she took, Rebecca would just keep giving and giving. Frightened by the strength of her own feelings, she put Meira in her crib and prayed that she'd stay asleep. She didn't. Meira was still wailing when her parents got home.

"I don't think I'm much of a baby-sitter."

"She's a spirited child. It's not your fault," Amanda said, but never asked again. Instead, a jolly, middle-aged woman named Svetlana moved into one of the small apartments upstairs and looked after Meira while rehearsals were going on. She toted Meira around under her arm like a log and seemed impervious to her crying.

The set is the same for all the Greek plays: a couple of flats, a couple of risers to indicate the entrance to the palace. They just need a coat of paint. Beyond that, they will work with whatever conditions they find in their various venues. Rebecca has got another set of flour-bags which can be sewn into sheaths for them to wear. But then there's the entrance of Medea at the end, with the bodies of her dead children, who – it is decided – are to be represented by hacked up and dirty plastic dolls. Rebecca collects a bunch of them from Value Village, the most distressed she can find. She brings ten to choose from and they decide to affix them all to the costume Amanda will wear when she makes her entrance for the final scene.

That entrance! The text says, "Medea appears above the palace on a chariot drawn by dragons." There must be a way to do this. It must be cheap, portable, and adaptable to venues of all ages and in all states of repair. The ideas put forward so far have all been jokes. They go from the simple and rough – perhaps a child's wagon, a shopping cart – to the impossible: maybe Amanda will arrive on a horse or in a vintage car. Rebecca sketches on the edges of her note-paper, contemplates the problem as she is falling off to sleep. There must be a way to give the illusion of flight.

In one of the Circles, Kevin says, "I woke up this morning thinking, 'Not much time left.' You know, my father died of a stroke when he was forty-five. I turn forty next month. A light really came on for me when I had that thought. I realize how much I've encoded that expectation of early death into everything I do."

Marlin prompts him: "Say more." Rebecca puts on an attentive face while she imagines what she could do if she had an enormous budget. There would be acrobats in dragon costumes, live musicians, projections. And Amanda would make the flying entrance in her chariot from the back of the theatre.

"You remember last week. Portia, I'm sorry to bring it up again. But last week when I talked about my attraction for Portia. Of course, you're a beautiful girl. Please don't take this wrong, but I know it's got nothing to do with you. It's a fear of looking in a mirror. Fear of seeing myself as I really am. I should be looking for someone my own age, but whenever I meet a young … nubile … irresistible young woman I forget about all the work I've done on myself over the years. I guess I just never wanted to grow up."

"Excuse me," Rebecca says, barely allowing a decent pause until

Kevin has finished his last word. "I have something to say."

They turn to her.

"I have an idea for Medea's big entrance. I'll be ready to talk about it next week."

Marlin grins. She's good; she's very good.

She calls Sylvia as soon as she gets home. "Thought you'd never ask!" Sylvia replies, and breaks into song. *"Look at me! Way up high! I'm flying!"*

"So you were in it."

"'No one has captured the essence of Barrie's unforgettable character so much as this young Peter Pan.' I memorized the review."

"Can you coach Amanda?"

"Well, I can give her an idea."

After half an hour of pacing, Rebecca dials the number she found on a brochure for the Canadian Opera Company. There are what feels like a dozen intermediaries to get through before she can speak to Serge. He is the technical director, with access to resources that are far beyond her reach. Waiting on hold, she remembers the air cooling her cheeks one late fall afternoon when they backed away from each other on Bloor Street, the flavor of cinnamon coffee still on her tongue. *"Demain,"* he had said. That was more than a decade ago. What made her think he would even remember her? But he does.

"So good to hear from you. How can I help?"

She is tentative at first, laying out her problem, but eventually loses herself in the description of the final scene of *Medea* and all she hopes it can be. This feels so good, sharing her idea with someone who thinks like her. With Serge.

"Great idea!" he says (where once he would have said it in French). "I'm going to put you in touch with Len Silverstone, a retired rigger. The best. And we can help you on this end with whatever else you need."

"Thank you so much!"

"Happy to lend a hand."

The conversation is over, but she can't stop herself from keeping him on the line. "How have you been?"

"Oh, we're fine! Work is tough, but I try not to get too caught up in the drama. They're only that age for a while. And you …?"

"I'm not — At least, I don't have —"

"Your company is doing important work in the schools, I hear."

"Yes! For kids to see this kind of cutting-edge theatre: it's amazing. I can't stop thinking about what it would have been like to see this work when *I* was a teenager. It would have changed everything. It's not a comfortable life, for any of us, but it's worth it." She is surprised to hear an explanation that makes sense tumble out of her mouth.

"You are still hungry, I see."

"Yes. I guess you could say I am. Thank you, Serge. Thank you for your help."

A few days later, she gets a call – not from Serge – but from Len. Her disappointment opens up a sink-hole of sadness in the otherwise delightful stretch of work she anticipates in realizing her staging idea. She tries to skirt those feelings, not asking herself why, or why the disappointment is so bad. Trying to understand would send her tumbling – she has no idea how far. Still, walking to the subway in the mornings, eating her lunch or brushing her teeth she finds herself asking something in the order of *Why not*? Not – *Why not me for Serge?* – the answer is his children – or at least –that he probably wanted them all along. But *Why not someone for me?* And *Why not someone who thinks of himself not as "I" but as "we"?*

She can't think of Marlin as the reason – he's with Amanda, after all. It's SenseInSound, and who she has to be in her work, and how it's shaped everything she is in the world. Who could possibly understand this? Who could possibly fit?

Rebecca falls in, then scrambles out of her sink-hole again and again until the demands of the show get so intense she can't tell whether it's fatigue or sadness weighing her down. And there's work to do. Serge provides everything it takes to design and build a portable truss that can be installed in a variety of settings, under ceilings that will vary in height. Amanda will fly from it, pendulum style. Rebecca borrows pipes, weights and cables, a winch so gorgeous she has to keep it at home for a week and eat breakfast with it on her kitchen table. Without consulting anyone on her decision, she arranges all her work on this project for Fridays, the usual times for Circles.

"You look like Ginger Rogers, Mummy!" says Amanda, and Sylvia, in wide-legged pants and worn but serviceable dancing shoes, executes a few arabesques.

"Shoes are a bit creaky, just like me joints."

Marlin paces morosely among the seats.

"Look, Len is donating his time here, I'm sure he doesn't have all day. Let's just see if this can work."

"Down to business," Sylvia calls.

They hook Amanda into the harness, and the harness to the truss. Amanda is 100 pounds to Rebecca's 180. Rebecca stands on a box, holding the rope as high above her head as she can, then jumps backward to the floor, all the time pulling it down hand over hand, as if climbing it. She lowers her own body until she is in a crouch. Then she anchors the rope to a stage weight by her feet. Amanda is counterweighted so that she cannot possibly drop very fast; still, the responsibility of her role makes Rebecca's hands sweat. She is glad for her leather gloves.

The first time up, Amanda flounders in the air, making Rebecca fear that she will lose control of the rope. When it comes time to lower Amanda, Rebecca secures the rope with her foot, then sets her down on the ground by paying it out slowly. Amanda claps her hands and laughs. Sylvia interrupts her daughter with a raised hand.

"Rebecca's done her job but you, my girl, have not done yours. *Your* job is to make it look easy. Take it again please. Ready?"

"Ready!"

"Think of something happy."

Len cues Rebecca and – with difficulty – she hoists Amanda.

"Something happy, I said."

Amanda giggles. "I can't think of anything just now."

"Well you shall have to. Right: again."

Rebecca lowers Amanda, then asks, "Ready?"

"Okay," Amanda says dubiously.

"Okay is not enough."

"Sorry."

"And nor is that. Think of being kissed, dear!"

Amanda laughs.

"All right then: gin and tonic."

Amanda lifts her arms in the air as Rebecca executes her move. She feels noticeably lighter.

"You're getting it. What shall we think about this time?"

Marlin calls out, "What is this, Walt Disney all of a sudden? The character has just come from killing her own children, Sylvia. I can't imagine your little spell is going to work."

Sylvia turns to Amanda and says, "Close your eyes, dear, and contemplate *murder!*"

Amanda raises her arms as Rebecca lifts her. It is as if she had lost half her weight. Amanda and Sylvia both burst into giggles. "Wheee! Amanda cries, "Look at me! I'm flying!"

Marlin leaves the theatre, thanking Len as he goes. As soon as the door closes, Len gives in to his own fit of laughter and he and Sylvia spontaneously sing a chorus of *"I gotta crow!"*

They work every day. The result is that for her final speech, Amanda is up in the air and able to move freely, clenching not just her fists but her whole body with the passion of her words, then standing straight and tall in the harness for the final lines. Rebecca's muscles begin to bulge in her arms and shoulders as she masters control of the rope. But this is just the beginning. There is still the tour to think about. They'll see their venues sometimes only a few hours before the performances. She'll train members of the cast to help, but cannot depend on anyone but herself. At nights, she imagines lifting Amanda gently up and feeling her weight before she ties off the rope. Sometimes, she imagines the harness failing, the truss buckling. Sometimes she imagines the rope slipping uncontrollably through her fingers.

"I need to share something." Kevin springs up from sitting on the floor, and moves about restlessly as he continues to speak. "I'm in love with Amanda. I can't get her out of my mind. I am sweating when we have our scenes together. I can't sleep. I am constantly … constantly hard."

"Whew." He says and stops. "That's the most difficult thing I've ever done, saying that. It felt good. Thank you."

Amanda sits with her face averted when Kevin talks. Rebecca noticed that he referred to Amanda in the third person. I love *you* is the usual phrase. I can't get *you* out of my mind.

"Okay," says Marlin. "Excellent, Kevin. That was a risk for you to take and we thank you for it. Let's inhabit desire. Everyone get up and find a space for yourself."

Rebecca grabs her notebook and backs out of the circle. She props it against her body, ready to take notes. Everyone scatters, pacing up and down or sitting cross-legged on the floor. Marlin takes Kevin's hand and leads him to sit opposite Amanda. Amanda and Kevin look into each other's eyes. Portia is also sitting nearby, and Marlin positions himself opposite her. The room is silent at first then begins to resound with soft, intimate humming. One voice can be heard above the others. It is Portia, who has begun to moan. Marlin stares fixedly in a way that appears to be pulling the sounds from her. No. Too much. It is too sexual, too exposed. Rebecca looks down at her feet until Portia's voice blends with the others'.

When she looks up again, a few of the actors are rolling around together in a heap. The scene is orgiastic, but all their clothes are on, and Rebecca, who has been observing these people for years, can sense their hesitancy and awkwardness. Then she notices Portia, still cross-legged, opposite Marlin. She has unbuttoned her shirt and sits with her hands supporting her from behind. Her mouth is open and her body undulates with each breath. Light shines off her tiny, pale breasts and emaciated ribcage. Soon afterwards, Kevin disentangles himself from the heap and walks over to her. He takes her hand and leads her into the shadows.

Rebecca backs away, her face burning. She encounters a small obstacle behind her. Meira. "Upstairs!" Whispers Rebecca. "This is for grownups. Up to Svetlana, now!" She scoops up Meira and glances around the workspace to see if Safra is around: thank God he is nowhere to be found. She rushes upstairs to find Svetlana, her face twisted with panic. "Do your job, will you?" Rebecca hands over the child and turns back to her work. The next week in Circle, Victoria announces that she doesn't feel she has an old enough soul to play Creon. Marlin listens, nodding, and thanks her. He casts Portia instead.

Rebecca holds the enormous wheel of a passenger bus. She loves having this machine under her control, riding high up off the road, maintaining just the right amount of tension in her hands. It is snowing again – not a full-fledged storm, but almost. She watches what little she can see of the road, intent. Fatigue presses in on her but she knows she can do it, can ferry them all through this weather and see them safely to where they are going. She is aware of her responsibility. A whole show rides in the bus behind her: sets, costumes, props. And all the actors, all those lives. Rebecca can imagine them, sleeping curled up or stretched out on various seats, covered with blankets and coats and sleeping bags, oblivious to the road's dangers.

Over the past few months they have gone on many short trips out of Toronto, to towns they can reach in an hour or two and make it back the same day. Often it feels like they never really leave the mega-city (as it's now called). The endless strip malls give way to ten or fifteen minutes-worth of country road before the next Tim Horton's or Boston Pizza appears. The boundaries of the city are blurring. One thing is clear, though: downtown Toronto is getting poorer. The headlines about school closings, hospital layoffs and skyrocketing rents have become commonplace in the past few years. Everything about Toronto has come to feel pinched and anxious, compromised. As they discover on these trips, the highway outside Toronto is maintained better than the city's roads. It is lined with housing developments stretching out for kilometers in the distance. Rebecca despises all this newness. When they get home, she takes a walk around her neighbourhood, relishing the sight of sidewalks strewn with butts and stray pigeon feathers, front yards full of abandoned furniture, run-down barber shops and variety stores.

Now, with the help of a touring grant, they have spent a total of two weeks on the road. Holding the wheel, Rebecca senses, with a kind of tingling in her back, the location of all her closest people. In the course of the tour they have all come to favour certain spots in the bus. Amanda will be a few seats back, alternately dozing and looking out the window with Meira nestled against her. Safra has two seats of his own. And in the three-seater at the very back, Marlin will be curled up with Portia.

Rebecca notices that someone had come to sit in the front seat. "Are you okay?" It is Amanda. "It's quite a night out there. Do you think we should keep going?"

"Sure," says Rebecca. "We'll be in Midland in an hour."

"You're such a good driver."

Rebecca smiles, enjoying the confidential tone of their voices. They are like two mothers whispering over an enormous crib. "Portia was great today," says Amanda. Rebecca smiles again. "Yes," she says, careful to pause before her answer, careful to leave out further praise.

"You were right about the antihistamine."

Portia woke up yesterday with red lumps on her face and ribs. Amanda feared bedbugs, but Rebecca suggested it was probably hives. An over-the-counter remedy was all it took to get Portia on stage. "Keep it Simple, that's my motto."

"What would we do without you, Rebecca? Listen, I'm sick of motels. Should we try to find a movie theatre tonight?"

"Better stay in. Tomorrow's going to be a big day. I have to get to the school by eight to have a look at the auditorium."

"I'll go with you. Marlin and I should go."

"Wouldn't be a bad idea."

Marlin has joined them. As he settles into the seat next to Amanda, Rebecca feels the connection between them ignite like an electrical circuit. Marlin is back: back with Amanda, with both of them. "What a night!" He says, "I'm glad you're at the wheel, Rebecca. You always steer us through the storm."

"Kevin, I wonder if you have something you'd like to say."

Kevin stands up in response to Marlin's invitation, but takes a long time to speak. When he does, his voice shakes and he extends both arms in front of him as if he were carrying a limp body. "I can't stop thinking about how vulnerable she was. Her life was literally in my hands. And what if we'd arrived just a few minutes later? One traffic jam might have killed her."

"Breathe. Everyone breathe through this, please. You got her there on time. That's what counts."

Yesterday morning they arrived early for their rehearsal, preparing for the two-week Toronto run of *Medea*. As soon as she lay on the floor, Portia started to cough, then to wheeze, then the wheezing became more laborious. Rebecca whispered to Kevin: "Take her to Emerg!" He did, but not a moment too soon. A tracheotomy was performed as soon as they arrived. The doctor told Kevin they should have called an ambulance. She could have died in the car.

Marlin says, "Rebecca has spoken to Portia's mother and she tells us she doesn't want visitors or calls. This is necessary transformation for Portia, for all of us. Snakes shed their skins; so do we, at times. Portia's body is giving her a clear message. Her time with this company is over. Each of us needs to find a way to let her go."

Rebecca's hands are shaking, but Marlin's confidence steadies her. At the end of the session, he calls on Victoria to replace Portia in the role of Creon.

"Rebecca, can you bring her up to speed?"

"Done."

"You *did* that? You *did* that in thirty halls all over Ontario?"

After their last Toronto performance, her old mentor, Bart Johnston, is waiting for Rebecca in the lobby. *Just don't come crawling back to me ....* She remembers his cutting words; she's never called him again for work. And she's proved him wrong about the company. Her loyalty has paid off. The show is a success. *She* is a success.

"Sure," Rebecca smiles. "Of course. What would you expect?"

"Nothing less, Hon. Nothing less. Now tell me, who was operating that cockamamie gismo that lifted your star in the air?"

"Me."

"How noble of you. My next question is, why are you running ropes?"

"I like to keep an eye on things."

"So keep an eye on things. But leave the heavy lifting to someone else, please."

"We don't have anyone else."

"Ah yes – the indispensability myth. Right up there with your Greek classics. You're a smart woman, Rebecca. You should be doing better for yourself. I'm not going to offer any more advice, but would you please call me when this cult finally implodes?"

Wanda's Words

A monthly blog featuring the voices of the young women at Wanda's Place

A message from Ginny Fontaine, Executive Director

Our March edition is in honour of Rebecca Weir, the distinguished producer of the annual *To End All Wars* festival of world theatre to Toronto. She's also a college instructor, who offered to teach our residents some carpentry skills because she found herself with too much time on her hands on the weekends! Well, she went on to start Power Tools, which journalist Rae Ellington called, "a sensible and empowering program that really works" in *Keep 'em Sick, Keep 'em Quiet*, her devastating expose on the upsurge of eating disorders among young women.

Despite being quite possibly the busiest woman in Toronto, Rebecca has never missed a Saturday with our residents as long as she isn't touring the world. Now, we're happy to announce that – as if she doesn't have enough to do – Rebecca will be joining Wanda's Board of Directors. I asked her for a quote but – shunning the spotlight as usual – she muttered something about hoping she could make a bit of a difference. Well Rebecca, you have, you do, and we know you always will. I'll leave the last word to one of our Power Tools alumni.

A.L. writes:
Thanks to Power Tools I am now a certified cabinet maker with my own shop and a staff of seven. I remember the first time I set foot in Rebecca's class. It was noisy and dusty. So much dust! I just ran out and sat in the hall rocking back and forth. But Rebecca came outside and sat on the bench with me. She said, "Just show up. That's all you have to do." So, I sat outside in the hall every week. One day she brought out a hammer from the shop and encouraged me to hold it. It felt good: heavy and hard and powerful at one end

and warm and well-used at the other. I wanted to get strong so I could swing it. And I went in the shop with her that day. And the day I used a hammer was the day I started getting better. You line it up – tap, tap, and you're ready. Bam! Bam! So true and straight. Not just eating away at myself in my own mind any more but putting that force out. Making something.

1998

Medea is done. Marlin is off on a meditation retreat and Svetlana has gone to visit her family in Ukraine. Arriving early one morning, Rebecca meets Kevin leaving the building. She blushes and barely greets him as they pass each other at the front doors.

Her project this week is to paint part of the basement floor, which means moving everything out of the way and running a Shop Vac for long periods of time. The more noise the better: anything to insulate her from whatever is going on between Amanda and Kevin upstairs. Rebecca crouches on the ground, pushing the nozzle into the dusty seam where wall meets floor. She does not notice at first that Safra has come down to the basement.

"What's up?"

Solemnly, he hands her a stuffed dog, one paw all-but severed, its button eyes hanging by threads. Clumps of stuffing bulge out of its chest. The toy has not just been roughed-up in a fit of temper, it has been deliberately destroyed.

"This looks pretty serious."

"I don't play with toys anymore."

His voice is husky; it is changing. But he could also be on the verge of tears. He does not move but looks from her face to the dog and back again. Rebecca takes out her sewing kit. She perches on a stool while Safra draws near, looking on. She sews on the leg, the eyes. She hands him the scissors and points to the thread where she wants it cut. She patches the holes in the body as best she can. When she hands it back to Safra, he does not take it.

"That's the best I can do, buddy. Sorry."

"I don't know what happened."

He continues to stare up at her. Rebecca gets it. She cleans out a box and puts the dog in it, places it on a shelf for Safra. The following week, the box also contains a few books and a toy train he was particularly fond of when he was small. Rebecca knows better than to ask him about the scabs she notices a few days later on his hands and arms. Bracing herself against embarrassment, she goes upstairs to see Amanda after Kevin has left the building.

"I notice Safra is having a few skin problems."

Amanda sighs. "I know you're supposed to let them work it out for themselves, but I don't have any experience with the whole sibling rivalry thing. It's a mystery to me. Anyway, she doesn't mean anything by it."

"By what?"

"She – well, Meira digs her nails into him – and you know kids. They're not always clean. I can't bring myself to tell anyone. His gym teacher called, thinking it might be contagious. I said he had a nervous habit and was picking at his own skin. I wish I knew what to do. You're from a big family, aren't you? How did your mother handle it?"

Rebecca wonders why she has not been keeping Meira's nails shorter – or better still, making her stop – but replies, "Oh, I don't remember much but I'm sure there were some bumps and bruises along the way."

In the coffee shop at the end of Rebecca's street there are always a few half-read newspapers lying on the counter. She has taken to reading Dorothy's *Wee Ones* column. There's an article on teething, another on toilet training, another on the best time to start daycare. This week there's a piece headed: "Little Angels?" accompanied by a picture of a boy about to hit another over the head with a nursery chair. The article is about bullying by siblings, about the damage done when parents excuse it.

The next time she sees Meira, Rebecca clasps her around the arms, picks her up so she can look directly into her eyes. She lets her drop a couple of inches. Meira laughs, but Rebecca glares at her until she stops. "We're not playing a game, Meira. You're five years old now, and I know you understand. I see what you've been doing to your brother. You think you're getting away with it because you're small. Well, I'm big, and I'm looking out for him, do you understand?"

Meira looks away.

"Do you understand?"

In Rebecca's arms, Meira feels small and manageable, and the knowledge comes to her suddenly: *she wants to feel this way.*

"I asked you a question." Rebecca turns Meira's body so that she can't help but look into her eyes. The barest nod.

"Out loud, please. Do you understand?"

"Yes."

"Thank you." Rebecca puts her down. Meira turns immediately and walks away. Dismissively? Surely she's not capable of that much complex thought.

We are like children.

Marlin meant innocent, without malice, but Meira is a child, and she's anything but innocent. *Someone has to do it.* For the sake of The Work and all it stands for, Rebecca must see this, manage it, and keep it to herself.

Garbage, she finds herself thinking. *How much garbage am I supposed to clean up?* More. Still more. Each day, the alarm rings and she gets up and goes into work.

Kevin tends to do most of the talking in Circles if Marlin does not prompt the others to speak. That's why Rebecca is surprised – then alarmed – when he remains silent during the first Circle after they return. And nor does Marlin ask him any questions. *You always steer us through the storm, Rebecca.* She plucks Kevin's sleeve as the others are packing up. "Can you give me a hand downstairs?" she asks, and, sorting through lumber scraps, hears the story: He's leaving. Won't be back on Monday. He was going to announce it in today's Circle then thought, "Why bother? These relationships are over. It's time to move on."

No. They need him. Rebecca knows what she has to do next. She thanks Kevin profusely for stacking a pile of boxes she could easily have managed herself, runs her hand down his back and asks, "Glass of wine?"

"You're very –" Kevin tells her three weeks later – struggling, she can tell, for a positive way to say it – "You're so *complete*. There's no place for me in all this." They are in a coffee shop, which seems horribly public, all of a sudden, with its wall of windows looking out on pre-Christmas crowds. She smiles at Kevin and watches the movements of his left eyebrow, which curves upward sympathetically when he speaks. He can take that eyebrow out into the world and attract other women, women who *do* have room for him in their lives, while she, with her mysteriously repellent "completeness," will remain alone.

For three weeks, she took him home to her house after the Journeys, three weeks where she blotted out thoughts of Amanda and Marlin. Blotted out thoughts that Kevin was doing the same thing. It worked. There was satisfaction in her body's obedience. In Kevin's, too. It seemed proof of the rightness of what they were doing. But then it was over. One night, she had to close her eyes to avoid being disgusted by the carrot-tinged tips of his fingers, the smell of his skin, infused with the garlic and kale messes he carried to rehearsals in mason jars.

He helped her by pulling back. "Think I'll just grab some sleep."

"Actually, it's an early morning."

"True, maybe I'll just get on my way."

In the coffee shop she forces herself to look out the window, away from that all-too-compelling eyebrow. A woman struggles across the road on a walker, the front and sides of which are draped with shopping bags. Rebecca gets up, endures a lingering hug from Kevin and goes home to dredge up a few tears. But Kevin has stopped talking of leaving. He has his dignity back. Rebecca's job is done, at least for now.

The International Federation for Regressive Progression®

About the founder

I'm a writer by day, a blues musician by night, a lay scientist, an aging hippy, an overgrown kid. Most important of all, I'm a stay-at-home dad to seven special children from all over the world. With their unique needs and abilities, they teach me to live in the Now. Along my wife, Dr. Naomi Cox, I run the International Federation for Regressive Progression®.

The wind beneath my wings

I remember my first encounter with Marlin Lewis. I was taking English Lit, dabbling in student productions when I heard of the unique voice and body work Marlin did out of an old Vaudeville Theatre in the east end of Toronto. I showed up one crisp fall day to join what Marlin called The Journey. Throngs of people were arriving. I had such an inflated idea of my own importance I was about to walk away rather than join such a big crowd. But I had glimpsed a beautiful woman and followed her into their journeying space. I don't know who this woman was, but if not for her I would not have entered and would not have stayed.

I expected Marlin to pay special attention to me. And of course, he did not. There were close to 100 people there, most days. Oh, I was cocky back then. Trying to make up for my insecurity with women, angry at my parents, blah blah blah. It was all so many words. As the weeks went on – and I surrendered to The Now – I began to see things clearly. I wasn't special. I wouldn't be special until I did something special in the world.

Marlin refused to charge for his services and refused to give his Work a name. He called his sessions Journeys, as indeed they were. Journeys within, and Journeys back to the world of our pre-verbal memories. The Journeys could be terrifying. They were expeditions into the wilderness of our selves. But he kept us all safe. Marlin eventually left us to fend for ourselves, but his Work – and the Journey — continue.

News
Balderson Medical Centre
April 20, 2012

For Immediate Release
"Regressive Progression® is set to make BMC Psychiatry a world leader in the treatment of mood disorders," Dr. Naomi Cox announced at a press conference today.

With the help of a generous grant from the SmartScreens corporation, BMC will launch clinical trials next year. The promising results already seen in Acquired Brain Injury (ABI) are thought to arise from the phenomenon of neuroplasticity, the ability of uninjured parts of the brain to take over the functions of the injured parts. RP® has been shown to activate lost functions by regressing the patient to movements normally made in infancy, and taking her or him through the stages of development again.

Mr. Kevin Purcell used the technique to heal himself from the results of a devastating stroke. He then went on to write the book *Lost and Found*. The book caught the eye of Dr. Cox – a celebrated neurologist – who fought for clinical trials. Now a staple of rehabilitations hospitals and patient support groups, *Lost and Found* has been followed by another book: *Regressive Progression®: Unraveling the Mysteries of the Brain.*

RP® follows on the work of Dr. Isaac Samuel, a German pediatrician forced to flee to England during the Nazi era. He used his knowledge of child development to work with Brain-Injured soldiers. Fleeing persecution, Dr. Samuel destroyed his papers before escaping Germany. At the press conference, Mr. Purcell has pains-takingly reconstructed his work and made it available to science again. Mr. Purcell refused to comment at the press conference but was visibly moved, standing with his hand over his heart as Dr. Cox accepted the cheque.

Lewis Facilitator® Training

The International Federation for Regressive Progression® holds facilitator trainings world-wide. Comprising a four-year, intensive program of Personal Journeying® combined with anatomy, phys-iology and the latest research in neuroscience, our Lewis Facilita-tors® have found work in clinics, hospitals and in private practice.

Please click the contact link for more details.

Lewis Facilitator®, Regressive Progression® and Personal Jour-neying® are service marks of the International Institute for Regres-sive Progression®.

PART III

Gesendet: 17/3/2012. 5:43 a.m.
An: director@graddrama.UToronto.ca
Von: AmAndAm@gmail.com

Betreff: The Truth

Yes, Dr. Charbonneau, that was me you saw on the subway a few weeks ago. Yes, I did start forward to speak to you across the gap between the platforms. And yes, I did tuck my chin in to my chest and dash away, embarrassed, when I realized what I was doing. You're an ideal confidante. Just as long as I don't have to meet you face to face.

I was in town for a wedding. At 2 p.m. on Tuesday, January 15th, I watched a plump and pasty redhead approach my daughter, who sat, draped in silk, in a chair draped in silk. She looked up at him, her face wet with tears. (I'd never seen Meira cry except when she wasn't getting her own way!) Yet here she was at her wedding, weeping with happiness like an innocent young girl. She *is* a young girl. Just turned eighteen. And the innocence? I guess she's doing her best to restore it. Gingerly and with shaking hands, the boy shrouded her face in layer after layer of fabric, taking time to make sure the folds fell just so.

Then I found myself crammed, sweating under the chuppah, surrounded by strangers in rustling taffeta. The boy squinted and craned his neck, peering through filthy glasses. My daughter was within touching distance, yet there were so many people between us. (Must put aside the suspicion that this was all orchestrated to hurt me.) When it was over I was given a moment to embrace her. She held me apart from her body. Then she was surrounded by her new family. I wished I had a veil, myself.

I was introduced to people. Cousins? Sisters-in-law? Packs of children, indistinguishable from one another, ran around on the lawn. There was a woman with four, five ... oh wait! Two more in the carriage and one holding on to the side. Then I noticed her unlined face. Was she even thirty? This will be my daughter's life.

"I want a family," Meira told me when she announced her engagement, "a big family. A *real* family." Children are irrevocable. More so than the metal stud she had driven through her tongue at sixteen, even the black "A" inscribed on her shoulder. (Removed without anesthetic, she announced proudly, driving in a spike of her own.) It scares me that she's limiting her choices, but maybe that's exactly what she wants.

There was no one from our side. Mummy and Daddy sent money. Safra was in production that week and could not fly up from New York. "If we'd had more *notice* ..." he remarked pointedly, as if I were the one who'd failed to invite him in time. I was proud of myself for waiting until he hung up before starting to cry. I didn't stay around for the dancing, or even the meal. (Where were they planning to seat me?) I went home, or what used to be home, the broadloom fortress of Mummy's and Daddy's love, and lay awake all night in the bedroom which they have kept, frilly, pristine, and utterly unchanged, since I was a child.

And a funeral. The very day after the wedding: a call from the nursing home. "Dorothy's taken a turn for the worse." My mother and I sat beside the bed. One more breath, one more breath.

"Where does it come from?" I asked. Mummy thought I meant Dorothy's determination, but I meant her breath. Where, in that deflated body, did she find it? We held her hands, moved her to her side and to her back again. Always the threat of an insult to the skin. It had become so thin, barely able to contain her. Whenever she woke, she swore at us. Angry, even at the end.

And then she was gone. Taking with her more memories.

The obit describes her as a daughter, wife and mother. Nothing about the books, nothing about the columns. Shiva at the home of her grand-daughter and her husband. (Didn't go.) I'm not mentioned, either. I'm being erased.

I flew home and got my poisoned journals down from the shelf. Found Dorothy in the pages. Thought you might want to know.

Yours truly,
Amanda M.

2000

When the fasten-seatbelt sign finally goes off, Rebecca can barely straighten her cramped legs. It's been twenty-two hours since she left her apartment, most of that time spent in chairs meant for people half her size. Then they have to wait and wait and wait for their cartons of gear, then go through customs, then there is the task of figuring out how to navigate the labyrinthine Charles de Gaulle airport. There's a shuttle to another terminal, which they crisscross several times seeking the train to Paris. At last, an overhead sign appears in the distance, showing they are headed the right way. One diminutive figure works her way ahead of the others. It is Kyoko, who dropped out of ballet school to join SenseInSound a few months ago. She turns a handstand on the concrete floor and lands neatly in front of the ticket vending machines. "Random! This is so fuckin' random, man!" she says, flourishing her wrists and sliding her head side-to-side in an imitation of Carmen Miranda. No one responds. Hordes of people file relentlessly past. Rebecca wants to pull Kyoko back as if she were a child who'd run into the road, but the crowd has hemmed her in. How did Kyoko get so far ahead of them all, anyway? Like a spirit, she is able to slip past obstacles as if she had no substance at all.

Rebecca, on the other hand, plods heavily along. They're not going to Paris, but must get to the *Gare du Nord* before taking another train to a town Rebecca can never remember except that it sounds like the name of a fish. A fish you would eat if you were really broke. Once they get there, there is no one to greet them at the station, and no one seems to have heard of the international theatre conference they are attending. Rebecca hands the organizer's phone number to a woman behind a grubby window, and mimes dialing a telephone.

"Mais c'est tout à fait clair, je crois."

"Just help me, okay?"

With a shrug, the woman begins to dial.

Hours later, she finds herself at a university campus, stretching out on a lumpy bed in a residence room, longing for sleep.

It is clear the airport and train station are all they are going to see of the city of lights. They will not see Paris, and nor, they soon learn, will they enjoy fine food and wine or partake of the small pleasures of daily life that are supposed to make Europe so much better than Canada. The dining hall has been decorated – slightly – in honour of the conference, with checkered table cloths on the long tables, and tea lights set in ashtrays, but they are the kind of tables with chairs affixed to them at cruelly uncomfortable angles and fluorescents glare overhead day and night. The wine is acrid, the coffee, weak, the bread, stale, and the meals consist of tough meat and reconstituted potatoes. The water is gritty. Even the bottled water.

They are scheduled to give three performances of their latest play, *Oedipus Rex*, and host workshops every morning for a week. In the evenings they can either return to their stark residences or meet in the room they call the Kafkateria. They choose the latter, drinking the free (if terrible) wine until they cannot not stay up any longer. There is none of the "interdisciplinary sharing" the brochure promised. Everyone stays with the people they already know, at the tables they staked out for themselves the first morning.

"Let's give this a miss." Marlin says, as they look over the program the next morning at breakfast. He's talking about *Les Soeurs*, the other Canadian company at the festival. They are scheduled to perform that night. "I think we should find a way to get into the city.

It is Paris after all." Rebecca smiles, relieved he's in tune with her. When she saw the blurb in the brochure, describing *Les Soeurs* as breaking the boundaries of physical theatre, she felt offended, as if the troupe had stolen something from SenseInSound.

"It'll be a breath of fresh air in this stifling atmosphere, and maybe we'll get a decent meal."

"Excuse me!" A short, trim woman approaches, introducing herself as Lorraine Charbonneau, a Ph.D. candidate from Montreal. She is at the festival to interview the participants. Would they mind if she asks a few questions? She has a digital recorder at the ready, as if assuming she will hear, "Yes."

"Jesus Christ," says Marlin. "Do you have to take everything from us?"

Lorraine looks at him, evidently so frozen with fear she is unable to put the machine back in her bag. Rebecca notices in the long silence that Lorraine is not all that young. A fine trace-work of lines is visible behind her glasses, and her short-cropped hair is seeded with grey. She is too neat, Rebecca decides. It looks like she's never had to contend with real life.

Marlin continues, "You academics have to feed on something, don't you? Publish or perish, isn't that how it goes? And so you prey on the people out here on the front lines, the people risking our blood and our bones for art. Amanda and I have been running this company for twenty years. We won't be able to send our children to university, though, because we're poor. Why should we answer your questions? Why should we give you something for free ... so you can further your career and we can starve? *Your* university won't hire us, will it? Will it, eh? I said, *Will it*?"

Lorraine says nothing, nor does she leave. What Rebecca first took to be an expression of fear is actually one of stubbornness. She is waiting him out. Seeing Marlin through a stranger's eyes Rebecca comes to a disturbing conclusion: his rages are getting worse. As he leaves, his feet seem to tangle. He almost falls, then rights himself. Lorraine continues to watch.

Now she addresses Amanda. "I noticed your name in the program. I hope you don't mind me asking, are you related to Sylvia Bloom?"

"She's my mum!"

"She was an actress, wasn't she?"

"In the fifties, yes."

"Sylvia's name keeps coming up in the research for my dissertation: *Genius in the Fog: The Forgotten Fifties Foremothers of the Contemporary British Stage*. She had this stunning expressiveness, according to the reviews. Audiences were in love with her. She worked with a director named Bobbie Lance – changed the face of theatre – now absent from the history books – what else is new? Anyway, Sylvia was Bobbie Lance's muse, you could say. All the plays Lance chose, all the innovations she made – everything was based on what Sylvia could do."

"That's not the way Mummy tells it."

"Really! May I call you when you get back to Canada?"

Amanda shakes her head.

"Maybe your mother would speak to me then. I'll give you my contact information." She takes out a notebook and begins to write with infuriating slowness. *Has this woman ever compromised in her life?*

She tears out the page, "Could you give this to Miss Bloom?"

"I'll … Lorraine, you need to understand this would upset my partner."

"Tell him … oh … never mind." Lorraine sighs and flops down in a chair. "I think I might not be presenting myself very well. Am I coming off as too – formal or stuffy or something?"

Kyoko laughs. "Lose the power suit, man!"

Lorraine unzips the jacket to reveal a T-shirt, the worn symbol for "woman" creased and flaking on her bony chest. "I got it at Value Village. I wanted to make sure I had something nice to wear for my presentation, but it's not that kind of conference, I guess."

"So what did you want to ask?" Kyoko says.

"I think –" Amanda breaks in – "I think we need to end this conversation."

"Please pass my number to your mother. I hope you will."

Marlin does not show up for the workshop that morning, or for lunch. Their plans to go to the city are in limbo, and Rebecca and Amanda agree that they must encourage the group to attend the performance of *Les Soeurs* after all. As the only other Canadians, their absence would be taken as a snub.

The play is called *Scylla and Charybdis*. Women are positioned in two rows on either side of the stage. Dressed in grey shifts, they make the sound of wind in all its moods. The rows lean toward each other as if magnetized, then pull apart. Rebecca knows that their simple but utterly controlled movements are the product of many months of work. Pairs of women break free of the rows and enact scenes: between mother and daughter, between sisters, between friends. Each pair has a fight over something worthless, a half-eaten sandwich or broken toy from the bottom of a cereal box. They fight in exaggerated slapstick, speak in complex couplets between the standing women, whose reaching movements threaten, at times, to entangle them and drag them back. Confusion mounts as the worthless thing receives more and more attention. Inevitably, they discard it and another pair of women takes their place.

During the last of several curtain calls, two women emerge to take one last bow together. One wears a body-stocking and has long grey cornrows collected in a bun on her head, adding to her already impressive height. The other, in a trouser suit, has a brush cut in the same steely colour. Their features are familiar, but their whole presentation is so striking Rebecca knows she would have remembered them had she seen them before. These are Gaëlle and Catherine Mercier: *Les Soeurs*. They bow and leave the stage with their joined hands raised in the air.

Rebecca lies awake, unable to get comfortable in her tiny bed, unable to stop thinking about the performance. *Les Soeurs* is made up of twelve people, just like SenseInSound in the old days. And the show draws on Greek mythology. The whole event feels like an

incursion into her own company's territory, all the more offensive
for its being well received.

And better.

It's funny, it's understandable. That's a relief in a festival of dull,
obscure plays. But there's more. The women moved together, but
they were all different. Their body shapes and skin-colours and
ages. They made SenseInSound look like ... an army? How can she
think that? Because – despite digging into their personal depths all
the time, there's something uniform about the actors in SenseIn-
Sound. For one they're all Caucasian (except for Kyoko) but there's
something more. Next to *Les Soeurs*, the SenseInSound actors seem
agitated. They're at attention, even when pouring out the most intimate emotions. Constantly alert. Let's face it: afraid. They're constantly afraid. And it shows. Year after year she has seen Marlin
relentlessly push his performers. They deliver things they do not
know they have inside them. But the women in *Les Soeurs* go further, and it looks easy for them. They're not scraping out the dregs
of their abilities. They're starting out with more to give.

She turns on her light and looks over the program, grunting when she notices the impressive collection of funder logos at
the bottom of the page. According to the description, Gaëlle and
Catherine Mercier, the producer and writer of the show are sisters.
Born in Haiti, they lost their parents to a car accident when they
were toddlers and ended up being adopted into different families
in Canada. Five years ago, Catherine lost a relationship and a job
in the same year. The crisis prompted her to go looking for her sister. Gaëlle wrote she had been living "without purpose" in Toronto.
Reuniting with Catherine helped her to figure out who she truly
was, inspired her to train as a dancer, though she was already forty.
Together, they travelled to Haiti and found their extended family.

"Gail!" Rebecca speaks the name out loud when she makes the
connection. This was Gail from SenseInSound, Gail, whose part
had been cut from *Genesis*. By bizarre coincidence, her friend back
then was called Katie, the long-lost sister, Catherine. It was as if
she'd been looking for her sister all along, even though she didn't

know she had one. But her face – it's not just that she has matured and changed her style. She is *there* – present in her own skin –not hidden behind a mask of tension.

In the program, Gaëlle has thanked everyone who so much as bought her a cup of coffee, but there is no mention of SenseIn-Sound. She has ignored the years she spent with the company and dismissed her time in Toronto as "without purpose." Yet clearly, she has been doing The Work. This is the only method which could give her troupe its exquisite harmony, the sense that every movement and sound springs forth organically, rather than having been created by any single human mind. More: she does not mention Marlin. The story Gaëlle tells about her own success is all about her relationship with her sister. Catherine has been her inspiration, the source of both her longing and fulfillment.

Gail and Katie showed no signs of disappointment when they were cut from their featured roles in *Genesis*. Rebecca didn't get it. Nothing seemed to affect them. Their moods were like a small weather system within the greater ups and downs of the company. And she didn't get why they were kept on, especially when they became her giggling, whispering problem. They were so caught up in each other she never knew whether she was getting her message across. Even sending them to different sides of the stage felt like prying apart two magnets.

But then came *Memorysong*. Gail invited Rebecca out for coffee one day after work. She apologized for acting so immature, and promised to help out after hours. Rebecca began to entrust her with a few errands and then some repairs. Meantime Katie carried on, blending, nondescript, into the rest of the group. Her attachment to Gail was the most interesting thing about her. Marlin booked extra time with Gail in an upstairs studio after class. Week by week, she transformed from gawky to graceful, from noisy to virtuosic. In the course of that year she became a diva with a voice that could pierce or thunder. She performed his gymnastic sequences seemingly without effort or fatigue. Yet for every ounce of encouragement he gave Gail, Marlin criticized Katie. "I want to hear *you*," he said many times. This only seemed to make Katie imitate Gail: in her clothes, her speech and gestures. Meantime, Gail grew more lovely and dignified every day.

But then came a rehearsal – Gail's last – when Marlin demanded she sing a line from a children's song, again and again.

"*Ring around a rosie, a pocket full of posy.*"

"No! Jesus Christ! *Give* me something! Every child hears that song. Surely you remember." Gail grew quieter and quieter, and eventually just stood there, barely breathing. *You people* ... What did he say? *You people have to get over* ... Something. Rebecca can't remember. Only that Marlin put his hands up on either side of his head as if in terrible pain. "I can't. I'm sorry. I can't do this. Will someone help?" He looked around wildly, his eyes resting on Katie. "Please," he said extending his hand in her direction. Katie stood up and began, tentatively to sing. Marlin nodded. "Listen to that! Listen to that!" he said to everyone – never looking at Gail. "You're hearing the truth."

Rebecca does not remember seeing Gail leave. All she knows is that she did not follow her. Marlin's pain eclipsed everything else. She thought about trying to call Gail afterwards but never got time.

Marlin is not with them the next morning. Kevin leads a workshop in which the European participants display stunning physical and musical prowess. They leave with nods and thank-yous in their own languages, but never a question and certainly never a word of praise. That night the talk at the SenseInSound table centres on how they shouldn't be presuming to teach at all. Everything they have been struggling to establish is mere foundation to these Europeans.

Marlin arrives just as their dishes are cleared away and they are opening another bottle of wine, speculating on whether SenseIn-Sound should have been focusing on classical training all along. He has a knapsack slung over one shoulder. He places it on the table. They fall silent, watching him walk over to the area *Les Soeurs* has staked out. Rebecca watches him tap Gaëlle on the shoulder, watches her rise, watches them embrace. Marlin takes her hand and grasps it as he speaks sincerely to her. Is he congratulating her on a performance he didn't even see? No. Marlin will be telling Gaëlle the truth: that she looks good. Gaëlle turns away from him, goes back to her wine and the people she is sharing it with. Rebecca admires Gaëlle's long, slim back, the agility of her studied movements. She also notices that Kyoko, whose attention never lingers anywhere for more than a few seconds, has not once taken her eyes from the scene.

Then Marlin comes back, opens his knapsack and distributes oranges and bananas to the SenseInSound group. He addresses them as if reading their minds, answering fears he has never heard them share. "The people live in small spaces in Europe. They can't respond generously. They will never tell us how much impact this is having on them. It's all about hierarchy. Class system. That's what it comes down to. Because we're not representatives of any university they're afraid to validate our work. But we're the most sophisticated artists in the place."

His voice is full, his movements relaxed. He is wearing jeans and a dress shirt: frayed and old, but a step up from his usual pajama-like outfits. The top buttons are open to display a neck that is powerful despite his small frame. Rebecca flushes, and she has a melting feeling through her whole body. Riding the ups and downs of his shifting attention is an abstract process. Simple attraction is a rare feeling these days, but it hits just as hard as it ever did.

"I met someone." Marlin says. "Someone new. He's here with *Dans Antonia* from Amsterdam, but he's not like the rest of them. He's got progressive ideas."

Beautiful is the word that comes to Rebecca's mind when she sees the man who approaches their table a few moments later.

"This is Jonathan Mayer." Marlin stands close enough to Jonathan that their sides touch. Jonathan's hair falls down his back in gold ringlets. His body is tall and lanky, graceful and strong. His face is strong, too, with wide cheekbones and a cleft chin, yet his soft skin gives him an angelic appearance. Jonathan's eyes range around the group. When he smiles at Rebecca she has the momen-tary sensation of looking in a mirror. They are the same height. It is a rare experience for Rebecca, even with a man. Like her, he has dark eyes and blond hair.

"Random!" Kyoko exclaims. "Are you guys long-lost twins or something?"

"Bit of an age difference to be twins. Anyway, he's better looking, don't you think?"

Everyone laughs, but Jonathan seems to take it all very seriously. He bows to Rebecca, palms meeting in front of his chest. Then he steps forward, reaching out a hand to each of the company mem-bers to shake.

"Jonathan Mayer. Pleasure to meet you. Very happy to meet you. I was in the audience yesterday. Very, very impressive. This is tru-ly something special." When Amanda's turn comes, he inclines his head toward her, hand over his heart. She nods in reply. Rebecca feels a change in the way she is standing. It was the way she felt after her session with Davis many years ago, the sensation of being light and balanced and easy on her feet. She closes her eyes and imagines herself being lifted by Jonathan, cradled. But then she opens them. She's still responsible for everything. She goes back to fussing about their route back to Paris, rehearsing each step in her mind.

Still, she isn't about to go up to her room with the newcomer here. She pours herself a glass of wine, offers one to Jonathan, which he refuses. He accepts a glass of water from Amanda, again with hand over heart. He talks about the troupe which hired him to com-pose and perform the music for their piece. "I make music to sup-port their dance – yet they act as if these were warring factions: as if one had to win and one to lose. And among themselves it is always a struggle to be on top. Even among close colleagues. Around them, I am lost. You know, yesterday morning on the way to breakfast, I fell. I am not normally a clumsy person, but I tripped over my own foot and bruised myself down my side. It has never happened before. I am divided from myself, being in this atmosphere."

They talk until late that night, enlivened by Jonathan's admiration. He asks them questions about SenseInSound and they all chime in with stories and anecdotes. Marlin sits back with his arms folded, smiling. Kyoko is unusually quiet. Then Rebecca notices her pull Marlin's sleeve while a few others are talking.

"That Sister Act thing."

"*Les Soeurs*."

"We saw it."

"Mhm."

"You should know what's going on there, man. It's a direct steal. Victoria said the head of it – Gayla or whatever she calls herself – she used to be with us."

"She was."

"Well she never said anything. You should make a lawsuit!"

"You can't copyright art."

"But now everyone's clapping for them. And they stole your method, man!"

The group has gone silent now, and Marlin's voice grows deep as he makes his next statement: "The Work is in all of us. Anyone can find it if they dig deep enough. Besides, I was Gail's teacher. My task was to give with an open hand."

Kyoko folds her arms and sinks her chin to her chest. Jonathan says, "This is a beautiful thought." Amanda says she is tired, and one by one they excuse themselves to go to their rooms.

Then it's the last day. While Rebecca packs, SenseInSound gathers for a Journey, along with Jonathan. He joins them for lunch afterwards. At the end of the meal he stands up and addresses them. "Excuse me, I wonder if I could have a moment of your time before we all go our separate ways. I have something I would like to say to all of you if you have a minute. Thank you. Thank you very much."

Rebecca has grown used to seeing Jonathan at their table. Marlin always sits next to him. Sometimes he whispers to Jonathan, who listens attentively, nodding. Rebecca cannot stop staring at them, drawn not only to the intensity of the men's connection but to the grace of Jonathan's every movement: the way he flips his hair back

over his shoulder, places a hand on his chest as if to press some remark of Marlin's to his heart. She is grateful for the way he seems to
admire Marlin, a wave she herself can ride.

Jonathan takes a long breath before beginning to talk. "I would
like to thank you for taking me on your Journey this morning. I am
a different man than when I got on the plane for France a week ago.
You know my parents were born in what we call the post-war-years,
and we had the shadow of the past on our household, many things
we do not speak of to this day. And all my life I have struggled with
these kinds of dark things. As a child I was very much into my studies as a classical pianist and then on to the further education in New
York, where there were a limited number of places and many people
who wanted them. Then came the years of auditions. You see, as a
musician I faced competition everywhere."

His voice catches, his face works; all the while his words continue to flow in perfectly composed sentences. "And I have to tell you
that this week, for the first time I feel I can express myself without
being measured and judged. I have been honoured to work with
you and"– he gestures to Marlin – "I'm delighted to say it will not
be the last time."

Rebecca's heart thuds. Marlin is nodding. He says, "We'll be going on to Berlin, to continue our work together."

"For how long?" asks Kyoko.

"For now." He turns and walks away, and Jonathan, after bowing
to them all with hand over heart, follows. Marlin has left her – left
all of them – as if they meant nothing to him. Just like she always
knew he would.

KYOKO CALLING!

I'm a mom, a cultural critic, a maker and interpreter of dances. And I don't see those roles as distinct from one another. I created this site to prove dancers can – and do – think for themselves.

KYOKO:

In this week's edition of my vlog, I get up close and personal with two women who give new meaning to the term "sister act," Gaëlle and Catherine Mercier, the Artistic Director and CEO (respectively) of *To End All Wars*, the annual performance festival that has given Toronto a leading role on the world stage. Gaëlle and Catherine, over the past decade, your company has blown it out of the park in terms of both its artistic and financial success. During the festival, *To End All Wars,* there are over ten thousand visitors who come in to the city, stay in hotels, eat, go to the museums, buy souvenirs. Can you account for …

BOTH:

(pointing at each other) It's her! (laughter)

KYOKO:

Let me in on the joke …!

CATHERINE:

Actually, let me turn the question back to you … why do artistic and financial success have to be separate?

KYOKO:

Well, the paradigm we see in this country is the valorization of either art or money. Absolutely corresponding to Bourdieu's autonomous and heteronomous poles. There's a whole constellation of cultural capital which goes along with receiving government subsidies for our work. Essentially with *not* being financially viable. We assume we have to make a choice between art and money, but it seems you've been able to set aside that dichotomy with *To End All Wars*.

CATHERINE:
We went into this wanting to create an event here, in this country
…

GAËLLE:
… city …

CATHERINE:
… that the whole world would talk about, and I think we've done that. Since the millennium – since *To End All Wars* – the play, I mean – wouldn't you …

CATHERINE:
That's right. Absolutely. The play was the first big success. And since then we've just followed the same magic formula, and watched it grow year over year. We bring the top people in from all over the world to collaborate with our homegrown talent, and we're investing, from an early age, in people who are settling in Toronto and wanting to get started as artists. And there's the programs in schools and community centres, so we're reaching …

GAËLLE:
… the next …

CATHERINE:
… the next generation. Exactly. We're thinking Now but we're also thinking long term. As you know, Toronto is the most …

GAËLLE:
…one of the most …

CATHERINE:
…if not *the* most …

GAËLLE:
… diverse cities in the world, but until To End All Wars, there were so many stories we never saw depicted on stage. This type of a project is made for this city. Now. I mean, to bring Noor in from Pakistan along with the likes of Hideki from Japan. And just to let them sit together for a year.

CATHERINE:
Two.

GAËLLE:
Eighteen months. And ask nothing. That long, long period where art can incubate. It takes a space such as we have, where people can live and work together.

CATHERINE:
It takes Leon Garten is what it takes!

GAËLLE:
Well, absolutely. Leon has the courage and the vision and the will-ingness to take risks and to commit.

KYOKO:
And the money.

GAËLLE:
Lots of people have money, Kyoko!

CATHERINE:
And they wouldn't risk …

KYOKO:
And he knows where to put it.

GAËLLE:
But also, he's committed. This is coming up on fifty years he's served Toronto audiences. Always coming up with something new. Looking around and seeing what's changing. How to keep up to date. It's like this man – it's all about *Now*, for him, you know. But at the same time …

CATHERINE:
Need to work for five years? No problem. You've got five years. You have Hideki, you have Noor and they say, "Let's bring in an orchestra."

GAËLLE:
And not just any orchestra!

CATHERINE:
He trusts them. And it's like – no! Don't need the orchestra.

GAËLLE:
Okay! Just the …

CATHERINE:
Clarinet.

GAËLLE:
Clarinet! Sure! Just the clarinet!

CATHERINE:
Pay everyone …

GAËLLE:
Keep the clarinet. (laughter) *What now? What now?* It's all about Now. That's art. And Leon lives that.

KYOKO:
That's Marlin Lewis talking.

GAËLLE:
That's lots of people.

KYOKO:
Aren't you denying your roots, Gaëlle?

CATHERINE:
She is not denying her roots, my friend.

GAËLLE:
We're talking about art.

CATHERINE:
You can't brand it.

KYOKO:
SenseInSound …

GAËLLE:
Nothing new …

KYOKO:
It was like an incubator for …

GAËLLE:
You can't copyright creativity.

KYOKO:
Marlin worked for two decades on SenseInSound and developed these methods and then you came in and …

CATHERINE:
Well, you didn't exactly have any qualms about …

KYOKO:
You came in and took what he'd risked basically his life for …

GAËLLE:
No one is denying Marlin's … contributions (laughter).

CATHERINE:
Let's go back to this incubator idea. An incubator, yes. For nigh-on twenty years. Leon bankrolled SenseInSound. Where else in this country do you find an entire company on staff with full benefits and salary, and no demands on them? Just create. Just create whatever you want, whenever you want, and I'll pay you. Where else? And something came of it. Something wonderful. But the risk was Leon's and he had the right to step in and put his own people at the top.

GAËLLE:
Well, it was Rebecca who made that happen. Anyway, look, he didn't kick anyone out. Anyone from the original group could stay. That's the stipulation he made when we took over. But they had to be willing to do the work.

KYOKO:
It was essentially a purge and you know it. Except for Rebecca. How do you work so closely with someone who was part of Marlin's old guard?

CATHERINE:
Look, Koyko! Would you get off Marlin? Rebecca is our producer and she's very good at her job. We don't all *sleep* together or anything …

GAËLLE:

It's a very simple issue. Rebecca was willing to do the work.

CATHERINE:

Hard worker, Rebecca.

KYOKO:

I guess we all agree on that.

2000

Three weeks have passed, and Marlin has shown no sign of returning. Rebecca is spending most of her time stripping linoleum from the back corner of the basement, the one area where it tenaciously clings.

Yesterday, Amanda caught her on her way downstairs. "Should I call my parents?"

Rebecca nodded. "We may need to. But let's wait 'til September."

"Are you ... alright financially?"

"For now," Rebecca lied. She had just agreed to teach a second course, but it won't cover her mortgage.

Some people have been gathering in the mornings for a half-hearted attempt at a Journey, but there are fewer and fewer every day. One afternoon last week, Kyoko appeared in the basement, saying nothing at first but loitering at the periphery of Rebecca's work room looking at all the shelves, drawers and cubby-holes she had set up.

"For God's sakes, what is it?" Rebecca barked, at last, rising from where she crouched, hacking away at linoleum.

Kyoko walked over as if approaching the gallows. She took a deep breath, preparing to speak, when Rebecca raised her hand. "You're leaving." Kyoko nodded, and the mangled story came out. She'd been offered a position with *Les Soeurs* after their performance in France and had initially said no. But then, with Marlin away …

"You guys are everything to me!" Kyoko said. "I can't leave this place!" She *was* leaving, though.

"Well, you know how Marlin feels about letting go."

Kyoko now launched herself at Rebecca, clasping her fiercely around the waist and almost lifting her off the ground.

"Okay, well, good luck," Rebecca said. She returned to her scraping. Kyoko remained, though. She indicated the room with a sweep of her arm.

"This is like, sick, man."

"Pardon?"

"I just want to tell you that you're totally OCD."

"Well, I wouldn't go that far …"

"I mean, In a good way! No one else would do this. You're one of a kind. Actors are like, totally random, you know? After me they'll find someone else and someone else and someone else." A deep breath. "But, Rebecca, you are the foundation on which The Work is built."

"Thanks."

"I'll never forget you. Goodbye." Kyoko grabbed her hand, pumped it – scraper and all – and walked away.

Next it is Safra who appears in front of her. She wipes her sweaty forehead with her wrist. Saying nothing, he waits for her to stand. He's holding a pair of sneakers. The shoes are a brilliant white, his expression, tragic.

"Nana says I have to get everything new."

"Shopping is the worst, isn't it?"

"I have to go to Switzerland."

"You what?"

"To Baccalaureate school. Nanna and Grand-dad say it would be good."

Rebecca's eyes fill, but she knows she must not let this show. She turns and gestures to some flats she has piled in a corner. "I'm doing some painting tomorrow. Help me out. That should rough the shoes up a bit."

"Thanks."

"Thank *you*."

"See you."

"Bye." Safra does not leave.

"Actually, I could use some help today."

Safra nods and finds himself some tools. Gravely, he dons the clean running shoes and they kneel down and dig away at the linoleum on the floor. When they're done for the day, they slop a bit of fresh paint over both their shoes.

Safra says, "I'll write." He's a kid, and not even her kid. He can't be expected to follow through. Still, the thought that he might stay in touch makes Rebecca feel like a thick corset around her chest has been loosened, just a bit.

It is violent awakening, the sound of the phone in the dark.

"Hi-dear."

"What time is it?"

"That's okay. Don't be scared."

"What are you talking about, Dorothy?"

"He's dead."

"Who?" Rebecca sits up.

"That boy will be devastated."

"Who's *dead*?"

"His father."

"Whose father? Are you telling me Marlin has died?"

"No-dear. Of course not. It's Marlin's father. Colon cancer. Half an hour ago."

Dorothy's voice is even, too even.

"I'll call Amanda and we'll get hold of Marlin."

"He can't live alone."

"I don't understand what you're telling me."

"He'll have to move back here. I know he doesn't like my husband, but he can't live alone at sixteen."

"Who are you talking about?"

"The boy-dear."

"Listen, what you're saying is not making sense. I will call Amanda and we'll try to find Marlin, okay?"

"Good girl. He always did inspire devotion in women. Surprising. Such an itty bitty pecker he has. Don't know where he got that. Abe was an idiot but he was hung like a bull."

"Dorothy, please!"

"Good girl. Don't be afraid."

"We need to get off the phone now so I can get hold of Marlin."

"*This is the very witching hour of night* … you know that speech, right? Things can happen at this hour."

"I'm going to hang up the phone now, okay?"

"That's when the spirits wake up."

"Dorothy, go to bed. I'm hanging up. Goodnight."

Rebecca lies awake, trying to decide what to do. If Marlin's father has just died, she must try to get hold of him. Dorothy seemed confused, maybe even drunk. Rebecca holds herself back from picking up the phone. Spreading panic will not help. *Even death needs a stage manager*, Rebecca thinks, and then: *I'd rather be managing a show.* As soon as she decently can, she goes to see Amanda and finds her in bathrobe and slippers, trying to get Meira out the door for school. Meira is wearing above-the-knee socks a short skirt and a bomber jacket. Amanda says, "Meira, you'll be cold!"

"I don't care."

"Honey, I feel like that's not warm enough."

"*Hot blooded, check it and see* … Svetlana taught me that song. She's a bad influence; I think you should fire her."

Too much to do. Too many things to take care of. Rebecca's mind is blank for a moment. Then she takes charge. "Meira, you need to put on some jeans and a sweater."

"Why?"

"Because you're in Grade Two, and you're dressed like a teenager."

"I'm gifted, didn't you know?"

"You're not a teenager and you don't want to hurry the process, believe me."

"Who says?"

"Meira, there's no more discussion. Change."

Meira spits in Rebecca's direction.

"Please, honey!" Amanda says.

Rebecca raises her hand to silence both of them. "Meira, change your clothes."

Pouting, the girl flounces into her room.

"Amanda, I'm sorry to show up at this hour but Marlin's father just died."

"His father?"

"Dorothy called me last night."

"His father died years ago, Rebecca, when he was Safra's age. That's when he went to live with Dorothy and her second husband, and everything went wrong."

"Dorothy called me this morning. Four."

"Not you, too! Last week she called my parents' place and scared the housekeeper out of her mind. It was the same time of night. I think she's losing it."

The phone rings, a blow to Rebecca's chest.

"Don't worry-dear."

"What's the matter?"

"Nothing-dear. The morning will be here soon. Only two hours. Then you can go pee-pee and by the time you get back to bed it'll almost be light."

"It's too early to make phone calls, do you understand?"

"I know you have enough to worry about with Sylvia and Leon and all the famous, beautiful people, little though they might need it. Don't worry about me, God forbid. I never asked anything of the little fucker."

"Dorothy!"

"All I wanted was my own career. And what did I get? Two broken marriages, and my own son hates me. And now I'm alone."

"Where are you calling from?"

"The floor-dear. I've fallen on the floor. Broken a hip. Broken hips, as you may know, are the primary cause of death among abandoned grandmothers. I'm lying in my own shit-dear. For three days in my own crap and piss."

"Give me your address. I'm calling an ambulance."

"6565 Kildare, Côte St. Luc."

"You don't live in Montreal, Dorothy."

"Such a smart girl! I live at St. Clair and Yonge but I might as well be at the South Pole-dear. I'm outside the orbit. The Gartens live ten minutes away but no one comes to see *me*. The sun shines out of their asses-dear. Do you ever think about it, how lucky they are? They look good, they have money, they have good taste, they are sooooo polite and nice, and by the way, healthy. And we – the rest of the world – we're diseased and crazy and we smell bad. And we wish they were them.

"Marlin is a smart guy. He sees that if he stays close to those Gartens, people will want to be close to him. They'll sit in a theatre and be bored out of their minds, and go to his classes and act like fools at his bidding, and call him a genius. Just because they hope a bit of that luck will rub off on them. Touched with the blessing of the holy Gartens. He's touched them alright. Insinuated that negligible *shmekl* into one of them and now they're joined for life. But those Gartens didn't bank on me. Take Marlin and you get his mother too. A package deal."

It isn't a broken hip, though Dorothy is found sorely neglected in front of her television set. Accompanied by Amanda, she arrives later that day in a cab, emaciated, her wig askew. She tries to run away when Amanda opens the cab door and Rebecca has to rush out of the theatre and seize her. With one arm around her shoulders, she leads her inside and upstairs to Amanda's apartment. Dorothy falls immediately asleep.

The dirty dishes and napkins are stacked in Amanda's kitchen. Dorothy has fallen asleep in the armchair where she ate toast from a tray on her lap. Meira goes to her room and Rebecca and Amanda sit at the table with cups of tea, trying to ignore the music blaring from behind her door.

"Is that okay?" Rebecca asks, discerning a string of obscenities in a rap song.

Amanda sighs. "I pick my battles. Can you stay a while?" Rebecca says yes, though she longs to get away from the pulsing bass.

"Back in a minute." Amanda returns with needles and a ball of what looks like very expensive wool. She plants a pair of glasses on her nose. The needles look bigger than Amanda's arm bones. She straightens out her work on her lap, frowning and counting stitches under her breath. Rebecca holds back from offering to clean up the twisted clump, which looks like it is intended to be a scarf.

"I miss Safra so much … You see your child every day, knowing how he feels and what he's up to. And then one day … gone! And I know that he's not thinking about me the way I'm thinking about him. He started out inside me. Part of me. And now …he's got his own life."

Rebecca nods. She does not mention she has been receiving daily emails from Safra. Yesterday: "Hi, Rebecca. Got a buzz cut this a.m. All that hair gone! Cooler in more ways than one. The air in this place is crystal clear. (excuse lame cliché) Everyone in my class is older than me and pretty rowdy, but I made friends with one guy so far (I think). There's a drama club. Thanks again for the knife I use it every day. See you at XMAS. Write to me. Thank you. Love, Safra."

"How are you managing with …?" Rebecca gestures with a tilt of her head in Dorothy's direction. Amanda answers with a shrug.

"The nursing home will be ready for her next week. Anyway, Svetlana does most of it."

"But you're good to her, Amanda." A spear of guilt – as always – about her own lack of patience and warmth. "I don't know how you do it, actually."

"Sometimes I feel like she's the only part of Marlin I can be close to." A pause, then Amanda blurts out, "I have no idea where he is."

Rebecca nods, concealing her shock at learning he has not communicated with Amanda either. Amanda dabs tears from her cheeks. "We were always," she puts up two fingers, and brings the other hand around to squeeze them together. "Like this. Side-by-side. Even though we had separate apartments. But it's different this time." Rebecca feels the sick panic that greets any revelation of Amanda's vulnerability.

"Remember when I went to New York after *South Pacific*? I think my parents were trying to separate us. But it ended up having the opposite effect. That trip changed everything for me. You know, there's a feeling you get when you're in front of an audience and things are going well. Something comes toward you – their attention – their love, basically. It's palpable. But as soon as I got to New York it was like someone had built a wall and I could not feel that attention any more. And I realized I'd lived my whole life in front of an appreciative audience. I'd assumed it was me, that my talent was making this happen but when I got to New York I saw that I had never earned that feeling. And there were others – so many others – who were so much better than me. My parents got me an agent there, introduced me to their friends. You know, they have deep pockets. I could have stayed for years trying to build something, but it was all very clear to me. I just wasn't good enough. I felt so alone. More than anything else I wanted to get rid of that feeling.

"And I did. A little visit to Marlin in Toronto and ..." she points to her belly. "The rest is history." She chuckles and shakes her head. "Mind you I was pretty happy when Safra turned out small-boned, like Marlin. Those were different days ... pre-AIDS. We were all over the place!"

"That's for sure," Rebecca answers, but that's all she says. All she'll ever say.

Gesendet: 5/6/2012. 11 a.m.
An: director.graddrama@UToronto.ca
Von: AmAndAm@gmail.com

Betreff: The Truth

Dr. Charbonneau,

After so many years, the dream never goes away: we are on a football field, stands full of people roaring, flashing their camera phones. I'm in the middle on some kind of ritual stone. Marlin is about to cut a hole in my throat. I'm smiling. I believe it will go better for me if I act like I want it. Or I'm trying to convince myself this is consensual by controlling the only part of it I can. When he cuts, orgasmic sounds come from my throat instead of blood. That's what the people want. The sounds are ripped out of me; I feel nothing but pain. The crowd always wants more. There's never enough.

I wake pushing the covers off. Another hot flash. I'm mouthing the word "NO!" but no sound comes out. All these accolades for Marlin on the Net. I read them and feel like there's something wrong with me. Something wrong with me in the bathtub. Something wrong with me walking down the street. Something wrong with me trying to put words on the page. Trying to breathe. I'm back to the time when Marlin had power over my well-being and I can't escape. I want to say something, tell someone. But who?

And what to say?

Marlin never hit me. Marlin never called me names. He never accused me of anything or controlled my comings and goings. He was the guy who called out other men for acting that way. Capital E equality. It was part of our Work, what we stood for. And yet he could – did – make me feel like I was worth nothing. He was at the centre of my life and if I lost him, I lost everything. And it went on and on. And on.

And suppose I do tell someone – I won't say "the truth" – but my version of it. Does that fix anything or does it merely feed your career, Dr. Charbonneau?

That sounds like something Marlin would have asked. After all these years, he's still inside me.

I can't do it. At least not yet.

Amanda M.

2000

It's the Friday before Thanksgiving, and everyone has taken the day off. Not Rebecca, though. Even though there's nothing to do but more basement clearing, she goes into work every single day. She is looking forward to having the building to herself, but Deverell is waiting for her when she arrives.

"What are you doing here?"

"Let's go for coffee," he says, putting an arm around her in his overly familiar way. She makes for the office and comes close enough to see that drawers are open, files scattered on the desk. There's also an adding machine, an old one, with tape spilling down to the floor.

"Deverell, you don't work here anymore."

He passes a hand around her waist and leads her away from the office. "Just come with me please."

"Fine!" Rebecca slips away from his touch and heads for the front door.

"Let's go to the Tango Palace. It's down on Queen Street."

"There's a Tim's in the mall."

"We'll drive to Queen."

"I can walk."

Rebecca chooses a narrow street so she can avoid Deverell's attempts to walk side-by-side. She leads the way at a fast clip, the question: *What's going on?* pushing forward in her mind, but she refuses to ask out loud. That would be helping Deverell and she wants to make things as awkward for him as possible. The coffee shop is full. A cache of customers is gathered around the pastry cabinet, admiring the profusion of cakes and squares.

"What would you like?" asks Deverell.

"Regular."

"Coffee?"

"*Yes,* I mean coffee!"

He goes to the counter to get their order. "Unsweetened!" she calls, before clambering around the overstuffed chairs to the one empty table in the corner.

He returns with their cups, collecting several packets of sugar on the way.

"So, how long are you going to stay around there?"

"Stay around?"

"That place. *Him.*"

"What's going on?"

"Martie Solomon is retiring. You know, she pretty much runs Theatre in Bloom, and has for years."

"What has that got to do with anything?"

"They never found anyone to take over from Martie. At least, not someone they like well enough. That theatre was inseparable from Martie. Theatre in Bloom will have to close."

"They have you."

"I'm nothing but a bean-counter. It's something you could have done, Rebecca."

"I didn't, though. Okay? And I still don't understand why we're talking about this."

"Leon's closing your little enterprise too."

"He can't!"

"Oh yes, he can!"

"We've been independent for years."

"Have you, now?"

"Marlin took over."

"And almost immediately approached his father-in-law for a loan, and the next year and the next. Leon said yes, of course. He's not going to let his family go without."

Rebecca performs calculations in her mind. There are the rentals, the grants, the classes, the donations she is sure are coming in from various wealthy students. How did this happen?

"The theatre belongs to SenseInSound!"

"The theatre belongs to Leon Garten, my friend!"

"Marlin has been buying the building from him."

Deverell shakes his head and sighs. "Okay. Let's *have* this conversation. Do you recognize the name Roberto Balducci?"

"Never heard of him."

"Freddy Grosvenor."

"I don't know."

"David Wong?"

"I don't know, Deverell. Why are you asking me this?"

"Well Leon has been bailing you guys out since Marlin declared his supposed 'independence.' But before giving you the really big, big bail-out Amanda is requesting in Marlin's absence, Leon asked me to go in and look at the files. And these individuals have all done 'contract work' for SenseInSound. A little research shows one's a herbalist, one's a past-life soul integrationist, or some damned thing. And then there's the officially-ordained-in-California practitioner of spinal straightness with a little Registered Trade Mark sign after his name. Oh, and the masseurs! All those masseurs!"

Rebecca shakes her head.

"That's right. Ever since Marlin has taken over the finances, tens of thousands of dollars have been going to these quacks. I have to hand it to him; for someone who scorns anything to do with business, he's a very good bookkeeper. It all goes under a generous budget line called 'Maintenance.' I want to see him in jail."

Marlin fudging the books. Marlin making appointments with practitioners she's never heard of. Being touched by strangers. Many strangers. This is too much, too much of Marlin she doesn't know. She must act like she knows what's going on even if she doesn't. If not to convince Deverell, then to convince herself. "He has the right to seek out alternative health care. We don't have a *benefits* plan, after all." Her voice comes out so sure and steady that it calms her own pounding heart.

"You're right. I hate to say it, but I checked them out. They're quacks, but they're real quacks. Anyway, he planted his seeds in the right place. Leon would never do anything to hurt his grandchildren. That puny bastard will get away with it."

"Amanda!"

"Well, she's not very happy at the moment. But trust me, she knows how to look out for herself."

Deverell drains his espresso. "Something to eat? He points to the cabinet of pastries, then turns to talk to Rebecca again. "Oh, I should have told you, there's a message at the office. A reporter. She wants to ask you a few questions."

"Ask *me* …?"

"It looks like one of Marlin's former adherents is going public about how he treats the women in the company."

"What are you talking about?"

"It's the mother, actually. A girl who worked with you guys ended up at death's door, apparently. Anorexia. She's never been the same since. After years of therapy she finally revealed some unpleasant details to her mother. Mom's kinda mad. Can't imagine why."

Portia. Rebecca remembers her pacing back and forth in the theatre, sipping from a water bottle while everyone else was eating lunch. "I encouraged her to eat. We all encouraged her to eat. And when she had that allergic reaction …"

"The term is anaphylactic shock. She could have died."

"We got her to Emergency as soon as we could."

"That's not the way she's telling it."

"She's lying."

Deverell shrugs. "So, tell that to the reporter."

"I used to bring her food at lunch-time, but she kept saying no."

"She's claiming there was sexual abuse."

"*What?*"

The rehearsal for *Medea*. No one asked – let alone forced – Portia to unbutton her shirt. And yet – letting go of inhibitions is so much a part of The Work. It is about finding parts of yourself you did not know were there. You have to be willing to do things you would not normally be comfortable with. At what point do you stop making a choice? Rebecca was there, watching. *Someone has to do it.* Her job was to hold on, keep things steady and in control. But what if the situation called for something different? At any time, Rebecca could have said, "Stop. This has gone too far." She didn't. And then Kevin, old enough to be Portia's father, took her by the hand and led her away. What happened between them in the dark wings of the theatre?

Implicated. Rebecca wants to get up and run – somewhere, anywhere, but feels trapped in a web of guilty panic. She longs to get back to Marlin and his certainty about The Work. At the same time she wants to go far away, back to – what? Her clean, old self, before The Work came along and spread its traces on every part of her life. Except that there's no such thing as *before*. Her connection with Marlin did not come from outside. It called to something fundamental within her, something her body knew, even though her mind did not. Marlin showed her how little she knew about herself, gave her access to memories she had forgotten. Marlin was her way to know.

"Portia's okay, in case you're wondering. It *is* her you're thinking about, isn't it? Not your*self*."

She has to steady her breath to answer convincingly, "I'm glad she's okay."

"Want my advice? Just ignore it."

"*Ignore* it?"

"Sure. It'll blow over. I doubt anyone will talk to the reporter, but worst comes to the worst, the controversy won't do you any harm."

"Are you trying to minimize –"

Deverell laughs, "Look who's taking the moral high ground all of a sudden!" He stands up. "They make amazing Nanaimo bars here. Want one?"

She thinks of Portia, the day she first noticed she was getting dangerously thin. She was sleeping, as she often did, in one of the theatre seats. Her T-shirt had ridden up, revealing a sharp hip-bone through translucent skin. Rebecca pulled the shirt down to cover it. Not enough. She did nowhere near enough.

"No food!" She answers. She takes a gulp of coffee, which burns her stomach. "Don't drink it like that." Deverell puts a hand on her arm, his voice full of a kindness she doesn't deserve. He hands her two packs of sugar and she dumps them in.

Sarah has designated herself the designated driver. While their mother prepares cranberry sauce and stuffing for the next night's dinner, she herds her sisters into her mini-van and drives the forty minutes to the Hôtel Dauphine on the highway. Rebecca was about to ask Audrey to join them, but Sarah said, "We need to bond, Mom. You don't mind, do you?"

Audrey said, "You girls go. I'll be fine."

The walls and carpet of the dining room are red, the tablecloths beige and covered in a layer of plastic. Rebecca and her sisters are the youngest people in the place, even younger than the waitresses who wheel the food over on carts, looking like they find it all an enormous bother. After dinner, they order Spanish coffees topped by whipped cream. The waitress looks puzzled when Sarah and Janice say they want "Virgin" Spanish coffees, and calls in a friend to interpret the sisters' increasingly elaborate explanations.

Finally, it looks like they've got their point across. Sarah says: "Well, then, let's talk." Janice nods knowingly. Rebecca has – as usual – been left out.

"About what?"

"Well, we all know you're very attached to The Property, Rebecca."

Rebecca is furious. Furious that Sarah, who once proudly called herself The Doberman of the Divorce Court, is adopting this sweet and conciliatory tone. Furious that she nonetheless seems to be expecting an argument. Fueled by the spiked coffee, she says, "Look,

Sarah, you don't have to put on your Parenting-101 voice, okay? I just want to know what the two of you have been talking about behind my back."

Sarah continues, "Rebecca, it's obvious that The Property is un-inhabitable and has been for years. We don't want to see our mother living that way when all of us are doing well enough to keep her in better circumstances."

"Mom's fine."

"Twice a year! Twice a year, Rebecca, you make it down here. If that. While Janice and I are back and forth every month even though we have very busy lives."

"What the hell is going on?"

"We need to decide where to put her."

"But she's perfectly okay where she is."

"Have you seen her limping around the place, closing off rooms with blankets like it's the middle of the Depression? She's going to need a knee replacement one of these days, and which of us is going to be able to drop everything for a year to look after her? Not you, I don't think, with your almighty schedule."

"It doesn't take that long to recover from knee surgery."

"Rebecca, I'm feeling very tense right now."

"Look, she's fine! She cooks, she shops, she gardens. Besides, she's got friends here."

Rebecca takes a big gulp of her coffee, then licks a mustache of whipped cream from her upper lip. It tastes good. And while the others were given a spoon, she was not. She leaves behind the conversation and surveys the table, crumpled napkins, lipstick-stained cups and soiled cutlery. She longs to clear this mess, sweep away the crumbs and re-set each place, lose herself in the task.

Somebody has to do it.

Clean up.

And *be* a mess, a problem for everyone to worry about.

At work, at home, everyone has a role to play, all the time.

"It's not a nursing home!" Sarah, assures her. "It's an assisted liv-ing facility. They have help on the premises. Fitness. Church. Golf.

Mom can still cook for herself if she wants, and she'll make friends. Maybe even get married again."

"That's ridiculous. It's just not an option."

Sarah turns to Rebecca. "Alright then. We know you've got activities that you care very much about, but Janice and I have responsibilities."

"Like what?"

"Adult responsibilities."

"You mean kids."

"Of course not, Rebecca."

"And those are the only responsibilities that count."

"You know I don't mean that."

"What *do* you mean, then?"

"It's just that you love it here. What if you moved back?"

Janice starts crying. "I'm the one!" she says. "I'm the one with no life!"

"Stop putting yourself down, Janice. You've got your writing!"

This brings a fresh outpouring. "What writing? All I do is edit diet books. My publisher's gone out of business. I can't get a grant to save my life."

"Listen," says Sarah. "I can buy you some time. Maybe you could use The Property as a retreat."

Feeling more and more helpless, Rebecca listens to the plan as it's formulated. They won't say anything until spring. In April, Janice will approach their mother about moving herself and her teenaged son to The Property. Sarah will subsidize Janice's writing while she looks after Audrey.

Then Janice says: "I've been thinking a lot about how it went when we were kids. I don't remember Dad at all. Do you?"

Sarah says, "I was twelve when he died. You should have memories before that, but my real memories start when we got The Property. The first day we opened the door. The place was so dusty. Old furniture lying around. After The Property the memories make sense; before that it's all just snippets."

Janice says, "Do you know how Mom even got the place?"

"Her aunt Judy owned it. Mom asked to stay there in return for fixing it up. Judy left the place to us when she died.

"Don't you remember anything about Dad?"

"It was a different life. A different world. It had nothing to do with the world we grew up in. I think that's why we can't remember. And Mom refused to talk about it. I used to ask myself if I was making it up, the picture I had in my mind of Dad. All we had was that old wedding photo. You know, when I started going out with George and we told each other our life stories I was amazed that he had so much history. The summers that they spent at the cottage, all their relatives. His whole past stretching out in one line.

"Mom completely lost it when he died. I remember her lying on the couch. It was kind of an olive green: I remember it vividly. She just lay there on that pukey couch, and I looked after everyone. I can't stop going over it in my mind. Someone must have dealt with the will or the insurance, but I don't remember Mom ever getting up. It was probably just a few weeks. Maybe even days, but it felt like years to me. Then one morning we woke up and it was: 'Get in the car, we're going.' And away we all went."

Janice shakes her head.

"I remember too!" Rebecca's voice leaps out of her. "I remember the couch. It was a blue couch."

"Green," says Sarah. "You were only four."

"She was on a blue couch. Same colour as her jeans. There was an afghan around her. She was shaking. I remember her teeth chattering. And besides, I do remember Dad, a bit."

"Rebecca, the couch was green. You can't remember that far back. I must have told you and you thought you remembered."

"I remember it!"

Sarah slaps her palm on the table, tears welling as she says, "Listen! I looked after all of you. *I* was the one who made sure you got to school. *I* was the one who made sure you had clean clothes and school lunches. It all came down to me, the day Dad fell off that ladder. If I hadn't done these things, we would have … well, we wouldn't have survived."

Rebecca does not answer. The warmth from the coffee has come and gone, and Sarah's outburst has drained her. Sarah has restored her role – all their roles – reflexively, as if righting a bicycle that is about to fall. Janice is patting her arm, handing her tissues and a glass of water. Rebecca looks down, feeling like yet another vital element has gone from her life. That memory of her mother on the couch was central to her, something she knew in her core. But she doesn't know this, or anything else, for sure. The green couch is as real to Sarah as the blue one is to Rebecca, but Sarah is louder and more determined. Maybe that's all knowing really is, having the force of will to make your own point of view prevail.

Her sisters' voices, the voices in the restaurant now blend and collide in the air around her. Rebecca reaches for Janice's spoon and scrapes out the inside of her cup, mixing the layers at the bottom before pouring the sludge into her mouth. She listens to her sisters' voices as she does Journeys at SenseInSound. The sweetness of Sarah's voice conceals a blade of aggression. And beneath that? A quaver sneaks in at the start of each phrase, the edge of a sob. Janice's throaty rumble sounds insatiable, reveals a deprivation that can never be satisfied.

And what about Rebecca? She's also part of the circle. Her familiar note is silence. She is afraid to disturb the air with so much as a breath. The pulse that animates this music is loss: sudden, overwhelming, irreparable. Looking up from the cup to the faces around the table, Rebecca feels sad. For all of them.

Life without The Property. Rebecca has to consider it if she's going to go through with her plan. She remembers Sylvia's words when she took Rebecca out for sushi years ago. Sylvia believed that her mother could never have left London. Is it this way with Audrey and The Property? No. Rebecca needs to believe she and her mother could have their silent companionship anywhere. She sits down with Audrey at the kitchen table the night before she's to leave. Together they have washed all the extra towels and sheets and put them in bags to protect them from mice. They have tipped the mattresses on their sides, put away the extra dishes and silverware. Now she can't put it off any longer. "Mom, I want to talk to you about something before I go."

"What?"

"I've been worried about you."

"Why?"

"You're here by yourself."

"You're not worried."

"You're right. It's the girls. The other girls have been worried."

"Well they shouldn't be. As you can see, I'm fine."

"I agree it's a little early to be talking about this, but they've got a point. You're miles from anything: the bank, the doctor, even the grocery store. It's twenty minutes' drive to the next house. You've got to think about the future."

"I'm thinking about it."

"I don't want you to feel forced into anything."

"Nobody's forcing me."

"What I'm saying is that if you're willing to move to Toronto you could have my downstairs apartment. I know it would be an adjustment but if you need help I'm right there. The others want to help, but ... well, I think they would drive you crazy, frankly."

Audrey sits for a long time, staring down at the table. At last, she says, "That's very nice of you. I never thought one of you girls would ask me that."

"Mom! Of course!"

"But it's not going to work. I wouldn't like the city."

Rebecca pauses, then says it: "What if I came here?"

"Your life is in Toronto."

"Everything's changing for me. I don't even know about my job any more. Maybe I should see what I can find around here."

"The house is sold."

Rebecca has the bizarre thought that they've all been trespassing for the past few days. "It can't be sold."

"Dixons down the road had twins. They need more space. I'm moving in July. There's a new apartment building for seniors. They have everything you need."

"How will we come and visit?"

"There's a motel not far."

"But how can you do this without telling us?"

"I'm telling you now."

"After the fact."

"I haven't moved yet."

"Well when *were* you going to tell us?"

"It's my life."

"No, it isn't. It isn't *just* your life."

"You're busy."

"But I might not even have a job soon …"

"Thanks. Thanks for offering to take me in. But I've made up my mind and I'm going to go."

Rebecca retreats to her room, fighting tears. She folds her T-shirts, sweaters and jeans into her duffel bag and shoves her dirty laundry into the pocket on the side. She keeps hoping Audrey will knock on the door and say something that will stop her from feeling so terrible, but the knock doesn't come.

"Look Rebecca," Audrey says the next morning as she's getting ready to go. "You know me. Once I decide something, I get on with it. That's the way I am and the way I'll always be."

"But we didn't have a chance to adjust."

"I'm not moving 'til the summer."

"I mean we *never* had the chance."

Audrey shakes her head. "I know the girls are all into this business of dredging up the past, but I'm not. All this talking is some kind of psychological fad that is going to pass and not a moment too soon as far as I'm concerned. It may not seem very – affection- ate – of me but the last thing I want to be is a burden. You girls have your own lives. And if you have a mess to clean up, Rebecca, clean it. Take care of your own work and let me do mine."

August 30, 2012

SEASON PREVIEW:
Cult or Cure, with Gloria Bianchi

This fall, *Cult or Cure* will continue to visit the close relationship between charlatanism and healing. First: "The Ups, Downs and Upside-Downs of Yoga" will ask whether Yoga is the new church. We'll look at the thriving industry of Yoga-wear, and delve into the history of Yoga, which has its origins not in Ancient India but in Swedish Gymnastics. "Cracking and Quacking" will introduce you to the colourful characters behind chiropractic. "Visualize this!" will unpack the art, science and fiction of mental imagery. "Ding Dong, Karma Calling! The Healing Arts as Pyramid Scheme" will show you the dollars and cents of working as an alternative healer in today's economy. Spoiler alert: don't quit your day job.

After all this and so much more, the season will wrap up with my own documentary: "The Starving Self." It's been over a decade in the making, because no matter how hard I tried, my daughter kept refusing to tell her story of abuse at the hands of a cult leader, fifteen years ago. She mistrusted her own memories. That was the terrible damage done by the cult. It would be easy to say that the story ate her up from within, but the sad fact is, she eradicated herself. Portia left us last year. She weighed 85 pounds. For years, I had longed to tell her story, believed it would free both of us if I did. But now I know I'll never be free. All I feel is a sense of responsibility to her memory. Portia, this one's for you.

2000

There is nothing to do but go back to work. Right now, that means cleaning the basement. She's about to go down on her knees and scrape up more linoleum when Marlin shows up at the foot of the stairs. Just like that, he's back. He is smiling, yet her gut stirs in fear. "Wow! Look at this. More studio space: we can rehearse down here!" She returns Marlin's smile and tries to feel only happiness at his approval. Longs for the feelings that used to motivate her. She cannot stop the word from coming into her mind: *mine*.

Mine because I've cleaned up the garbage.

She says nothing, continues to scrape. Marlin comes closer. "You stayed away so long at Thanksgiving," he says.

"My sister *summoned* us for a family meeting." Marlin's silence, as always, acts as a mirror, making her aware of her own attempt to deflect responsibility. Her own cowardice. Why doesn't she call *him* out for disappearing for weeks on end? What comes out is: "My sisters were in from all over the country."

"And of course your family has always been so wonderfully close."

"I'm sorry."

"I had hoped we could spend some time together. I need you here, Rebecca. I'm not – well you know what I think of doctors. But I'm going to need to know who I can count on in the next little while. And clearly ..."

"My mother needed me to help clean up. I couldn't come back."

"Couldn't or wouldn't?"

Her thinking is eclipsed by the anger in Marlin's voice.

"Couldn't or wouldn't, Rebecca?"

You just checked out! I had no ideas of your plans, she wants to say, yet she knows that Marlin has stepped outside of logic. He has set himself against her, will find a way to oppose her no matter what she says. All these years she's avoided his rages but she's observed their momentum. He won't give up until he breaks her down. And he knows how to break anyone down.

"Rebecca? Won't you even do me the favour of an answer? It's the least you can do, I think, after all these years."

I'm done with you. The words present themselves with every ounce of force she has. She forms them silently and almost shakes with the effort of holding them back. But saying them means stepping outside of something, the very universe she has inhabited for almost seventeen years. It is cold outside, and very dark.

But it's Marlin who speaks. "All these years I've been waiting, because I believed if I stayed around long enough, I could get a commitment from you."

Rebecca thinks of the way she laid everything about herself open to him from the start: her body, her emotions, her time. He continues, reading her thoughts in that uncanny way he has. "I know! I know you keep busy with your painting and sawing and your endless notes, but that's not what I mean. I'm talking about *commitment.* From your heart."

"But I thought ..."

"Don't tell me you don't remember! The body doesn't lie, Rebecca. I couldn't get enough of you when we first met."

For the first time ever, he has acknowledged their being lovers. With the mention of it she is back on her pullout couch during one of her interminable nights of waiting. Except this time, her wishes are coming true. She is hearing words she longed, all that time, for Marlin to say. It is as if he were touching her in the way she has always wanted so badly to be touched.

But he is not touching her, and has not for many years.

The truth is weighty. She heaves it up word by word. "You went back to her."

"Why do you think I did that? It was obvious that everything came second to your work. And you're still pushing me away. Pushing all of us away. You're surrounded by people who want to get close to you and yet you squirrel yourself away with your lists and your tape and your safety pins, telling yourself you can't. Listen, Rebecca – you think I do – what we did – with just everybody? You and Amanda were – well, you've been the only ones. Ever, frankly."

Memories of her years with SenseInSound crowd in on her. All the times when she felt alone, was she actually holding herself apart? The times when she felt helpless, was she actually the one in control? She does not know. She does not even know how to know. She needs someone else to tell her. She needs Marlin.

"Sooner or later you have to commit, Rebecca. You have to let go and start to live."

Live: that's what the rest of the world is doing and she is not. The word encompasses everything from dressing better to having children to knowing what career she wanted when she was a kid.

"Well obviously there's no point in me sticking around," he says. "I'll see you when I see you."

That night, Rebecca lies awake feeling as if her spine were dissolving into the bed. Her doubts about Marlin and The Work. All of these seem foolish to her. Not only foolish, shameful. She doesn't have the right to think beyond the horizon of what she knows: SenseInSound, Marlin. She has to keep trying to get that right.

Rebecca paces her living-room, gulping coffee, as she dials the phone.

"Deverell O'Neill, speaking …"

She jumps in, not bothering to identify herself. "The theatre belongs to SenseInSound."

"Good morning to you, too."

"We did all the work on it. At least I did. That has to count for something."

"No one's disputing that, but Leon owns Gerrard Space: the bricks and mortar."

"I've got an idea.

"For going into more debt?"

She imagines Marlin looking up to her, nodding and grinning. Marlin taking her hand, telling her: *You've saved this company*. She glows with the thought. She will tell Marlin he needs to be free to concentrate on his projects. That his role will be exclusively artistic from now on. He'll have no desire to discuss why financial control has been taken from his hands.

"No, actually. This is a moneymaker. And the best thing that's happened to Toronto in a long time."

Deverell is silent.

"Okay: Leon closes the big theatre, scales down, moves the new operation to Gerrard Space. Toronto leads the world when it comes to multiculturalism. Why not in theatre, too? We develop shows by local playwrights from all kinds of backgrounds and host visitors from other countries. There are workshops and conferences. The first show is ..." She presents her idea in a rush. A lie? A speculation? A hope? She must make this work. "It's a collaboration with a composer from Berlin. And here's the personnel: Me as Producer, you as General Manager. And –" (quickly) "Marlin to direct the plays."

"Pardon me?"

"I'll be in charge. We can just contract Marlin by the show."

"You are utterly single minded. Did you hear anything of what I told you last week?"

"Leon's going to be supporting him one way or the other."

There's a pause and then, "I hate this."

Rebecca waits, invoking Marlin's technique of going silent, until she knows she's won. She speaks quickly, before the last bit of confidence drains from her voice. "So, we'll talk about money next week."

Before Deverell can answer, she hangs up the phone, imagining Marlin smiling at her. Still, she cannot get rid of an image that rose unbidden in her mind when she said "personnel" – Gaëlle and Catherine Mercier, as they appeared in France, raising their joined arms, kissing their free hands and holding them out to the audience before taking a bow. Rebecca's heart races. *There are some mistakes you can't fix, Rebecca.* Once upon a time, she treated Gaëlle as if she were inconsequential, inconvenient. There is no reason Gaëlle should ever speak to Rebecca again.

There are seven people on the Journey. That number includes Jonathan, who is staying in one of the empty apartments upstairs. Marlin sits on a chair with the others cross-legged around his feet. His arms are rigid, hands gripping his thighs. Rebecca fears an explosion of rage, yet he wears a beatific smile as he waits for people to quiet down.

"I never had a father," he says. "And I was angry about that. Angry at my father himself for being a simple, uneducated man. Angry at my step-father for being so rigid.

All I wanted was a father's time. His touch. And I took it out on the people I cared about the most. It's time to give that up."

Marlin is apologizing. Or coming as close as he's ever done. He's reflecting on himself. Sharing something as intimate as can be. Everyone is rapt, some are weeping. Rebecca is unmoved. Refusing to commit. Rebecca is wrong.

"I put my longing for a father in a box. I labelled it Isaac Samuel and I worshipped it. Hid it away. But like everything else, it was impermanent. And it's the women in my life who showed me that. My mother, my wife, my daughter. And all of you women here in the room. Thank you."

He bows his head.

All of you women. Rebecca feels like she has been struck in the chest. Yet this has to be enough for her. After all, she only gave part of herself.

After a silence, Marlin says: "But enough of the old. I believe someone expressed discontent about our productions of the classics? 'No more fucking Greeks' were your exact words if I remember correctly." Marlin lets the laughter go on for a while before settling the company with an outstretched hand. Rebecca notices the deliberateness of the action, his hand pulling away from his torso as it lifts. It is a graceful movement, but controlled; he might also be trying to stop it from shaking. "Well, we're done with the Greeks for the time being. It's time to let go of relics of the past. To move on. To something much bigger."

Marlin waits for the applause to end. "We're back to creating something of our own again. This time, with a script, a set, and music. More of everything. The working title of our show is *To End All Wars*. Nearly ten million lost their lives in World War One. Young men, men not much older –" he takes a deep breath and says the rest with a break in his voice "– *than my own son* were conscripted to feed the ravenous killing machine. Children, in other words. As we all know, that bloody conflict paved a golden pathway for the Fascists to enter Germany.

"This was the war where my great grandfather did not fight. He was one of the few men of his generation who did not, in their lifetimes, commit murder. And yet he believed himself weak. He never got over the shame.

"You've heard of the Christmas truce, perhaps. The boys (and they were *boys*) came out of the trenches and celebrated together for one day, then went back to kill and maim each other the next. What possessed them to form relationships with their fellow men, then ignore what was in their hearts and hurl themselves into the fray? It was separation of mind from body. Simple as that. If they'd listened to their bodies, they would have stopped the killing then and there.

"The Christmas truce will be our basis for the next show. We don't know much more than that, except that Jonathan Mayer will be part of our process. Jonathan and I have been creating a duet. We've been living in close quarters, a hothouse of creativity. We've been getting up at all hours of the night to work, going without food sometimes, all to unsettle our patterns and break down the psychological defenses of habit. To find the fundamental truth inside us. We've wept and laughed together. Together, we explored the intimacy of violence, tried to get to the depth of what makes men fight. And what makes them love."

Throughout this speech, Amanda sits cross-legged in the circle with the others, her head bowed, face obscured. Rebecca notices the sharp bones of her spine. In the past, she would have heard all the new ideas before they were presented to the group. She would even have developed them with Marlin. Clearly, not this time.

Marlin and Jonathan begin back-to-back, leaning on each other. Marlin sits on an exercise ball, and Jonathan holds himself as if sitting in a chair, but there is no chair there. Instead, his strong thighs support him. He stares at himself in a mirror, which is off to one side. Still looking in the mirror he begins to stand while Marlin gradually slides to the ground. Marlin creeps along with the lizard-like movements they used during *Genesis*, while Jonathan steps on various parts of his body. Yet he is always looking in the mirror, admiring himself. Rebecca is horrified by Marlin's weakness. His arms seem to have trouble bearing him forward. Jonathan places his feet on Marlin's body with a care that Rebecca finds spellbinding. His superior strength tamed, the ability to hurt, unused. He portrays an oppressor, yet his skills save him from being one. She can see the intimacy between them. Their relationship is beautiful, yet crushing for the way it excludes her. Gradually, Jonathan climbs on the ball and stands up, taller and taller. He must have been coached endlessly by Marlin to achieve that degree of balance and strength, coached by someone who can no longer do the moves himself. He walks on the rolling ball like a circus performer, cursing with syllables that could be German, but are not. He mimes whipping Marlin, who grows weaker and weaker. When Marlin stops trying to raise himself, Jonathan flounders, then falls.

Jonathan gradually gets up, abandoning the mirror, approaching Marlin now. He tries various lifts. Eventually, he cradles Marlin like a baby and walks away. He stands Marlin on his feet and the two men return, holding the mirror to the watching group.

"Jonathan, I wonder if you'd like to start the discussion," Marlin says.

Jonathan nods and closes his eyes for a long while before beginning. "I greet you, and thank you for welcoming me," he says at last, hand over heart. "About the piece, there is not much to say, except that working together on this was a new experience for me, and a very beautiful experience, since I had honestly never before felt so close to another human being. This is a sad thing because it includes my relationship with my parents, and with the women I have thought I loved, but it's true. Something in me has broken open. I feel ready for true closeness.

"I think of this as a complete process, from beginning to end, like a season. One of these experiences that could not last long because it is so intense, but one that changes your life. I'm grateful to have worked so closely with Marlin, and now I'm very grateful to be part of your company. You will be my family here in Canada, and I hope you will call me by my family nickname, which is Natto. I look forward to working with you. Let's see what the next season will bring."

Marlin nods emphatically in agreement, and almost cuts Jonathan off when he says, "Yes, that's right. It's the beginning. The beginning of something. What you saw was simply a draft. We need to work on it together a lot more. You all know about that."

A section at the back of the basement holds all the large items which over the years could not be taken up the stairs and out the front door: overstuffed chairs, couches and box springs, a refrigerator and two freezers. How did anyone get these things down here in the first place? During Deverell's tenure, Rebecca had the back doors widened and a new set of stairs put in leading up to the alleyway in the rear of the building. Still, the junk has sat in the basement for years. Tomorrow, a haulage company is finally coming to take it away.

Rebecca changes from her work boots to flexible sneakers so that she can kneel by a patch of linoleum that she is gradually working free from the planks underneath. She hears rustling, then banging in the alleyway outside. Garbage cans? It must be raccoons. Rebecca gets up stiffly. She opens the double doors into the renovated stairwell. The bins are undisturbed and there are no animals around so she climbs the steps to check the alleyway. It is dark, lit only by the windows of neighbouring buildings. To her left, a shape moves. She can't make out what it is, only that it is big. It seems human, yet it is distorted by a huge, misshapen head. Her heart thuds. She cannot take her eyes from it. The bulky shape divides, its large head becoming two small ones. There is the silhouette of a nose and lips, pushing urgently forward. Rebecca knows this urgency. These are Marlin's lips, in a moment of desire. *You think I do this with just everybody?* This is not Marlin reeling someone in, trying to get a better performance out of them. This is Marlin, in love. Then there is a violent movement, a pushing away. The two figures separate and stand facing each other. The other man is Jonathan. He stands with his back against the wall, looking up at the sky and breathing hard. Marlin takes a few slumping steps, then breaks into a clumsy run.

"I'm sorry!" Jonathan says. He kicks at the wall behind him with his heel and slaps a hand against his forehead. He turns and calls to Marlin's receding figure: "I am sorry. I am not that way!" Marlin stumbles and falls, first against the wall then all the way to the ground. Jonathan rushes over and kneels by him, hovering a hand over Marlin's prone body. "Be careful. Please, do not do this." Marlin tries to get up but seems to get his limbs tangled and falls again. Jonathan guides Marlin to a sitting position then stands up himself and offers Marlin a hand.

"I'm sorry. I'm really sorry but you have to stop doing this. It is not this way with me. You have to believe it, okay?" Marlin stands, with Jonathan's help, then shakes him off and lurches down the alleyway. Rebecca recedes and closes the new, blessedly silent door behind her, locks it, then puts on the chain. She leans with her full weight against the door, knees bent as if to keep out an unwelcome force on the other side. She braces herself harder and harder, arms wrapped around herself, jaw clenched. She begins to shake, a movement that starts in her viscera and radiates outward. Her teeth chatter, her ankles and calves quake. She is alone, yet not. It is not *only* her, shaking; someone else is sharing her body, the past has come to meet the present, inhabiting this moment with her.

Audrey: lying on a pilled blue couch. Her arms are wrapped around herself, her chin tilts to the ceiling and she resists, then gives in to bouts of shaking. There's a percussive sound as her back teeth knock against each other. Rebecca, the little girl, runs away. Rebecca the woman pushes herself forcibly away from the wall. She begins to pace, leaning one elbow on the opposite arm, gripping the hair in front of her forehead then shaking out her hands. This is Marlin's gesture. Her vision is patchy. She feels possessed. And she hears something Marlin would say, except that she is saying it to herself: *make some noise!* She dredges up a deep grunt of rage, then an even deeper one, as if all her effort just now in peeling up the stained linoleum could be made into a sound. She is.going to kick something; she knows it, and in the scant moment left before her body acts on its own she forces herself to move away from the brick wall and toward the carcass of a chair with one broken leg. She kicks the chair again and again, each time with a roar, and it rolls into the middle of the room, shedding horsehair and splinters.

She feels the power in her leg, the chair, broken and cowering with every blow. It is Marlin she imagines kicking, his arms wrapped around his chest, his shoulder diving for the ground, head tucked over in an attempt to protect himself. Marlin, as she saw him just now, crumpled in the damp alleyway. Weak. She hated him that way.

Not until two hours later, after she's cleaned the mess in the basement, after she's locked the doors and set the alarms and taken the subway home, does she feel the throbbing in her toes. Sitting in her front hall to take off her socks and shoes, she looks away to avoid seeing how swollen her foot is. She limps to the bathroom and immerses it in water, feeling faint when at last she looks down at the purple blotches spreading, the middle toes separated at an unnatural angle. Sitting on the edge of the tub, she rocks to calm herself, and hears her sobs echoing around her on the bathroom tiles.

"It hurts," she wails. "It really, really hurts."

It has always hurt. It will only ever hurt. It will hurt to be without Marlin; it will hurt to stay. She doesn't know which is worse, but it's over, anyway.

Tensor bandage
Epsom salts
Tylenol
Packaged soup
Oranges
Thank you.

The doctor prescribes her three weeks of home care and eight of physiotherapy, during which she must not work. Not work. She writes lists for the visiting homemakers. All she needs are a few supplies and sleep. Sleep.

Messages: Deverell: has she got enough to eat? Yes of course she's got enough to bloody eat. There are oranges and coffee and sliced ham. Another message: he has left a casserole on the front porch.

Vic, Connie. Not Amanda. Never Amanda. The messages say Marlin has fallen, broken a hip. They want to keep him in hospital. They can't discharge him. There's something wrong that caused him to fall in the first place. They can't let him go home. Where is Rebecca? They're worried about her. They need her. No one knows what to do.

She must fix this. She surges out of bed. Her foot is an alien, bloated weight at the end of her leg. She feels every jarred bone and tendon. She drops back down again, curls on her side. Sleeps. Dreams she has committed a crime and must make a getaway. She is in the driver's seat of a car with the top down. There's a child holding her arms out. The girl reaches for Rebecca, her mouth stretched out in silent distress. Rebecca turns deliberately, steps on the gas and speeds away. Sometimes it is Meira standing there, sometimes Portia, sometimes it is Rebecca herself, as a child. She's culpable. For leaving. For staying. For abandoning. For betraying. For saying yes. For saying no.

The basement will flood! The mail will build up! Marlin needs her! Again and again she wakes to the prison and protection of her pain. Lets herself sink into sleep. And then the calls taper off.

Marlin Lewis Memorial Page
November 12, 1946 – March 30, 2002.

Posted by Bill Stronach, on the tenth anniversary of the death of a great teacher.

Marlin was suspicious of words, and at no time do we sense the rightness of this belief more than now. Words cannot express our love for this artist, teacher and friend. His work was his life and his life was his work. His colleagues were his friends and his friends were his family. He was a bold, uncompromising genius and anyone who met him came away changed. It was not always an easy Journey with Marlin but if you took it, you came away feeling like you were finally, fully alive.

About Bill: I have been doing counselling for individuals and couples for two decades. Along with my wife, Connie Herbert, I offer weekend intensive workshops for couples: "Now at the Breakfast Table," "Now in the Bedroom," "Now at the Bank." My memoir, *The Breath of Genius*, is available on Amazon.

Comments:

Connie Herbert: Ten years, already. How can it be? Marlin you left a great gap in our lives.

Victoria Fodor: So glad to see Marlin's community gathering here on FB. Ironic but somehow right. God, I miss him.

Catherine Kinnear: I thought you would be with us forever.

Trevor Smith: One session with this great man changed my life.

Atherton: What happened?

THE WORK

Catherine Kinnear: Something to do with his brain. Or his feet. He couldn't breathe.

Greta Wong: He came to our office once. I don't even remember what he did with us; it was a blur. But I asked for a raise the next week and got it!

Catherine Kinnear: Yes let's all stay in touch.

Fred Rodrigues: Does anyone have pictures?

Kyoko Watanabe: Alright, guys. Enough. First of all, who the fuck are you? And secondly, where were you when Marlin was sick?

Gillian Easterbrook: He came to our class in grade 10. Now I'm a physiotherapist.

Norman Fulton: Forever in our hearts.

Kyoko Watanabe: He. Is. Dead.

Catherine Kinnear: A meetup, maybe.

Norman Fulton: I want to say it was 9/11 and then he fell and didn't come out of the hospital. Or did he fall before 9/11? It was fitting.

Kyoko Watanabe: You people attended one class at Senseln-Sound and you are his family all of a sudden?

Chelsea Franks: That's amazing, Greta. I wonder how many people took a session with Marlin and went out and did what they needed to do afterwards? We felt it in our bodies and we couldn't ignore it any more.

Kyoko Watanabe: What I want to know is, who put him in that shit nursing home? Shit shit shit. That's what it smelled like in there and so did he. No one cleaned him. No one touched him. No one stayed with him. He used a machine to breathe. Meantime, his work was a success. This page smells like shit.

Victoria Fodor: Is Rebecca Weir on FB?

Connie Herbert: She is everywhere but.

Tech Word Ho: Weir is totally the man. Hot!

Fabian Derkson: The world was ready for *To End All Wars*. The towers fell, the show was built. Uncanny.

Norman Fulton: Totally. A necessary collapse. Marlin would have said so!

Catherine Kinnear: Or maybe a TUMBLR.

Kyoko Watanabe: Everyone took from him. No one was there for him. He just smiled when he saw me and closed his eyes. Next day he was gone. You are hypocrites.

Victoria Fodor: Where are the kids?

Deverell O'Neill: Kyoko come on. Nice death scene but where were you those two years he was at Sunset Haven? You were riding the success of *To End All Wars*. I had no time for the man but at least I'm honest. We owe him that.

Bill Stronach: We should all get together some time.

Catherine Kinnear: We really should.

2001

"Rebecca? It's Christine, here. From the office? I've got a few things to go over with you if you don't mind stopping by this week."

"This week?" Rebecca searches her mind for who the caller might be. Has she missed a doctor's appointment?

"Some time before classes start."

Oh yes, Christine. About to fire her for being too severe. They liked the substitute teacher better, obviously. She emails Christine's secretary. Sets up an appointment.

Doing a good job is its own reward. They need to learn that.

These are the words she goes over in her mind, preparing to have to defend herself, as she knocks on the door. She has wrapped her foot too tightly. She imagines her toes turning black inside her boot, having to get them cut off at the hospital. She hears vicious barking on the other side of the door, startling her so much that she feels faint. Okay, she's nervous. But it will all be over soon.

"Terror! Blood! Leave it! Just a sec."

The barking quiets as a frazzled Christine answers the door. "Sorry. Please come in. I don't keep the muzzles on when it's just us girls in here."

The room has been draped in velvet curtains, the institutional fluorescents replaced by floor lamps. The desk has been pushed off to one side and a couch and two chairs shaped like high-heeled shoes are arranged around a triangular coffee table. Christine curls up on the couch. She gestures to one of the chairs. Rebecca perches on it.

"Like the office? It's Felipe's work." Christine giggles. "I'm always encouraging him to develop some interests outside of the kids."

Rebecca's boss wears a red bustier with what at first glance appears to be a black mantilla over her shoulders. But it soon becomes clear that the lace pattern is etched into Christine's skin. Christine pours coffee from a carafe on the table. "Almond milk?"

"No, thanks. I take it black."

"How about some agave nectar?"

"Black's great, thanks."

Christine picks up her laptop and begins scrolling. "How are you?" she asks.

"Good. Good. Just like new," she lies.

"Fabulous. Now, let me see what we need to discuss ..." She sighs. "It's going to take a minute. Meantime, check out our Christmas shots!" She gestures toward an album with pictures of two girls in blue velvet dresses at the base of a Christmas tree, their arms around the unmuzzled dogs. There are pictures with an older couple, with Christine, with their shy father turning his face from the camera.

"Here we go. Oh! Oh, dear!" She clucks her tongue soothingly. "Oh my goodness. Well, it looks like we had a letter from a parent. Aww, that's terrible!"

It's happened. Rebecca straightens herself in the diminutive chair, wincing as she shifts her hurt foot. She thinks of the girl who arrives ten seconds before class every day, dressed in stilettos, who once asked to miss school for a *week* because she was organizing a baby shower. Rebecca did not even dignify that one with an answer, just stared at the girl until all her arguments ran out and she retreated in tears.

"I can't reveal the name of course, but it looks like he ..." she covers her mouth. "Like this *person* experienced some stress in your class last year, 'due to the negative view of job prospects for stage managers.' Goodness me!"

Frowning, she looks up at Rebecca, who is now on her feet, clenching her jaw as the dogs growl.

"The student's father is a member of the Board of Governors, I'm afraid. Oh, Golly! I don't like to do this …"

"It's a hard job, Christine. Theatre is hard."

"Well …"

"No need to be nice. Just go ahead and fire me. I'm sure everyone felt more *comfortable* with the sub you brought in. I want to see that letter in black and white that says teenagers can give orders to people who started work in this business when they were in diapers!"

The dogs are flanking Christine, slavering and barking as best they can with their muzzles on. "Girls! Off!" With a red-tipped forefinger, she directs each rump down to the floor. "Could you please sit down, Rebecca?"

"Why?"

"Because I'd like to ask you something."

"About lowering of standards for instance?"

"Sit! I mean, please sit down."

Rebecca lowers herself to the chair.

"Do you enjoy your job, Rebecca?"

"Enjoy it?"

"Yes. Enjoy it."

"It's not about that."

"What do you mean?"

"Because theatre isn't about that."

"Hm!" Christine makes a surprised grunt.

"Because life isn't about that."

"Oh!" Christine pats the couch to invite the dogs to climb up beside her. Stroking the heads that now clamour to be touched, she bites her lip and stares at her bookcase.

"Are we finished?"

"Goodness gracious, I hope not!"

"Well, I'm sure you can send the paperwork by email."

Christine pauses then asks, "What is it like?"

"What?"

"Teaching when you don't enjoy it. Working when you don't enjoy it."

"It's just something I do."

"Hm!"

"Not everything in life has to be fun."

"So why do it?"

"Someone has to."

"But do you *want* to?"

"It's my life."

Christine gets up and begins to pace, hands behind her back.

"I have to give this some more thought."

"Well you don't have long. My class starts next week."

"And you'll be teaching it as wonderfully as ever."

The relief Rebecca feels makes her catch her breath.

"But the complaint …"

"Oh, that! Never mind. I'll talk to him. Rebecca, listen, you've given me an idea for a paper I'm writing on artists in the academy. It just occurred to me that there might be a generational difference between the boomers and the millennials. Maybe even something to do with trends in funding. May I interview you some time?"

"Thanks, I mean: Okay." Rebecca's stomach feels watery. "I should go."

"Yes of course. Sorry to keep you. Just …"

"What?"

"Ease up on the kids, okay?"

"Sure, okay. Thanks."

Either her height gives her away, or the telltale flecks of paint on her clothing, but the waiter seems to be expecting Rebecca. "In the corner, Ma'am," he says. When did she become a Ma'am? And who drinks in a place like this? The Roof bar at the Park Hyatt is eighteen floors above the city, overlooking the university campus and the shopping district. Rebecca feels uncomfortable among the unblemished table tops and white napkins. She glances out the window at the rush-hour traffic and takes a step away from the windows, wishing she were back in the basement.

"I'm meeting someone …" The waiter points to a corner table where a woman sits reading, leopard-patterned glasses perched on the end of her nose. She's sipping a martini and reading a book. Martie is dressed in a boldly cut jacket constructed of yellow, orange and red patches. There is a green streak in her hair behind one ear; otherwise, it's all white. A thin braid originates at the nape of her neck and hangs down over one shoulder. She looks up over the glasses, grins, then rises to reach across the table and shake Rebecca's hand. The glasses fall on their length of chain to clink against an enormous silver pendant around her neck.

"Hi!" The word comes out confident and generous, as if it were an extension of her smile. "Joe!" She calls to the tidy, bespectacled man behind the bar. "Told you she'd get here eventually! What's two decades between friends?"

Joe laughs and asks Martie, "What will your friend be drinking?"

Martie appraises Rebecca: "Scotch."

"Well, usually I stick with beer." Rebecca already feels put out, having Martie order for her, and the conversation hasn't even begun.

"We'll start her on a nice Glenmorangie. Easy sipping."

Rebecca cuts in, "Way too sweet. Bring me an Ardbeg."

Joe nods. "Very good."

Martie grins and Rebecca feels embarrassed, realizing that Martie probably intended to provoke her. But after a sip of whisky, extended with a precise amount of water, it bothers her less. She wonders if she's going to be able to pay attention to what Martie has to say without being too distracted by the flavour she's been missing for twenty years.

"I like a woman who knows her whisky. Who taught you to drink?"

Rebecca smiles at the memory. "Guy by the name of Ian Hope. Years ago."

"Hope Against Hope! I love him! Serious drinker. But he did

brilliant work. He lost his nerve, though. Wasn't a pretty sight. You've got to keep working or you're done for." She gulps her martini. "Scary thought!"

Rebecca nods. This woman understands her. She tells Martie about the job she had driving Ian around, how that led her to Gary Curtis and Bart, about the performance artist, the ketchup, the Quonset hut. Martie's laugh booms through the bar, and Rebecca prickles with discomfort as she imagines the attention of the whole room focused on her. And yet, choosing her second whisky from the menu, she imagines Ian guiding her hand, smiling at her as she aces this test of her character. *My Amazon.*

"How was your meeting today?"

"With Christine?" (As if she had any others.) "Great! Great! Just getting up and running again. I've been ... on leave." She gestures to her foot.

Martie nods. "That's too bad. Listen, Doll. I want to tell you something. Do you understand the word *mensch*?"

"I've heard it ..."

"Okay, I'll tell you the definition: Leon Garten."

Martie sounds like she's about to tell Rebecca what to do. Anger conflicts with politeness as she answers, "Wonderful guy."

"You're right. And you work for him. And you're lucky. So, when Leon offers you something it's a good idea if you just say thank you, and you take it. You take the opportunity and do your best. Your very best."

"That's what I do every day."

"Sure, Doll. Listen, you're playing with big stakes here. Leon – this is Leon *Garten* we're talking about – saw potential in you years ago and you treated it like one more ketchup gig. He's supported you like – quite frankly – a daughter, and he's been screwed over by your whole organization year after year. After you never called me – I told him he was crazy but you know what he said? 'Anyone that loyal, I want on my team.' That's how much faith he had in you. Leon: I love that man. And Sylvia, too. And they adore their daughter who has been breaking their hearts for forty years and continues to break their hearts and will probably go on breaking them. I hate to see it. And there's Medusa or whatever the little demon seed is called. Is she off the tit yet? It never seemed right to me, this business of breastfeeding them 'til they're allowed to vote, but then I'm just a dried up, childless old crone. What would I know?"

Rebecca smiles and tips her glass at the "crone" remark. Anything to cut through the bleakness of worry which has shadowed her ever since Meira's birth.

"The Gartens don't deserve to live through this, but they have been, and they still are. I don't want to leave Leon, but – let's just say the time has come." She holds up her book so that Rebecca can see the cover: *Let's Go Turkey*. "June has plans. And after thirty years of putting up with me in this business, I owe her. We want to hit the road in September. God willing you've got many good years of work ahead of you, so next week, I will arrive at your doorstep. And, Doll, you will learn to work."

"Are you saying I don't know how to work?"

"Good intentions. But I suspect not."

"What are you talking about? Do you know how many hours I've spend in that theatre?"

"You know how to run, and so far, you've got enough energy for it. But you don't even know what work is."

"I'm exhausted all the time."

"Well, then I guess you *don't* have enough energy. Let me ask you a question. If you need an extra hour to finish something, what do you do?"

"I stay! I'm there sixteen hours a day."

"I rest my case. Your very, *very* generous patron has given you a building to use, any time you like. You have no schedules, no deadlines, no board of directors, no unions to deal with. As a matter of fact, all your employees are members of the same cult. You've got everything your own way. You've never worked in a professional theatre in your life."

Rebecca cannot formulate a reply. She is drunk, and Martie has got the better of her.

But I am fighting.

I want this.

"With me you will do things once, you will do them properly, and you'll go home after eight hours. No overtime until production week."

The thought of having that much free time makes Rebecca want to get up and run away. But where? She takes a gulp of scotch.

"Got someone nice? For what I have in store you'll need someone who can cook."

Rebecca blushes. There have been many casseroles on her steps over the last few weeks. And today, a card inviting her to enjoy the next one at Deverell's place. Whenever she thinks about that card, her stomach clenches. How can this possibly work? And yet – she realizes – *I want it to.*

Martie laughs. She points a severe finger in Rebecca's direction. "Doll! Don't mess this up. Leon and Sylvia will be happy, and I'll be happy, and June will be happy. And your nice partner will be happy to have such a sexy girlfriend if you'd get some adult clothes and cut your hair. And I think you'll be happy too. And if you're not you've got a very, very big problem."

"You're treating theatre like it's some kind of corporate job."

"Dolly-bird, listen to me: you have a chance at being in charge of a major centre for theatre with the backing of one of the most powerful impresarios in the world, with his most trusted producer as your mentor. You get to keep your anti-war idea, except that you get to make it bigger and better. And you get to keep your precious building. You're not exactly losing anything."

"But I am!"

"Sure. Bitter, twisted people, anxious little plays that no one enjoys or understands, no publicity, more actors on stage every night than in the audience – "

We had full houses for years, but anyway … "No! It's more. It's – I feel part of something I believe in, that we all believe in together."

"What is it that you believe in?"

Rebecca's throat feels like it's closing. She wants to say "SenseIn-

Sound," but she really means Marlin, and she can't say that to Leon's closest colleague. "Theatre," she manages at last.

"Doll-baby! Sweetheart! You're not losing that!"

It's not theatre it's the *willingness* to believe in something, to the point where she would give her whole life to it, the way she has to the company. She tries again, "These days ... With this – transition. Everything feels so grey, so empty. I mean, what next?"

"Puh! Puh! Puh!"

Martie makes a spitting gesture from one side to the other. She raises her hands as if to stop the conversation. Looking over her glasses at Rebecca she pronounces, "Good things! Good things for all of us."

Gesendet: 15/8/2012. 4 a.m.
An: <u>director.graddrama@UToronto.ca</u>
Von: <u>AmAndAm@gmail.com</u>

Betreff: It's over

Yes, Dr. Charbonneau, I was in Toronto again. Yes, I was ignoring your calls.

I'm surprised you didn't show up to the unveiling of Dorothy's headstone. So many people were there! It was like the memorial Marlin never had. Anyone who had worked with him for a day or two showed up, talking as if they'd known him for years.

Rebecca was there. Not for long. She retreated almost immediately to stand by the gates of the cemetery, as if she couldn't bear to approach the stone. She was with a man! Was it? Could it be? Yes. Deverell. He came over, gave me a cursory hug, said she was "taking a little time to herself." Wedding ring. Thud to my chest.

Meira's new family arrived. She wasn't with them, which told me one thing. I'm to be a grandmother again. To a child I may never know. *A real family.* I felt the stab of separation in the midst of being happy for the life she'd chosen, a life where she'd never feel as lonely as I did at that moment.

Her mother-in-law arranged the unveiling, giving me only a week's warning. Natto was on tour in Japan. Safra cancelled at the last minute when his son came down with an ear infection. "Bubbie would have wanted it. Children come first … *She's* the one who taught me that." No holding off the tears this time. He waited for a while then reminded me with excruciating gentleness that he was at work.

I caught up with Rebecca at the reception afterwards. She looked stunning and I told her so. As always, she was dressed in black, but a different black. She looked – well – like she'd arrived. She smiled and began to drift off, but I could not let her go. I needed to find out, right then, how she'd left Marlin and why. As if hearing her say it would free me, too. I grabbed her arm, too tightly. "What happened?"

She blushed, and stammered, and I saw that *What happened?* meant something very different to her. "You were gone. We didn't know if you were coming back." She said. I was snatched back, decades, to a time I can barely remember. Remember what happened, that is. I remember the feeling very clearly indeed. It was of not being good enough. Of trying, trying, trying to be loved.

"You might as well have asked me to." This was a new Rebecca. Solid, rooted to the spot instead of slipping away. She was here to see me or have me see her. Thriving. Over him. Over me. Over us. All the trouble I had finding the jealous rage to play *Medea*! We dug scrupulously through my history, and finding nothing, blasted down to the bedrock. We questioned my parents' marriage, the home where I grew up, leaving fault lines of doubt that have yet to heal. And yet that particular kind of rage kept escaping me. My most carefully guarded secret. The nut that would not crack. My solution was to imitate my daughter. At three, her biggest tantrums coincided with Safra's story-time. Night after night I produced howls and shrieks that inspired audiences to grip my hands afterwards and tell me I had given voice to the truth of betrayal. I felt like a fraud. It was mimicry. Pure and simple. There was no story-time for anyone else when I was growing up. I had no idea how that felt. But it was there at the reception. And it is now.

The worst of it is that I wanted Rebecca at that moment. Wanted to rest my weight against that tree-trunk of a body. But she had gone to stand with her husband. She was leaning against *him*, not being leaned-against. I watched her shoulders heave and saw the way he stroked her head and rocked her, whispering in her ear. She straightened herself, took a few breaths free-standing and strong on her feet. Then they left, arm-in-arm. I wanted to get between them. Become the centre of her story again.

Dr. Charbonneau, I'm ready. You will need to come here. We will need to speak in the afternoons. Mornings I write.

Yours truly,
Amanda M.

Request For Funding

November 12, 2012
Dr. Lorraine Charbonneau
Chair, Department of Drama
University of Toronto

Budget

Air fare Toronto/Berlin: $1,000
Accommodations: $2,000
Per Diem: 20 days x $100/day: $2,000
Ground transportation: $250
TOTAL: $5,250

Project description

The notion of an invented tradition, as described by Eric Hobsbawm and Terence Ranger (1) applies, not simply to nation-building, but to the construction of groups who gather for the purpose of self-development, always around a charismatic leader. My research to date has focused on chronicling one such movement, which began in the early 20th century and persists – as my study will show – to the present day. For want of a better term I shall refer to it as the Samuel Method, but its adherents refer to it as The Work.

The training is rigorous in its pursuit of a form of authenticity which it terms to be "the truth." However, as Philip Auslander reminds us: "The body is no more purely present to itself than is the mind and is therefore no more autonomous a foundation for communication than verbal language" (35-6). What may appear authentic is nothing more than a construct.

Invented traditions, according to Hobsbawm and Ranger, arise "when a rapid transformation of society weakens or destroys the social patterns for which 'old' traditions had been designed" (4).

In the face of instability – not only socio-politically, but at the level of the individual in the face of the ego-challenging practices they advocate, leaders tend to portray themselves as part of a tradition, chronicling their own discipleship and situating themselves in a lineage of similar practitioners. A commercial element is often involved, as the role of entrepreneur/healer/teacher/performer becomes more and more common.

My books, *Genius in the Fog: The Forgotten Fifties Foremothers of the Contemporary British Stage* and *Breath Pause: The Role of Trauma in Early Twentieth-Century Voice Pedagogies* dealt with two generations of the Samuel Method, looking back to England in the 1950s and early 20th century Germany, respectively. *The Tyranny of Now: The Misogynistic Annihilation of Narrative in Contemporary Body-based Performance Practices* is a historical study of Toronto's SenseInSound theatre company.

Ironically, this present-day phase of the Samuel Method has been the most challenging to research. Though the participants are all living they have been unwilling to grant interviews. The only means of research has been advertising materials from members of the original, core group. However, at long last, I have gained access to three key sources. Dr. Dorothy Samuel, sister of Isaac Samuel and a prominent child psychologist and writer, has bequeathed his notes and papers to the McGill University Library. I have been the first to access this collection. Rebecca Weir, the company's producer, has housed her archive of (copious, if difficult to decipher) production notes at the Humber College Library. Additionally, the ex-partner of the company's leader has agreed to do a series of interviews. She has kept journals since the inception of the company and is writing a novel based on her experiences.

Works Cited

Auslander, Philip. "'Holy theatre and catharsis," *From Acting to Performance: Essays in Modernism and Postmodernism*. London and New York: Routledge, 1997.

Hobsbawm, E. J., and T. O. Ranger, editors. *The Invention of Tradition*. Cambridge University Press, 2012.

THE END

ACKNOWLEDGEMENTS

This book has been hard work and has taken me a long time. I could not have completed it without a lot of support.

My first thank-you goes to my husband, Rolf Meindl, for creating the home where my imagination could come out of its hiding place at last. Also, for reading the manuscript multiple times, sniffing out typos, telling me when it was getting boring, and countering my cries of "It's no good!" with a quiet, "Yet!"

I am grateful to the Toronto Arts Council and the Ontario Arts Council Works-in-Progress and Writers' Reserve programs, with recommendations from Quattro Books and Tightrope Books, as well as to the Humber School for Writers, Timothy Findley/William Whitehead scholarship.

I have benefited immensely from the advice and guidance of David Bergen, Nino Ricci and Robyn Read. My time at the Sage Hill Writing Experience with generous comments from Nino Ricci, proved a turning point in shaping the story.

I have rewritten this book so many times it has sometimes felt like throwing spaghetti at a wall and seeing what stuck. Actually, it was more like throwing drafts at my friends and seeing what they could tolerate. Thank you to the many, many people who have read parts of this manuscript. Special thanks to Suzanne Alyssa Andrew, Gail Benick, Lorne Blumer, Patti Flather, Dayle Furlong, Lisa

Guenther, Andrea Johnstone, Diana Kiesners, Heidi Reimer, Julia Steinecke, Leona Theis, Nancy Wesson, Kathleen Whelan, Molly Wills and Catriona Wright, and to the Toronto Salonistas for sharing information, support, inspiration, resources and celebrations. Thanks to all my friends for bearing with my angst over the years. Thank you, Gila Schwartz, for throwing your immese smarts and experience behind my promotional efforts.

My parents, Hetty Ventura and John Gould, and my grandmother, Mona Gould never got to see me have a book in the world, but their sometimes-compatible brew of persistence, imagination, gumption, subversiveness and dedication to craft still flows in my veins. Shirley and Ted Franklin, Elisabeth Raab Yanowski: you're still sadly missed, but present every day in the encouragement, love and gracious example you sowed during our time together.

Some generous individuals have read the whole thing, some, more than once! Thank you, Andrew Daley, Terri Favro, Brenda Hartwell, Alice Kuipers, Rolf Meindl, Rebecca Rosenblum and Julia Zarankin for reading, and reading and reading.

I sought out advice from several esteemed theatre professionals in researching this manuscript and got – not only answers to my questions – but solid editorial feedback as well. Sincere thanks to Paula Danckert, Nancy Dryden, Maria Popoff as well as to Laura Cournoyea and Michel Gagnon. Any errors are my own.

Thank you, Netta Johnson, Anne Brown, Lisa Murphy Lamb and Julie Yerex of Stonehouse publishing for believing in this book, "getting" what I was trying to say, and bringing it out into the world.

And finally, this story was dreamed up on many long walks through the neighbourhoods of Toronto. I have lived here most of my life, have known it as the place where you had to fill out a form to buy a bottle of wine, and as the place where thousands filled the streets to protest cuts to public services; as Toronto the Good and Toronto the Gridlocked. I love it for all its contradictions and layers. But people have been living and creating on this land for millennia before my ancestors arrived. I would like to acknowledge the traditional stewards of this land, the Huron-Wendat, the Seneca and the Mississaugas of the Credit River and all the recorded and unrecorded nations who have lived here. Thank you to the many Indigenous artists, teachers and elders who live and work here today for sharing your wisdom, stories and creations, and for continuing to teach us settlers – with undeserved patience and generosity – how to be better guests.